I Put a Spell on You

Sarah Vance-Tompkins

I Put a Spell on You
Copyright © 2021 Sarah Vance-Tompkins
All rights reserved.

ISBN: (ebook) 978-1-953335-24-1
(print) 978-1-953335-27-2

Inkspell Publishing
207 Moonglow Circle #101
Murrells Inlet, SC 29576

Edited by Yezanira Venecia
Cover art By Najla Qamber

For
My Fairy Godmothers

SARAH VANCE-TOMPKINS

CHAPTER 1

Rule #1: A fairy godmother never makes an appearance until her skills are desperately needed.

Not every fairy's tale begins with "once upon a time."

Mine didn't begin until the day The Fairy Godmother's Rulebook arrived in the mail. Up until then my life was a monochromatic drudge, punctuated by a few moments of black, white, and complete G-rated shades of gray. After the book arrived, my life transformed into a highly color-saturated Technicolor fur-reak show like The Wizard of Oz.

I didn't think I was special. I was, in fact, almost completely invisible, afflicted with a slow metabolism and a paralyzing fear of birds. Not that it matters now, but at the time I didn't believe in poison apples, glass slippers, or happily-ever-after endings. Nor did I have any idea that your fairy godmother never shows up until you are completely desperate.

Truly. There wasn't any room in my little world for magic of any kind.

If I knew then what I know now, I wouldn't have been so surprised when my ringtone startled me awake at a quarter after six on that foggy morning in LA.

To be honest, when my mother's number popped up on my iPhone, I wasn't feeling all that desperate. I was actually feeling pretty shitty and hungover. I hit the ignore button and let her call go to voicemail.

I rolled over and attempted to go back to sleep, but the movement was too much for the contents of my fragile stomach. I could feel the bile rise up in my throat, getting dangerously close to spewing all over my sheets.

Ugh. I was so dying.

Kidding. Not kidding. I wished I was dying.

My head hurt as if it was a melon being split open with a santoku meat cleaver. Every hair follicle on my head throbbed, and the tips of my ears itched as if I'd been exposed to a particularly virulent strain of poison ivy. Even my toenails ached.

At the time, I assumed my painful symptoms were being caused by the copious amounts of red wine I'd consumed at my pre-birthday dinner with my best friend, Josie. I'd never had more than one glass of wine in my life, and now I knew why.

The inside of my mouth tasted as if I had eaten cat food just before bed and during the night an evil dental hygienist had used one of those air spray tools to dry out my mouth, leaving the smell and flavor of rotting cat food behind. I desperately needed to swish my mouth with something industrial-strength. Like Lysol.

My need to rinse out my mouth was ever so slightly less significant than my need for five more minutes of sleep. I plumped my pillows and tucked the fluffy down comforter under my chin. Just as I was drifting back to sleep, I remembered my intake appointment with Emily Bernstein, PhD. I jerked awake and looked at the clock again, willing it to be twenty after five instead of twenty after six.

I blinked. And looked again. Squinting through my lashes.

Nope. Not happening. No magic.

I bounced up off the bed and stumbled into the bathroom. Splashing cool water on my face, I ran my fingers over the aching tendons in my neck. As I worked out the kinks, I was surprised to discover two painful lumps between my shoulder blades on either side of my spine.

What the what? Now I had some kind of disgusting back acne. I'd just turned twenty-one, but I had a longer list of ailments and complaints than a person twice my age.

I pulled a dark gray Free People herringbone dress out of the laundry basket and grabbed my favorite rag & bone booties out of the chair where I'd left them the night before with my purse and work tote.

A heavy fog had rolled in from the Pacific Ocean overnight, hanging ominously in the early morning air as I waited for an Uber in the gated driveway of my parents' house. From my point of view, high atop the Hollywood Hills, the only building eerily poking through the mist was the castle-like Chateau Marmont on Sunset Boulevard.

A phenomenon the local weather forecaster called "May Gray" had been holding the greater Los Angeles area hostage for weeks. Gray skies. Gray sidewalks. Gray buildings. The monotone color palette dominated the city.

It was depressing.

I closed my eyes and let my head fall back against the cloth upholstery in the back seat of the Uber car. There was nothing I wanted more than to cancel my appointment, but it was too late to do it without being charged. And I was too cheap and too much like my dad to pay for a service I wasn't getting.

I used up three birthday wishes while we were stopped at the red light at Sunset and La Cienega, hoping Dr. Bernstein would call and have to reschedule my appointment.

Just my luck, my birthday wish didn't come true.

At least not yet.

Going to therapy wasn't my idea. Dad frequently

shared how bleak his outlook was for my future with whoever would listen. After getting recommendations from his golfing buddies, who were all very sympathetic to the fact that his youngest daughter was a "late bloomer," he selected Dr. Emily Bernstein, a career guidance specialist, to put a fire under my ass. Dad's first assistant, Glenda, set the appointment and pushed a reminder about the date and time into my iPhone calendar via email.

It was my father who was willing to pay someone to find some ambition for me, but it was my BFF Josie who insisted I get some professional help.

"You're not happy, Aviana. That's all we talk about. How unhappy you are," Josie declared loudly over cinnamon-scented bowls of beef broth at the trendy 9021-Pho in West Hollywood. She flipped her long raven hair over her shoulder and fixed me with a look of mild disgust. "The restaurants where we discuss your unhappiness change, but the level of your unhappiness never does. Honestly, I don't think you should turn down the opportunity to discuss some of your concerns with a trained counselor."

I wasn't completely convinced, but girlfriend had a point.

Stumbling out of the car in front of a tall office tower in Century City, I paid the Uber driver, took the elevator up to the fifth floor, and exited into a well-appointed lobby. Two spectacular table lamps on an antique console table created dramatic lighting in the plush waiting area. This appointment had to be costing Dad a chunk of change, as he paid all my deductibles and this doctor wasn't in-network. I pushed the button to alert Dr. Bernstein to my arrival and took a seat on the striped sofa across from an ornate mirror.

Is it a one-way mirror? Am I on camera? Am I being watched?

Confronted by my own reflection, I fidgeted. Another restless night without sleep had left me with a little Cindy

Lou Who hairdo. Which wasn't a good look on an eight-year-old, not to mention a chick just turning twenty-one. I'd tried to make my pinkish-blonde mane look a little less Seuss-ian by tucking my hair behind my ears.

Whoa. Just wait one minute.

Had my ears always been as pointy as a Christmas elf?

My self-assessment was interrupted when Dr. Bernstein appeared with not a hair out of place. I immediately recognized her as a pant-suiter in the mold of Hillary Clinton, fully accessorized with a Hermes scarf at her throat and what I guessed were obscenely expensive Italian leather loafers on her feet. She looked like she would be giving a keynote address at the United Nations later the same day.

"Aviana Willowbrook?" she asked.

Instinctively, I raised my hand as if she was calling attendance in homeroom. Flustered by my unkempt appearance in comparison to hers, I got to my feet, smoothing down the rumpled skirt of my dress and buttoning up my cardigan in an attempt to cover the creased fabric as I followed her down a long hall of closed doors.

Dr. Bernstein's office had a view of an atrium at the center of the building. It was filled with plants dead and half-dead from never seeing the sun. I knew their pain. I lived in Southern California, but I hadn't actually seen the sun in months since I usually went into work early and stayed late.

I sat down in one of the two big leather chairs in the center of the room and tucked my purse into the chair next to me. My phone vibrated, but the short burp told me it was just an email. No need to spring into action.

Dr. Bernstein picked up a notepad from the coffee table and sat down in the chair across from me.

"All right, Aviana. Let's get started. On a scale of one to ten, how would you describe your stress level today?"

"About a six," I said without thinking.

"It's seven o'clock in the morning and you're already revved up to a six?" She looked alarmed.

"Is that bad?" Now was definitely not the time to mention my sleep-working activities.

"What do you think?" she immediately responded. I hated it when people answered my question with a question.

"I don't know." I was still stuck on the first question.

"What do you do to manage your stress? Do you meditate?"

"Oh, hell no," I said, I guess a little too quickly because Dr. Bernstein gave me a look.

"Why do you say it that way?" she asked.

"Meditation just isn't my jam." I shrugged. It was, in fact, something my mother was totally into. I didn't see her very often, but when I did, she wafted in and out of rooms on a wave of patchouli-scented air in expensive Lululemon yoga clothes.

"Do you know anyone who does meditate regularly?" Dr. Bernstein prompted.

"My mother," I said under my breath. Dr. Bernstein made note of my response. "But I don't know her very well. My parents divorced when I was five. My mom moved back to Los Arboledas, and I grew up here. In Beverly Hills."

When I was younger, I pretended Mom had a dark secret that my father was using to blackmail her into letting him have full custody of me. I fantasized she was an international spy or an infamous jewel thief. It made the reality of being abandoned by her a little less heartbreaking.

"How often do you see your mother?"

"Two or three times a year."

"You don't think she's had much of an influence on you or your behavior?"

"No. Not really. Honestly, I've made my peace with my relationship with her. I was raised by my father and my stepmom."

"Your father?"

"He's an entertainment attorney. They call him 'The Whale.'" No one who was anyone in Hollywood ever called Hal Stern by name. He was the biggest fish in the shark tank.

Dr. Bernstein's mouth fell open. "Then your stepmother is …"

I nodded. "Madeleine Stern."

"The head of the Monarch Motion Picture Studios?" she asked, sounding impressed. "How wonderful it must be to have such powerful parental role models."

I bit my tongue and gave her a toothy smile instead.

"Do you like her?" she asked.

"Madeleine? I like her just fine."

"How old are you?"

"I'm twenty. Twenty-one," I corrected. "Today is my birthday."

"Happy birthday," she said. For a moment, a hint of warmth and compassion was visible behind her eyes, but it was gone as soon as she blinked. Without another word spoken, she scribbled two more paragraphs of notes on her pad. Her voluminous notes regarding my birthday kind of freaked me out.

"Do you think that's significant?" I asked.

"Do you?" she challenged.

Gah. I held my mouth in a tight smile and shook my head.

Dr. Bernstein quickly returned to the format of her prepared questionnaire. "Do you have any brothers or sisters?"

"Two. Stepsisters. They're twins," I said. Valerie and Vanessa were identical twins with totally different personalities. The only thing they shared was an uncanny ability to succeed in their chosen professions.

Valerie had worked as a runway model in Paris as a teenager until she realized she was more than a pair of mile-long legs and a pretty face. She had a flair for fashion and was now one of Hollywood's most sought-after young costume designers. She was also engaged to Nao, a music producer who only went by one name and just made Billboard's top-ten industry power list.

Vanessa won her first spelling bee in third grade. She owned all academic challenges from that point on. She graduated valedictorian from high school and went Ivy League for undergrad and law school. She returned to Hollywood triumphant and was starting to earn her own reputation as a killer lawyer in the shark tank.

"Vanessa is my boss," I said.

"Really? Do you like working for your stepsister?"

"She is a benevolent dictator," I said with a straight face.

My answer caused Dr. Bernstein to write furiously again for what seemed like at least two detailed single-spaced pages.

"On average, how many hours a day do you spend at the office?" she continued with her questions.

"No more than eight." Oh, yes. Let the tall-tale telling commence. This was my one true gift: my ability to stretch the truth like Silly Putty.

"Is that the truth, Aviana?"

I nodded. I couldn't say "yes." If I said it out loud, it would be a bald-faced lie, and I wasn't that kind of liar. I was more of a you-may-have-misunderstood-my-facial-tic kind of liar.

My phone vibrated again in my purse; it was the intermittent pulse of an incoming phone call. I didn't want to take the call when I was in the middle of lying to Dr. Bernstein about how much I worked, so I tried to ignore it and didn't hear the question.

What had she asked me?

"Yes?" I hesitated. I figured I had a fifty-fifty chance of getting the answer right.

"I sense you're not telling me the truth, Aviana," she

said.

"About how much I work?" My panic was increasing. I never worked less than twelve hours. I had a very strict schedule. I was in the office every day by almost eight in the morning, and I didn't leave until almost eight at night. Five days a week.

"Yes," she prompted, her pen poised over her notebook.

"Okay. I work twelve hours a day." Why did I think going to therapy was a good idea? I knew people who had been in therapy for years and still weren't happy.

"Is there any possibility of advancement in your current position?"

"No. I'm never ever going to law school," I said. Despite the kind words of praise Vanessa frequently lavished on me, she didn't think of me as an employee as much as an indentured servant.

"What is your dream job, Aviana?"

Dream job? "I've never really considered it," I said, lying like a rug. My father had been hounding me about my career plans since I was six. He gave up on me when I was in high school.

I was a good student, but I never excelled at any subject. I didn't have big dreams. No musical ability. Too shy to be an actress. I wasn't artistic or creative. I didn't like to cook. Math, no. Religion, no. Politics, no. Science? Don't even. My only essential skills added up to a job with someone else's name in the title. All I really wanted was to belong to something or someone special, but I didn't think I could hope for both.

"Let me ask you this," Dr. Bernstein said. "Are there any aspects of your current job you do enjoy?"

"I like helping people. I'm a good problem solver. I'm organized and I'm able to keep track of the small stuff that trips up other people."

Her face screwed up in a way that made me think she'd been recently sucking on lemons. "But you don't have any training, like college or trade school classes?"

My shoulders sagged. "No."

She didn't make one mark on the page before firing off her next question. "Do you have a hobby?"

"Define 'hobby,'" I said.

"Something you do for pleasure," she said.

"I read." I couldn't help but say it with skepticism since lately I had been downloading self-help books in order to fall asleep. I wasn't reading for pleasure. I was reading to fight insomnia.

"Are you lonely?"

Lonely? Me? Was she kidding? The only long-term relationship I'd ever had was with loneliness. I was intimately familiar with the kind that made you feel as if your insides had been scooped out and you were nothing but a hollowed-out jack-o'-lantern with a crooked, carved-on smile.

"Yes," I said quietly.

Dr. Bernstein wrote a long, detailed note. "Are you dating?"

"No." My cheeks blushed with heat. I wasn't dating in reality, but in my imagination, I was deeply involved with Nash Nolan.

He was one of those Nolans. That's right, my crush was the heir apparent to Nolan Hotel Group—five-star hotels and resorts that set the standard for luxury brands around the world. Dad had represented the Nolan Hotel Group's legal interests for many years.

Not content to rest on his laurels, Nash had tapped into the zeitgeist of what the modern business traveler wanted in luxury accommodations and put it all into an app. He was dragging the hotel business into the twenty-first century.

Tall, dark, and impossibly handsome, he was a computer coding geek who wore large dark-rimmed glasses in need of frequent adjustment. Whenever he was in the office he was constantly pushing them up the bridge of his nose, and every time he did, my heart fluttered.

Too much of my time in the office was spent fantasizing about him, but I wasn't prepared to tell anyone about us. No one would understand, especially, I suspected, not Dr. Bernstein, so I held my tongue.

She went back over the pages and pages of notes and then studied me carefully before she spoke again. "So, what I'm hearing you say is you're currently living at home with your parents, working at a dead-end job, and you don't have a personal life. Is that correct?"

I nodded. Was it possible that after only one visit the good doctor had been able to pinpoint a solution to all of my problems?

"Wonderful!" Dr. Bernstein seemed genuinely pleased. "I think we've found the perfect place for us to start our work together. Unfortunately, we've run out of time for today. We'll have to begin your journey to happiness next Monday."

Journey to happiness? Are you kidding me?

I don't have time to wait. Any spark of hope was extinguished. My shoulders sagged. I honestly believed sharing the intimate details of my life would relieve me of some of the burden I was carrying.

Dr. Bernstein must've sensed my despair. She closed her notebook and patted my knee. "Being happy isn't a destination, Aviana. It's a journey. One we're going to embark on together." She gave me a card with her office number on it. Then she did the thing with her eyes that made her resemble a compassionate person ... if only for a millisecond. "I want you to know you're not alone. If you need me for any reason, call me. I'll do my best to get back to you within twenty-four hours, but if it's a life or death emergency, you should hang up and call 9-1-1."

"9-1-1?"

"I hope it doesn't come to that." She inclined her head.

"Me too." I got to my feet and backed out of the room, feeling self-conscious and emotionally naked.

Shuffling down the long hall of closed doors, I was more depressed than I had been when I arrived, feeling desperate and out of control.

As soon as I crossed the threshold of Dr. Bernstein's office, my cell phone rang again. I glanced at the caller ID. It was my mom. I wouldn't be able to avoid her phone calls forever. I knew why she was calling. She called every year on my birthday, but I was dreading her call this year.

Aviana, darling, how are you? Are you happy?

With other people, I could fake my way through an answer. But my mother wouldn't let me get away with a simple yes or no. She was the original artist, a true genius when it came to fabricating fiction from fact. As an expert liar, she never let me get away with telling her anything other than the truth.

What could I say?

It was my twenty-first birthday, and I was seriously unhappy, but I didn't want my mother or anyone else to know.

How am I?

I'm seeing a therapist because I'm a grown ass woman and don't have a clue about who I want to be when I grow up.

I decided it would be best to let her call go to voicemail. I'd deal with her when my head wasn't throbbing like an open wound, but just as I was about to do so, my fingers slipped and I hit answer instead of ignore.

"Aviana." A woman with the breathless lilt of a movie star murmured my name. She had the kind of vaguely European accent used by Katharine Hepburn and Madonna. "Happy birthday, darling. I'm so glad I finally got a hold of you. Your mother has been absolutely desperate to talk to you."

Did I mention my mother talks about herself in the third person?

"Is everything all right?" I asked. "I know you tried to

reach me early this morning."

"I'm fine," she said. "I was worried about you. How are you feeling?" It was a terrible connection. I could barely hear her above all the white noise and static. "Aviana? It's your mother? Are you still there?"

I was spared any further interaction when my mom's call dropped. Almost like magic.

Finally. One of my birthday wishes had come true.

SARAH VANCE-TOMPKINS

CHAPTER 2

Rule #2: A fairy godmother embraces knowing "happily ever after" is her purpose, not her future.

The law office of Stern, Fayed, and Lopez was just a short walk from Dr. Bernstein's office. There were a few other early birds in the law office most mornings, and Bart from the mailroom was standing next to my desk trying to decide where to deposit the morning mail delivery. The bin marked "inbox" was too obvious for him. Instead, he deposited a pile of business-sized envelopes and some manila envelopes with files that had been messengered over from another law firm onto the center of my desk. It was my pet peeve, but I didn't want to lose my temper so early in my day, so I bit my tongue.

"*This* came for you," Bart said. He acted put out by the effort of lifting up a large heavy parcel from the mail cart. "Postage must've cost a fortune. It weighs like ten pounds."

"You couldn't put it in my 'inbox' with the others?" I sounded snippy, but I hated the way Bart acted as if he was upper management and I was a janitor.

"It's addressed to you personally. Were you expecting

anything?" he asked.

"No, but it's my birthday."

"Really?" he muttered under his breath. "I think it's a book." Just like that, the surprise of getting a gift disappeared. "You're going to have to sign for it."

I dispensed with the signature line on Bart's clipboard and took a glance at the parcel wrapped in plain brown paper and tied up with white string. The address was in green ink with old-fashioned handwriting created by the scratches of a quill pen. I didn't recognize the return address. It wasn't in English, and the letters were smudged. Instead of a computer-printed stamp in the upper-right hand corner, there was a colorful puzzle of a half-dozen expensive-looking foreign stamps.

The package was a mystery I didn't have time to unravel. I had legal documents to proofread and contracts to execute. And nothing was going to get done when I had such a splitting headache. I shoved it into my tote bag underneath my desk.

During my morning coffee break, I escaped to the parking garage, where Josie and I sat with our bare feet propped up on the dashboard listening to the first track from the new Billie Eilish album she'd gifted me for my birthday.

Josie had stopped at the Sprinkles Cupcakes ATM in Beverly Hills on the way over and picked up a triple cinnamon cupcake with cream cheese frosting and Belgian dark chocolate topped with fluffy coconut shreds. We wolfed both of them down in a manner of minutes.

"How'd it go with your new therapist?" Josie asked, licking frosting from her fingers.

"The good news is, she says she can help me." I sounded hopeful, then I made a face. "The bad news is she wants me back on Monday. Twice a week. I must be far gone."

"There's nothing wrong with you." Josie shook her head. "She just got a peek at your dad's bank account."

"No doubt he'll demand a return on his investment." I laughed. "What am I going to do with my life? I don't have a clue."

"I don't either," she soothed. "And I just finished a college degree program."

"Have you gotten any response from the last batch of resumes you sent out?" I asked.

"No. As far as I can tell, my resume is invisible."

I blew out a blast of frustrated air. Josie had been living paycheck to paycheck and her financial struggles were stressing her out. "Something good will happen. I just know. At least you can take pride in knowing you got into school on your own merit. Your dad didn't have to donate a baseball stadium or anything." We were convinced that even with Vanessa's high grades, Dad made a generous donation so Vanessa could get into her number one choice for law school.

"There is that ..." Josie paused for a moment. "Still, the world seems like a scary place right now."

"I know. I'd handle it better if I didn't feel like crap." My voice cracked, and I let my head fall into my hands. My headache was not improving. If anything, it was getting worse. Way worse. And now my neck and shoulders ached as well. "I think I may be running a fever. Does my face feel hot?"

Josie pressed the back of her hand to my forehead. "A little. You may have a very slight fever. You should go home and get some rest."

I'd never taken a sick day in my life, and I certainly didn't think a little neck and shoulder pain changed that, but Josie had always been a bit of a hypochondriac.

"You know, you've got two big bumps back here," she said.

I ran my fingers over the tendons in my neck and down toward my shoulders, kneading the two lumps on either side of my spine. They were much more pronounced than they had been in the morning.

"What is it? Does it look like spider bites?" I asked.

"No. More like …" She paused for a long time before completing her description. "Horn buds."

"What?" I was mortified. "Are you kidding me?

"No. I'm serious. It looks like you have horn buds." She sounded a little too matter-of-fact. "You know, baby cows aren't born with horns. As they are maturing they grow horns from little buds that appear on their foreheads."

I tried not to let her see me roll my eyes in exasperation. Josie had spent every summer of her life on her grandparents' farm in Iowa. She was forever comparing the movie stars she spotted going about their business in Los Angeles to farm animals. She had side-by-side photos on the bulletin board in her bedroom of Anne Hathaway and an ostrich she insisted was the Academy Award winner's doppelganger.

"And you think I have these *horn buds* growing out of my back?"

"Yes. Or something like it." Josie took another look at my back. Her face crumpled as if she'd seen a brutal murder in a horror movie. "It looks painful. No wonder you're not feeling well. You really should go home."

"So what? You think I'm like a baby cow?" I almost laughed.

"I'm saying you're not normal. Tell your sister you're taking the day off to seek medical attention." Josie was concerned. Of course, she was. She would stay home with a paper cut. I made a mental note not to ask her any more health-related questions.

I checked my watch. It was almost ten o'clock when Vanessa usually made her appearance in the office. I put my feet back in my boots and got out of the car. "I need to get back to my desk."

"How are you celebrating tonight?" Josie asked, leaning out of the window as she pulled away.

"The usual. With the fam. At Mr. Chows." I waved

good-bye to Josie and hustled back across the parking garage.

I had just settled back at my desk when the double doors connecting the main office to the lobby burst open. Sunlight flooded the space, I shielded my eyes from the glare and noticed the other assistants paused from their activities.

My wicked stepsister was dressed as if she were the Duchess of Sussex in Westminster Abbey on Easter Sunday as she cat-walked the corridor next to Mila Winters, Vanessa's office best friend. She was the attorney who handled most of Nash Nolan's legal affairs.

They were the office cool chicks who prowled through the halls of the law firm as if powered by their own personal soundtracks. Vanessa took it one step further, channeling Beyoncé, she looked as if a wind machine was keeping her perfect beach waves tousled off her perfect face.

They moved in a choreographed hip-hop dance, leaving the administrative assistants and support staff scurrying like rats on the Titanic to get out of their way. Vanessa stopped by my desk to pick up some files and her messages. She was wearing a flirty navy skirt and sailor top with a pair of Giuseppe Zanotti espadrilles.

"You look fantastic," I said.

"Thank you," she answered brightly. She was a good lawyer, but compliments about her looks truly warmed her heart. She loved to hear she was pretty. Her twin was, after all, a former supermodel. Despite being super smart, I think Vanessa always felt as though she was lesser than.

As Vanessa made her way to her office, the phone started ringing. Instinctively, I picked up the handset and tucked it under my chin to continue multitasking. "Nessa Stern's office."

"Aviana? It's Mom." I expected her to admonish me for not taking her calls on my cellphone, but she didn't pause to take a breath before she started peppering me with questions. "You haven't by any chance gotten anything unusual in the mail, have you?"

"I got something this morning," I said. "I think it's a book."

"Crap," Mom muttered under her breath. "*She* never listens."

I pulled the brown paper-wrapped book out from under my desk to look at it again. "Did you send it to me?"

"No, darling. Your mother isn't *that* ridiculous. Did you open it?"

"No. I honestly haven't had the time," I bluffed.

Taking the scissors out of my top drawer, I cut the string tied in knots then gently folded back the brown paper wrapping. No surprise. It was a book. Fine dust covered the hand-tooled leather binding, the weighty tome was at least five inches thick and a foot wide.

"THE FAIRY GODMOTHER'S RULEBOOK" was written in gilt-edged calligraphy along the spine. Holding the musty old book as far away from my body as possible, I didn't know what to make of it. Other than it was very old and resembled a book of nursery rhymes.

I wrinkled my nose. "It's a children's book."

"No," Mom said. "It's not. It's definitely not for children."

"What is it, exactly?"

"I can't tell you now. I know you're at work. We'll have to talk later," she said. "But I wanted to check and see how you're feeling."

"I'm fine," I lied, pressing fingers to my aching temples. "I mean. I've got a slight headache. That's all."

"Oh. Oh, no." She sounded way more alarmed than she needed to be.

"It's nothing, Mom. No worries. I'm fine, but it's really not a good time to talk."

"Oh, I'm so glad I caught you when you had a moment to talk." She was completely oblivious

Gah. How was I going to explain the exact opposite was true?

Just then Vanessa suddenly appeared at my desk. Her eyebrows furrowed. "Is that a personal call?"

"I have to go," I said into the phone before slamming the handset down into the cradle. Vanessa had stepped out of a meeting with a group of studio executives in the main conference room.

"How can I help you?" I asked.

"I need you to run down to the file room and pick up some documents." She handed me a yellow Post-it Note with a series of numbers haphazardly scrawled on it. Her handwriting was terrible. *Dad should've busted out his checkbook and sent her to medical school.* I hustled off to catch an elevator to the second floor.

When I returned, *The Fairy Godmother's Rulebook* was open on my desk. No one was nearby, but the old vellum pages were open to reveal a woodcut etching of a fairyland scene faced with a thin slice of tissue paper. In the etching, a group of fairies floated above the ground in a circle around a regal-looking woman in a ball gown as they balanced a bejeweled tiara on her head.

Having had enough of it for now, I slammed the book shut and a cloud of glittering dust rose from the pages, making me woozy and giving me the sneezes. When I recovered from the sneezing fit, my ears itched as if I had poison ivy.

No surprise.

If the old book had anything to do with Mom, I was allergic to it and its contents. I stuffed the book back into my tote under my desk. Best to be forgotten. As soon as possible. I didn't have time for fairies ... or fairy tales. I didn't believe in them when I was a little girl, and I sure as hell wasn't going to start now.

"*The Fairy Godmother's Rulebook,*" I muttered under my breath. "As if."

Opening a new Excel document, I followed the procedures in the administrative manual for creating a new deal memo. Within seconds I was completely absorbed in my task, so I was caught off guard when a stranger appeared next to my desk.

"I saved you a slice."

I glanced up from the spreadsheet on my computer. A girl I'd never seen before had a paper plate filled with ice cream cake in her hand. In the relatively sheltered world of Stern, Fayed, and Lopez administrative assistants, she had to be brand spanking new.

"A slice?"

"Of your birthday cake." She smiled and offered me the plate.

Petite and slender as a ballerina with long dark hair and a shy smile, she was close to my age. Her almond-shaped eyes were outlined by thick lashes that made her look like an animated forest animal who might dart off to the safety of a forest glen at any time if startled.

"Mint chocolate chip ice cream with chocolate cake and frosting," she said.

"That's my favorite."

"We forgot it's your birthday until after we were done singing."

"No worries." Knowing my daily intake of calories had come from cake and nothing but cake.

Once she had done her part of delivering my slice, the girl made herself busy at the desk near mine that was usually occupied by my dad's second assistant, a position filled by a rotating cast of characters. She studied me with a curiosity so intense I was too self-conscious to keep eating. "Are you..." she hesitated. "... by any chance, related to Liliana Willowbrook?"

Shivers went up and down my spine. I wiped frosting from my lips before I answered. "She's my mom."

"Ruby Ramirez." She put her small hand out for me to shake. She had a surprisingly firm grasp for such a tiny person. Her dark gaze so intense. There was something otherworldly about her eyes. "I'm from Los Arboledas."

"Really?" I was surprised. "I don't think I've ever met

26

anyone from Los Arboledas other than my mom. Why did you move to Los Angeles? Are you dating someone down here?"

Ruby laughed then added rather cryptically, "'Happily ever after' is my purpose, not my future.'"

I didn't understand, but I didn't want to pry any further into the personal life of someone I had just met. I hoped our conversation would end right there, but Ruby's eyes sparkled like gemstones. "Your mom is a living legend in Los Arboledas."

Oh God. Please don't let her tell crazy stories in the office.

"She is one of a kind," I agreed with a fake smile. Now was not the time to air my dirty laundry.

"People from all over the world know her and come to Los Arboledas to see her." Ruby appeared to be immune to my sarcasm.

"Are you sure we're talking about my mom? She's a yoga instructor."

Ruby's laugh was bright, like notes on a musical scale. "She's so much more, and she talks about you all the time."

"For reals?" Again, I was surprised.

I couldn't remember ever being alone with Mom. During our brief visits, my dad always acted as a buffer between us, as if he was reluctant to let us be alone together. But how do I explain my family dynamics to someone I've just met? "She and I ..." My words halting and uncertain. "We're not ... close."

"I figured. Since you grew up here." Ruby unleashed a warm smile. "But you do look like her. A lot."

"Really?" It wasn't true. Mom looked like red-haired Christie Brinkley with lilac eyes like Elizabeth Taylor. She was spellbindingly beautiful. And I look like me. No one but a delusional stranger would ever guess we were related.

"In the eyes." She waved her fingers in front of my face as if performing a magic trick.

I smiled brightly, wondering how to bring this conversation to an end. "The rest of me is all my dad." "The Whale" would never be described as handsome, and neither would I.

Due to the mercurial personalities of both my dad and his assistant, Glenda. I didn't have the heart to tell her no one who ever occupied that chair ever stayed more than a few days.

"Are you Dad's new second assistant?"

She nodded. "But I'm just a temp. I won't be here long."

Truth. I smiled at her sheepishly. She seemed too sweet to be trapped between a rock and a hard place, which is the best way to describe Dad and Glenda.

Anxious to get away from Ruby's awkward inquiries, I grabbed a packet of stale ramen noodles from the bottom drawer in my desk and went into the break room to heat some water, hoping I'd also run into Keir Bell and Paul Jameson.

Keir was in contract administration. Paul worked in business affairs. The two divisions were on opposite sides of the building, which meant their paths hardly ever crossed. Keir was an office early bird, and Paul was one of the owls who stayed late every night, burning the midnight oil.

Six weeks ago, I noticed they were both reading *Brussels Hustle,* an epic love story about two diplomats from enemy nations who hook up hours before one of the despots they work for is murdered during a coup d'état.

I was certain all that was needed to create a romantic connection between Paul and Keir was a gentle nudge. So, I brought a copy of the book into the break room. I guess my luck had turned for the better, as they were both in the room. just as I had hoped.

"Hey? Is this your book?" I asked. Both of them turned to look at me.

"No. It isn't mine," Paul answered. "I only read ebooks."

I nodded to Keir. "But weren't you reading *Brussels Hustle?*"

"I finished it months ago," he said. "I love La Farrar. I've read all his books."

"Me too." Paul was looking at Keir as if he'd hung the stars in the sky.

"You know, La Farrar's new book is out next week," I added, hoping to encourage their conversation, but neither one heard me. The spark of interest had already been lit, and they didn't care that I was still in the room. Keir and Paul had settled at a table near the windows. Their eyes locked together.

I could feel it even from the other side of the break room. It was a bit like being trapped between the Millennium Falcon and the Death Star when the tractor beam was turned on. I had to escape, so, once they were done cooking, I took my noodles and ran.

To no one's surprise, Vanessa was waiting for me when I got back to my desk. "Where have you been?"

"I was on a break."

"Seemed super long." She huffed while checking the time on her iPhone. She didn't like to be kept waiting. "Be sure your time sheet accurately reflects it."

"Absolutely." I nodded. "Is there something you need?"

"I'm out of the office for the rest of the day," Vanessa said, speaking in a hushed tone. "I have a meeting on the Sony lot." She glanced over at Ruby. "But I'd like to keep it on the down-low. I'll be reachable on my cell until four. After that, can you handle any issues that might come up?"

"That's why I'm here," I assured her.

"Can you also pick up my dry cleaning on your way home?" she added as an afterthought. "I'll let you drive my car." She dangled her car keys from one finger in front of my face.

I snatched the keys from her hand. Not being at the

mercy of Uber during rush hour traffic in Los Angeles was a gift too great to ever decline. "I'm happy to do whatever you want."

"Thank you, Aviana." She spoke softly and was almost sincere. "I really do appreciate you."

Without any fanfare, she turned on her heel and disappeared down the long hallway leading out to the lobby elevators. I figured she might be doing some last-minute birthday shopping, so I didn't pry any further about her evening plans. Just in case I unwittingly spoiled my own surprise.

Despite my physical ailments, I was suddenly feeling very upbeat. Tonight, I'd celebrate with my family. Madeleine didn't cook, but she did have the number of every celebrity chef in town on speed dial, and she could cater the heck out of a dinner party. She considered it a matter of pride to make sure a cake was ordered from the best bakery in town days before any family birthday event. I closed my eyes and fantasized about chocolate ganache with buttercream frosting while I finished filing.

"How are you celebrating tonight?" Ruby asked, interrupting my sweet daydreams of sugary treats and frosting-covered baked goods.

"Beg pardon?"

Her question startled me. I wasn't used to having a conversation at the office focused on me.

"Your birthday?" Ruby reminded me with a warm smile. "Do you have plans with someone special?"

"No." I laughed ruefully. "With my family."

That's when reality smacked me upside the head like a frying pan.

All this time I'd been operating as if having a birthday dinner with my family was a foregone conclusion. The truth was, no one had made firm plans to celebrate with me tonight. In fact, no one in my family—other than my crazy mother—had called me all day.

I dialed Vanessa, but her cell phone was turned off. So,

I called Valerie's office to see if she knew anything about my birthday dinner. Val had no filter and couldn't keep a secret for all the money in the world. If someone had mentioned a family gathering for my birthday, she would tell me. She wouldn't be able to help herself.

"Val Stern's office." Her assistant picked up on the first ring.

"Hi. It's Aviana," I said. "Is she in?"

"Let me see if I can grab her for you." She put me on hold but returned a few seconds later. "I'm sorry. I can't get her. Do you want me to leave word?"

"Please. Can you ask her to call me when she gets a chance?"

"Sure thing," she said. "But I'm not sure if she'll be able to return your call today."

"For reals? Where is she?"

"Yooooouuuu knooooow …" she said, stretching out her words. She sounded exactly as I did when I was lying faster than my imagination could keep up. "I'm not sure, but I'll give her the message." She dropped the phone before I could say another word.

I dialed Madeleine's office, and then hung up. I didn't really want to talk to either one of her well-meaning assistants. I toyed with calling her on her cell phone but then decided against it. My stepmom wasn't demonstrably affectionate, but she hadn't ever been unkind. Over the years, I think she'd tried harder to be a good parent than either my father or mother. She had been there with me on the first day of kindergarten, and she had taken me to get my first driver's license.

A text acknowledging my birthday was *de rigueur* for Madeleine. I wasn't expecting anything with "X's" or "O's" from any of my family, but something along the lines of *HB2U! See you at Chow's.*

She was detail-oriented and über organized, and she had a team of assistants to help keep her on track. It wasn't like her to forget any events or family occasions.

"Hey, Ruby. Is my dad still in the office?" I asked.

She looked at me with wide eyes. "He left hours ago. Said he would be out of touch for the next few hours."

Huh. That was unusual, but still, Dad and Madeleine must be expecting me just to turn up at Mr. Chow's for my birthday celebration.

I checked the clock on the wall behind my desk. I would have to hurry to make it to the restaurant in time. I looked around the office. Dad's new second assistant and I were the only ones there. The rest of the support staff had already gone home for the day. I didn't think anyone would notice if I left a little early.

It was my birthday after all.

CHAPTER 3

Rule #3: A fairy godmother always asks, "Who needs my kindness most today?"

When I arrived at Mr. Chow's, I gave up the key fob for Vanessa's luxury sports car to the valet as if it was a rental—carelessly tossing the keys at the first guy who came toward me in a red jacket. I then hurried through the golden doors to find the bar full to overflowing. Groups of people lingered in the lobby, waiting to be seated. I pushed past them all and presented myself to the maître d' like I was a VIP.

"I'm meeting my parents for dinner," I said.

"Your father's name?"

"Hal Stern." I swear the entire restaurant went silent.

"The Whale?" he confirmed with all due reverence. "Right this way."

Without referencing the reservations tablet, the maître d' led me to a large table in the main dining room. It was not Dad's regular table where he and Madeleine could see and be seen. It was much larger.

A ripple of excitement shot through my body. Vanessa and Valerie must both be planning to show up. Having them included in the party would keep my father from focusing his attention on me and my lack of ambition. He was generally unable to speak about little else in my presence. This was a gift in and of itself ... and a welcome relief. I slid into the leather banquette and made myself comfortable.

The waiter arrived with glasses of water on a tray. "Can I get you something to drink while you're waiting for the rest of your party to arrive?"

"I don't suppose you have any ibuprofen on you?" I asked. "I'm kidding. I'm fine." My head still felt as if it was being split in two. I had been hoping for a sip of champagne tonight, but the last thing I needed was a drink. It would be like pouring gasoline on a fire. "Can I get an iced tea?"

He nodded and disappeared.

"Miss?" I looked up to see the maître d' hovering over the table. "Your stepmother canceled your family's standing dinner reservation for this evening two weeks ago. As you may be aware, she doesn't tolerate mistakes. Can you tell me how many will be in your party this evening?"

"But it's my birthday," I asserted. "We're always a party of five. I don't understand."

"Say no more," he said with a wave of his hand. "We will make all the necessary arrangements."

When the waiter returned, he brought an iced tea, a small tidbit plate with four ibuprofens, and a bowl of fried wontons with assorted dipping sauces. I loved this guy. I made a mental note to add some cash to Dad's tip at the end of the meal. He was a notoriously lousy tipper.

My spirits lifted. I was almost ebullient. Maybe I *was* getting a car for my birthday. After all, it was my twenty-first ...

I gasped.

Forget the car, Zara Wakefield was at a table on the other side of the dining room. She was one of the few celebrities I followed on Twitter. She had her own television show on HGTV and coordinated events with Michael Voltaggio and Gordon Ramsey. I'd seen her on *The Today Show* just last week broadcasting live from her store, Wisteria Wholesale.

She was the modern hipster bride's answer to Martha Stewart, and she was only in her mid-twenties. She was an amazing wedding and event planner. One of my favorite online guilty pleasures was scrolling through Pinterest images of the idyllic rustic weddings she'd styled. She set the trends the rest of the world followed.

Built like a cat with a dark cap of black hair, Zara was simply gorgeous, and happily sharing an egg roll with a broad-shouldered hottie. At least I assumed he was hot. Judging by everything she designed, Zara Wakefield wouldn't settle for anything less than absolute perfection, and there was no way a guy with shoulders like that could be anything less than perfect.

I leaned forward in my chair to get a better look at him. His profile was familiar, but I couldn't place him. All of a sudden recognition knocked the air from my lungs.

Nash Nolan.

Zara Wakefield was enjoying the company of my crush and his family. I recognized his dad. He was one of my dad's golfing buddies. And his mom … well, I could tell Nash had obviously gotten his sweet smile from her. She had the same shiny chestnut hair as his as well.

From across the room, the sound of Zara's tinkling laughter blending with Nash's baritone was like a gut punch to the stomach.

Ugh.

This wasn't how I thought my birthday dinner would be. In desperate need of reinforcements, I called my dad's office and got his answering service. I called the house phone, but our housekeeper didn't answer. I tried calling Dad and Madeleine, and then Vanessa and Valerie on their cell phones, but my calls went directly to voicemail as if all their phones had been switched off.

Forty-five minutes and an order of firecracker shrimp later, I declined the dessert menu and ordered a vodka martini. It was gradually sinking in that my family wasn't joining me. And just when my nightmare couldn't get any worse, it turned truly dark.

My waiter brought a slice of birthday cake to the table with great fanfare as a long parade of waiters followed him singing a chorus of "Happy Birthday" in phonetic Mandarin. Zara and Nash joined the other diners in the main room of the restaurant singing the birthday song, mumbling over the part of the lyrics where my name should be inserted.

Most of the restaurant staff dispersed as soon as the song was done. My waiter set five candles afire on top of the cake and pushed it over to me. "Make a wish."

"I don't think so," I replied. "I don't believe in magic or hocus-pocus-y stuff."

"Make a wish," the waiter insisted.

When I looked up, Nash was watching me. His full lips curled up at the corners into a smile, softening his angular features. His eyes focused on me. He was so dreamy that I was almost unable to tear myself away from his intense gaze. Fortunately, my phone vibrated inside my purse, and I huffed a sigh of relief.

Finally. Someone in my family had realized their terrible mistake and was calling to beg my forgiveness. I answered it without checking to see who was calling.

"Are you having fun?" Josie asked. How's the party going?"

My stomach dropped twenty stories when I heard Josie's voice. Fighting back tears, I gulped air before I could form words. "I'm at Mr. Chow's. I'm alone. And they just brought the cake."

"You're throwing a solo birthday party? In a place like Mr. Chow's? That's really pathetic."

"And Zara Wakefield is here," I said. "With Nash

Nolan."

"The travel app guy? Didn't you used to have a major crush on him?"

"Did. Still do," I insisted, overwhelmed by mixed emotions. "Not to drift off-topic, but where do you think my family could be?"

"Maybe they're planning a surprise party," Josie suggested.

"You'd think they would've called with some instructions by now," I said.

"But they know you never leave the office early, and if they call you and tell you to come home, it'll be ruined."

"That's why all of their phones are turned off," I said with a tone of mounting excitement in my voice. I was so Nancy Drew.

"Exactly," Josie agreed. "I'll meet you at the house."

"A surprise party," I said after clicking off. My heavy heart lifted. I had always wanted to be the guest of honor at a surprise party. It was all too marvelous for words.

Dad and Madeleine lived in the part of the Hollywood Hills known as the "Bird Streets"—an enclave of multi-million-dollar homes with amazing city views built on twisting and winding streets called Blue Jay Way and Skylark Avenue. Which was somewhat ironic because I was scared to death of birds. It was the wings. When they flapped, it totally freaked me out.

The ultra-contemporary house was dark when I punched the security code into the gate and pulled into the circular driveway. It was unusual. The house was completely still. No one, not even our housekeeper, Gardenia, was home.

Maybe the celebration was out in the back yard. Dad and Madeleine had built the best outdoor entertainment area money could buy in their tiny cement-lined back yard. It featured a black-bottomed infinity pool and breathtaking views of the city lights. But a quick glance told no one was in the garden.

Josie rolled up a few minutes after I did and rang me to open the security gate for her. I hiked around the front of the house and met her in front of the four-car garage.

"No one is here," I said.

"You've got to be kidding me. Are you sure it isn't just that the valet has done a really good job of hiding all of the cars?"

"I'm sure. Even Gardenia has the night off." I stood in the backyard spinning in a circle like Maria Von Trapp in the Swiss Alps with the sinking feeling that no surprise party had been planned. I was numb that I didn't even notice when my phone lit up with an incoming call.

"Your phone is ringing," Josie said.

I checked the caller ID. "It's my mother. She's been calling me all day."

"Did you talk to her?"

"Just for a minute," I said. "But I really … I'm not … I can't … deal with her today."

"I get it," Josie said, putting a supportive arm around my shoulders. All I wanted to do was go inside and tuck into bed, but I didn't want to seem ungrateful. Josie had been just as hopeful as I was about a party at home. "We must celebrate properly. Twenty-one is big deal. You have to eat cake, sip champagne."

Josie found the keys to my dad's wine cellar in the knife drawer in the kitchen, and after spending some time checking out the most expensive vintages, she picked out two bottles of French champagne. I didn't protest. It was my birthday after all.

We settled at the big table in the dining room. Josie relit the five candles on top of the slice of cake from Mr. Chow's and pushed it over to me.

"I already made my birthday wish," I said.

"What did you wish for?"

"Nash Nolan," I said, my cheeks heating with

embarrassment. "Sort of."

Josie rolled her eyes. "You might as well have wished for world peace. That's not going to happen either."

"Please, Josie, don't sugarcoat it for me. Give it to me straight." I giggled. There was no way I was going to be forced to make another birthday wish.

"Make another wish, but this time be more realistic. And don't tell me what it is, or it won't come true."

This was so hard. What did I *really* want?

A love? A life? A family? A career? Honestly, I'd settle for being able to find a purpose in this crazy-ass world. Who uses up a birthday wish for that?

"Go on," Josie insisted with dollar signs dancing in her eyes. "If you're going to wish for money, make sure you're very specific about the dollar amount."

It took me a long time to focus. In the end, I wished for my own happily ever after and blew out the candles in one go. As soon as the flames were extinguished, my phone buzzed again.

"You should've wished for your mom to stop calling you." Josie reached across the table to hit the ignore button on my phone for me.

"What makes you think I didn't?"

Josie washed down a bite of the cake with a big gulp of champagne out of a glass that could've been a comfortable home to four large koi fish. I sipped the champagne, but I couldn't finish the cake. I was overtired and a little nauseated again.

Out of nowhere, perhaps because she was tipsy, Josie blurted, "Have your ears always been pointy? You look a little like an owl."

"For reals?" I shook my head.

"Sorry. My bad. Now is not the time for criticism of any kind." Josie knew about my aversion to birds. She actually seemed contrite, which really wasn't her style.

My ears were itchy and my shoulders were achy. All I wanted was to go to sleep. Josie must have sensed it was time for her to go because she started gathering her things, including the second bottle of champagne, which she tucked under her arm.

I locked up the house and drifted back through the kitchen to my room. When I was in high school I'd taken over the room off the kitchen that had been used by our former au pair. I liked keeping a little distance between the rest of my family and me. It was a small room with tiny windows looking out to the brick wall around the neighbor's house, but it had its own bathroom and small private patio.

Before I tucked in, I took one last look in the mirror. Josie was right, my ears did make me look a little like a garden gnome in the bathroom light, but I was too tired to care as I pulled on my pajamas and tumbled into bed.

The house was so still. It was eerie and a little ... well, a little frightening. It was as if my entire family had been beamed up to another planet by aliens.

My forgotten birthday was completely forgiven. I was moving on to becoming seriously alarmed about my family's disappearance.

Had they been in an accident? Should I call the police and report them missing?

My anxiety kicked in, and I began to wonder if I would be a suspect in their disappearance? What would I wear at the press conference? Would the reporters notice my pointy ears and horn buds? Would I look guilty on camera? If so, could I style my hair to look less culpable?

Exhausted by my overactive imagination, I put my head down on the pillow and was asleep within seconds.

My dreams were filled with visions of dancing cupcakes and an assassin squad of long-winged owls who kept swooping down to attack my hair and face with their talons.

I don't know how long I had been asleep, but when I woke up, my cell phone was vibrating against the mattress. I managed to pick it up right before it went to voicemail.

"Aviana, darling?" It was Mom. I had to give her extra points for her tenacity, but seriously, it was after midnight.

"Mom." I was feeling churlish. "It's really late. What do you want?"

"We need to talk." She fired right back.

"Okay. I'll call you back when it's not the middle of the night." I ended the call without another word.

The next morning, I stretched awake then kicked off the covers and rolled over on my back, grabbing my fuzzy purple blanket and a couple of pillows from my bed. I pulled *The Fairy Godmother's Rulebook* out of the tote bag I'd left in the chair next to my bed and dragged it all with me out to the sofa in the living room.

Sitting on Madeleine's big white sofa was a big no-no. One of her long-standing house rules was "no sweats in the living room." She didn't own a bathrobe or "believed" in loungewear, and she was of the opinion that sweats in general were "filthy." I usually confined myself to the six thousand dollar vintage Eames chair. But not tonight. Wrapping myself up in the fuzzy blanket, I opened the book and settled back against the toss pillows.

Thumbing through the pages, I hoped to find a note or inscription inside to identify the owner. No such luck. I did find a lot of notes written in the margins. The handwriting varied—some tight and small—and was barely legible. Other words written with i's dotted with little red hearts were more distinguishable. The book must've passed through many hands over the years. I ran my fingers over the paper's marbled endpapers. The frontispiece featured some friendly woodland creatures, in a dark forest, gathered around a woman admiring her reflection in a cheval-looking glass propped against the wide trunk of a tree. I flipped past the table of contents to a list of rules and what appeared to be a code of conduct for fairy godmothers.

A fairy godmother joyfully embraces the knowledge "happily ever after" is her purpose, not her future.

Someone had quoted that recently.

Who? I couldn't remember.

I tried to keep reading, but the musty smell of the old book was like a sleeping pill. Or maybe it was glittering dust stuck in between all of the pages. Within seconds, I fell into a deep sleep.

The next time I stirred, the house was still and dark. *The Fairy Godmother's Rulebook* was open next to me on the sofa. Mesmerized by the pattern of lights dancing across the ceiling from the pool in the back yard, I came to the dawning realization I wasn't alone. Someone was in the house with me.

Maybe I was dreaming, but every time I came close to being fully conscious I had the terrifying feeling I was being watched. I tried to sit up, but I couldn't. It was as if I'd lost the use of my limbs. I kept drifting in and out of sleep. Then a shadow moved over me and soft hands brushed against my face. I couldn't move, and no matter how hard I tried, I couldn't make a sound.

"Look at her ears," a man said in a hissing whisper.

"She's almost reached full maturity," a woman whispered in response.

A pair of hands gently pushed my hair back over my shoulders. A hand lightly touched my shoulders, gently moving over the raw, bumpy skin protruding out of the middle of my back.

"She's fledgling. It won't be long now," a woman whispered once more. "No more than forty-eight hours."

I struggled to become fully awake. It was as if I had been drugged. I laid on the sofa paralyzed with fear until I slipped back to sleep.

My stepmother would not approve of my fuzzy blanket fort, but she had disappeared, and so, as far as I was concerned, had her rules.

CHAPTER 4

Rule #4: A fairy godmother never exposes her magical gifts to the world of non-believers.

I woke up just before dawn in a puddle of sweat and feathers. One of my down pillows must've exploded in the night. I swept up the feathers along with the pillow I suspected was leaking and put the whole mess in the trash in the kitchen.

A gray mist still blanketed the city. Although I couldn't see it, I knew traffic was moving on the streets below our neighborhood. Traffic in LA was the one constant you could always count on.

Dad and Madeleine hadn't come home, and Gardenia wasn't here. It was all so very strange. She was usually puttering around the kitchen, but this morning it was quiet. Gardenia was obviously better informed about my own family's schedule than I was. It was very disturbing.

Where could they be?

I was drifting in and out of sleep when the sofa cushions began trembling from an incoming call on my cellphone. I blindly patted under the blanket to find my phone.

I sat up and held the phone close to my ear. "Hello."

"Aviana, dear, it's Madeleine." Her voice was as sweet as honey.

"Are you all right?" I blurted. My voice cracking with emotion.

"We're fine, darling. Everything there okay?" She sounded bright and light.

"I'm fine," I said. "But I tried to reach you and Dad yesterday, and I got worried when I wasn't able to connect."

"I know. We were on the plane." She was very matter-of-fact.

I couldn't comprehend her answer. It was as if I missed a memo. "I didn't know you were going out of town. I couldn't reach Vanessa or Valerie either."

"Yes. We all had our phones turned off."

"Valerie and Vanessa are with you?" The information she was providing didn't make any sense.

"We rented a seaside villa in Cabo San Lucas. Didn't your father tell you?" She laid the blame for any and all confusion I was having squarely at Dad's feet. "He was supposed to tell you."

"No," I said. "He didn't say a word." Was she kidding me? Dad never talked to me. Not if he could help it. How could she not know that we didn't talk? After all, she was the only conduit of communication the two of us had over the past fifteen years.

"Do you need something, dear?" she asked. "I wasn't sure why you called. Your messages sounded a little ... desperate."

I was speechless.

My family, who I had feared were dead for the last few hours, was, in fact, alive and well, drinking margaritas and eating street tacos on the Mexican Riviera while I was home celebrating my birthday alone.

"No," I said after a long pause. "No, Madeleine. I'm fine. I wanted to check in, you know, to make sure you're all okay and you had a safe trip."

"Oh, that's so nice of you, dear. We're all fine. Your father and Vanessa are going to play golf this afternoon while Valerie and I go shopping."

"Sounds fun."

"This trip was your father's idea. He thought it would be nice for us to get away, you know, before Valerie gets married and Vanessa gets a big promotion—while it's still just the four of us." Madeleine was speaking very fast, as if telling me the truth this way would be like a Band-Aid being ripped off, and it would hurt me less. It didn't. "Of course, we were going to include you, dear, but Vanessa insisted you don't take time off from work. She says it gives her comfort to know you're in the office when she isn't."

"Of course it does." I spoke through gritted teeth remembering how Vanessa had slipped me her car's key fob on her way to "a meeting" as if she was doing me a favor. I was shocked that even Vanessa hadn't let on about the trip, rather let me think she'd been on a work assignment. Not to mention how she used my own work ethic against me.

Grrr.

"It's so lovely here," Madeleine continued without taking a breath. "So idyllic. You'd love it."

"I'm sure I would." If only I'd been given the opportunity to come along. A tropical vacation? "What's not to love?"

"I'll tell your father I spoke with you, unless you want to speak with him yourself? Did you have something to tell him?"

I had so many things I wanted to say to my father. Every day for the past twenty-one years, he never skipped going into the office. If only for a couple of hours. And now on my birthday, he finally takes a vacation and goes to Cabo. Without me.

"No, Madeleine, I have nothing to say to Dad." There

was no way. Right at that moment I didn't think I'd be able to string together anything other than two-word sentences beginning with a four-letter word and ending with "you."

"All right then. When we get back you'll have to have dinner with us at the house and tell us all about your counseling appointment. Dad will want to know if he's getting a return on his investment, and you don't have to work late every night, Aviana. We're free any night next week, I think, except Wednesday. Wednesday is our 'date night' at Mr. Chow's. We have a standing reservation, just for two. Tell Gardenia which night is good for you. She knows our schedule.."

Then she hung up without saying goodbye.

I threw my phone across the room, where it landed safely on top of the buttery leather upholstery of the Eames chair. I marched into the powder room and grabbed a box of Kleenex, balancing on the edge of the sofa, anticipating a storm of tears. But the crying never happened. It was almost as if I didn't have any tears to waste.

Not for Dad. Not for Madeleine or for either one of my stepsisters.

It wasn't news to me that I was "Aviana Willowbrook" and Vanessa and Valerie were both "Sterns." I had always thought it was odd. I was his daughter by blood. "Willowbrook" was my mother's maiden name, and my parents were married when I was born. "The Whale" had adopted Valerie and Vanessa and given them his last name. By all rights, I should be a "Stern" too.

Why hadn't I ever questioned my role in my family?

The truth was staring me right in the face. I wasn't a part of this family. I was my mother's daughter. They were a family of four, not a party of five. A perfectly matched set. I was the unwanted add-on. All these years I'd been wrong. My role in the family wasn't Cinderella. I was the other one.

I was the wicked stepsister.

It was a long time before I mustered the energy to face the day. I retrieved my cell phone and did something I'd never done before in my life. I called in sick. I had no idea it was so easy. I left a message on the Human Resource Department's voicemail saying I wasn't feeling well and I wouldn't be coming in to the office. It sounded totally legit to me. I poured a big cup of coffee, filled to overflowing with cream and sugar. Dressed in my favorite sweats, I went back out into the living room.

For the next twenty-four hours I didn't answer my phone and ignored all incoming texts. I ordered pizza for lunch and Thai for dinner. I had it all delivered via Postmates. I ate ice cream out of the carton. I binge-watched all of my guilty pleasure television: *Terrace House*, *Dr. Pimple Popper*, and *'90 Day Fiancé*. And I did it all while wrapped up in a cotton candy cloud of bliss in my forbidden blanket fort on Madeleine's twenty thousand dollar ice-white sectional sofa.

Friday morning, I woke relaxed and rested, but without any motivation to return to the office. Take a four-day weekend? Don't mind if I do. The rest of my family had gone on a luxurious five-day weekend in Mexico, why couldn't I spend four days at home? It took less than thirty seconds to leave another message on the oh-so-convenient HR voicemail. When my phone rang two hours later, I was in the middle of a game of Minecraft. I picked up without checking the caller ID.

"Aviana? What is going on?" Vanessa demanded. "Where are you? Why aren't you in the office?"

"I'm home. I'm sick." I faked a cough for emphasis.

"Seriously? You're never sick," Vanessa said.

"I am today. I'm really, really sick."

"Okay. Well, I was really, really counting on you to be in the office while I was gone so you could get some things done." Vanessa prattled on with a list of tasks for me to work on. "And could you respond to—"

"Could you hold on a minute, Vanessa? I need to take this phone call."

"Don't you dare—" Vanessa began, but I clicked over to the other line without waiting for her to finish.

"Hello?" I said with a forced smile, knowing it was my mother.

"Aviana? Is everything okay?" she asked.

"I'm fine. I'm fine. Just busy," I lied.

"You always are. I worry about you; I am your mom."

"I know. I … thank you." I stopped myself. I was going to say "I love you," but I wanted to be honest. I hardly knew her. *How could I say I loved her?*

"How are you feeling?" she asked.

"Not bad." The bumps between my shoulder blades were bigger than ever and my ears itched, but I had decided to ignore my symptoms.

"I hope you're taking care of yourself. You know when you get on a plane, how they have the safety video telling you to 'adjust your own oxygen mask before helping others?'" she asked. "It's not just good advice for airplanes, Aviana. It's good for real life too. You need to tend to yourself before you can help other people."

I started to cry. I wandered out to the kitchen to get a Kleenex out of the box Gardenia kept on top of the refrigerator.

"As long as you are happy and doing well and enjoying your life—I am happy," she said. "I won't bother you anymore, Aviana. I promise."

"I'm fine." I was sobbing with tears and snot falling down my face.

"Aviana, I am your mother. And I am a much better liar than you are. I know you're not fine."

"Okay, I'm not fine. I'm seriously unhappy," I said. "And I haven't been happy for a long time, but Dad thinks you're crazy, and I don't feel like I know you well enough to tell you the truth."

There. I said it.

"I know, darling," she said. And to my surprise, she didn't sound shocked or angry. "It's all my fault. I'm so sorry. I want to tell you so many things. There is so much you need to know."

"It's okay," I said. "I shouldn't have gotten so angry with you. None of this is your fault."

"It is all my fault, Aviana. I take full responsibility for the way you're feeling right now."

"No. It's me, Mom," I said as I wandered through the kitchen and into my small bedroom. She shouldn't blame herself for my inability to grow up and find a purpose. "I've been in a holding pattern. I need to make some career choices. I'm twenty-one. I can't goof off anymore."

My call waiting beeped again. According to my caller ID, it was my other sister, Valerie. She was usually the voice of reason. Maybe she'd offer a plausible explanation for why they had all gone off to Mexico without me.

"Can you hold on for a sec, Mom?" I clicked over to the other call before she answered. "Hey, Val. Hold on. I'm wrapping up with my mother."

"It's not Valerie. It's Vanessa." She was so angry, she hissed her words like a snake. "I'm using her phone because I knew you wouldn't pick up if you knew I was calling, you big fake faker."

Oh, the irony. "Hold on."

"Don't put me—" she started to say before I clicked back to Mom's call. I honestly had nothing else I wanted to say to Vanessa.

"Mom, are you still there?"

"I'm here, Aviana," she responded. "But please, promise me you won't put me on hold again."

"I promise," I said.

My headache was back, unbearable pain throbbing at my temples. I ran my fingers over the tendons in my neck and down toward my shoulders, kneading the tender flesh.

The two lumps between my shoulders were now the size of crabapples. I dropped to my knees on the floor and howled in pain, unable to censor my yelps.

"What's wrong, Aviana?" Panic made her voice rise by several octaves.

"I think I'm dying." It was a bit hyperbolic, but my mom was fussing over me. Not gonna lie, I was enjoying it a bit.

"What's happening? Be specific."

I stumbled over my own words. "I've got this terrible headache. It won't go away."

"For how long? How long have the headaches been going on?" Her voice was shrill.

"I don't know, a couple of weeks, maybe."

"Anything else?" she asked. "What are your other symptoms?"

"Headache. Itchy ears. Back acne. And I've been having trouble sleeping," I said.

"I see. That does sound bad."

"Yes." I was relieved she recognized my symptoms. It didn't matter that she didn't have a medical degree. Or that my dad said she was crazy. She was my only family … at least it felt that way at the moment. "The lumps on my back have gotten so huge, and they hurt so much. I think maybe I should go see a doctor."

"No," my mom shrieked, her tone more serious than it'd ever been in my life. "No. Aviana, no matter what happens, you mustn't go to the doctor."

My mother doesn't want me to see a doctor? What kind of parenting is that?

"What else can I do?" I asked. "I'm sick. I could be dying."

"Is your father there? Put him on the phone."

"No," I said. "He's not here."

"What about Madeleine?"

"She's not here either. They're gone."

"What do you mean 'they're gone?' Where is your

father? I specifically told him he had to be with you on your birthday. This is *the* year. Are you telling me he wasn't there?"

"They went to Mexico. Just the four of them. Stepsister not included." I spoke with my teeth gritted so I wouldn't tempt any more tears of self-pity.

"What about your birthday? How did you celebrate?"

"I had dinner alone," I said. "No big deal." I lied.

"Why didn't you tell me?" Mom stuttered with indignation.

"Why would I tell you? I hardly even know you," I lashed out, unable to prevent myself. She was the only person around to inflict my anger on.

She took a deep calming breath. "I understand you're upset, Aviana. You have every reason to be. Being alone on any birthday can be very upsetting let alone a milestone birthday like your twenty-first. But I don't think you need to go to the doctor." The tone of her voice had completely changed.

"But I'm probably dying." I sounded like a spoiled, petulant child, but I didn't care. There will be no one with me when I take my last breath. I would die alone. I wanted my mother to feel bad.

Should I clean up the living room and get my affairs in order before my family gets home and finds the body? Or should I let them deal with the mess when they get home?

"You're not dying, Aviana," she said. "Your life is just beginning."

I sat down on the edge of the bed and put my head between my legs. I was hyperventilating. I had lost my filter. "How can you say that? You don't know anything about my life."

"You have a point." She sounded patient. "Maybe you need to take time off work."

"I called in sick yesterday. And again, this morning."

"Good," she said. "That's a big step in the right direction. Why don't you come up for a visit? Los

Arboledas is lovely this time of year. You can relax and we can celebrate your birthday. Together."

"I don't think so," I said. "I'm not really feeling up to it."

"There are things I need to tell you, Aviana. Things you must know," she said. "Before you get any further into …"

"Further into what?" I asked.

She didn't answer. I could hear her breathing, but she didn't speak one word.

"Mom, I'm waiting," I prompted. "Give me a little clue. Some kind of hint. I need a reason to trust you. Anything in that department would be appropriate here."

"I really think we need to speak, Aviana. In person," Mom implored. "Come to Los Arboledas and bring the rulebook with you."

"Mom, it's just. It's not possible."

"I'm being completely honest, no matter what your father has told you. You need to be here. We haven't got any time to waste."

"You seem to think that I want to hear what you have to tell me. That I might enjoy a trip to Los Arboledas. And that is where you are wrong. I don't."

"Aviana, listen to me …" Mom was persistent.

"No. I don't want to hear what you have to say. And more importantly, I don't *care* what you have to say."

"This is a matter of life and death, Aviana," she urged, "We haven't got any time to waste."

I involuntarily rolled my eyes. I couldn't help it. Mom was being so heavy-handed with the drama cover-stick.

"Look. If I'm being completely honest, I don't know you. I don't want to hear what you have to say."

"But…" She struggled to respond, and I cut her off.

"No buts, Mom. Seriously. If you really wanted me to listen to you, you shouldn't have abandoned me when I was five."

"That's not true." she protested. "I didn't leave you

without a fight. Your father has been lying to you."

I shook my head. "It doesn't matter, Mom. I can't do this."

"But ..."

"I'm not coming up there, Mom. Not now, not ever. And there is nothing you can do or say to get me to Los Arboledas." Before I was able to get another word out of my mouth, I heard the tones signaling someone waiting outside the security gate at the street. "Someone is here. I have to go."

Thinking it was my pizza from Mulberry Street, I pressed the star symbol to let them in. Then I found my wallet and walked to the front of the house.

I opened the door and was shocked to see the person standing on the welcome mat. I didn't know what to say.

What was she doing at my house?

CHAPTER 5

Rule #5 A fairy godmother knows the limits of her powers.

"What are you doing here?"

My dad's temporary second assistant, Ruby Ramirez, was standing on the welcome mat. I honestly never expected to see her again in my life. She was, after all, just a temp.

Ruby didn't answer right away. She was having trouble maintaining eye contact, peeking over my shoulder at my blanket fort in the living room.

"I brought Valerie's dry cleaning. You forgot to pick it up the other day. So, the cleaners delivered it to the office. I thought I'd bring it by the house. You know … just in case."

"Just in case … what?" I asked.

She looked stumped. "In case of … an emergency?"

Her answer made my eyebrows go up. She was sweet and guileless, but she was so obviously lying.

When Ruby smiled, it was as if she'd been living in an animated cartoon with a happily-ever-after-ending her entire life—but her eyes were taking in every bit of visual information in the house behind me. I took a step forward and closed the door over.

"Thanks," I said.

I was anxious for her to leave, even though Ruby didn't seem threatening in any way.

I started to close the door, but Ruby stuck her shoe in the door. "Wait."

"You need to go," I said, pushes the door closed.

"But I need to ask you a question," she stammered.

"What do you want?" I was willing to give her the benefit of the doubt.

"How are you feeling?" she asked.

"Who wants to know?"

"You've been out of the office for two days." She studied my face … my ears.

"I'm feeling much better. Thank you again for bringing Valerie's stuff. I'll buzz you out through the gate."

There was something different about her. Something I couldn't quite put my finger on. I didn't know her at all, but I felt like she had me under her spell. I wanted to be as far away from her as soon as possible, and yet I didn't want to be rude.

Just as I was about to close the door on her, all of the stress I'd been carrying around for weeks returned in full force. It manifested as a sucker punch to the stomach. The pain was so sharp it dropped me to my knees.

"Aviana? Are you there?" Ruby shouted from the other side of the door, about to let herself into the house.

"No," I shouted. I was still on my knees. "Please, Go away."

Tingles of ice shot through my fingers, up my arms, freezing my torso. My breath was slowly being squeezed out of me, and I couldn't expand my lungs to breathe. There was nothing I could do. My body was wracked with convulsions, I shuddered uncontrollably.

The tips of my ears burned as though they were on fire and the spit in my mouth was sticky like glue. My cheeks were so heated, I looked like Clifford the Big Red Dog.

I gasped for air, my breath coming in short bursts. The splitting headache I'd been fighting for the past few weeks, came back and forced my eyes closed. The bumps on my back were actually raised to a point now where they were pressing through the fabric of my shirt.

I was struck by a sudden stabbing pain between my shoulder blades. It was so sharp, I twisted my body like a contortionist in search of the knife I was sure had to be protruding from my back.

I opened my mouth. I wanted to shout for help. I wanted to scream in pain, but I couldn't. All I could do was moan. It was the sound a wild animal makes when it's hurt and injured and caught in a trap. Then out of the corner of my eye, I saw something or someone inside the house moving.

It was Ruby. She'd followed me back inside the house.

"Aviana? You're going to be all right. I'm here. I'm here for you," Ruby said. She was the last person I wanted to see, but I was desperate.

"I need a doctor."

"I'm going to help you," Ruby said. "You can trust me."

"There's an urgent care on La Cienega, two blocks up."

"It's going to be all right," she soothed.

Another wave of nausea flooded my body. I closed my eyes, waiting for it to pass, but it didn't.

I raced to the bathroom just in time to be sick. Every morsel of food I had eaten in the tranquility of my blanket fort left my body in a hurry. When the violent contractions of my stomach finally came to an end, I flopped onto the floor, my body was spasming and shaking like a freshly caught fish. Pressing my face onto the cool tiles in the bathroom, I wished for it to all be over soon.

"Do you need anything?" Ruby asked.

I needed a cold washcloth and some Pepto-Bismol. Not necessarily in that order. "I'm fine," I whispered.

"Please go away."

"You're going to be okay," she soothed. "You're emerging from Chrysalis." She was speaking in a foreign tongue.

"Emerging from what?" I asked.

She checked over her shoulder once or twice. Her nervous behavior was infectious and caused me to look around as well. We were alone.

"Chrysalis," she repeated quietly.

"I don't know what you're talking about," I said.

She looked down at her hands, becoming fidgety and nervous. "My bad. I didn't know you didn't know. I thought your mom would've explained a bit …" She stopped herself and re-grouped. "I'm sorry. I don't know what I was thinking actually."

"Something dreadful is happening to me," I said. "Can you get Josie? The number is in my phone. Tell her I need to go to an urgent care."

Ruby didn't make a move. "You're going to be okay," she soothed.

Why didn't she understand? Panic set in, and I couldn't breathe once again. I dropped to all fours, panting like a dog.

Just when I thought things couldn't get worse, a sudden rush of air came behind me. Feathers showered down around me.

"What is happening?" I shrieked. "What is happening to me?"

She reached for my hand. "Hang on," she said. "It's going to be okay."

God, could she say anything else? It certainly didn't feel like everything was going to be okay. I'm dying here …

A moment later, someone screamed. Bloodcurdling screams. It was another moment or two before it became clear the person screaming at the top of their lungs was me, and it didn't take me long to realize why. Ruby was transfixed by whatever was waving above my head.

"Wings," she said. "You have wings."

"Wings?" Confused, I gathered all of my strength in order to look in the mirror. The air space above my head that was usually vacant was now filled with a pair of feather-covered wings.

I had wings. They were real. I had wings.

I don't know how long I stood in front of the mirror staring at my own reflection.

"What is happening to me?"

I dropped to my knees, desperate to get away from them, but they came with me. Bashing me in the head over and over again. I screamed every time they flapped over my head.

Up until two days ago, I didn't think my life could get any more miserable, but this ... this was worse than anything I could've imagined.

Having horn buds on my back was bad. But wings? I couldn't think of anything worse. Me. The chick with the phobia about being pecked to death, or even worse, flapped to death by a wild pack of winged creatures actually was one.

This was my worst nightmare come true.

I took a deep breath, and then another. Nothing chased away my anxiety. If anything, it intensified. At this rate, I'd be hyperventilating in a matter of minutes. I was unable to control them.

Feathers, bits of skin and sinew rained down around me. It was the last thing I remembered before I hit the marble floor in the front hall.

Unconscious.

When I woke up, Ruby was sitting next to me. She handed me her phone. "Your mom wants to talk to you."

"Mom. Something is wrong. I need help."

"Aviana, there's no time. " Mom said. "Come to Los Arboledas, and I'll explain."

"No." I was being stubborn.

"You can't deny who you are." She was being calm.

I ended the call and shoved the phone rudely back to Ruby. She took it without a word. I got to my feet and stood in front of the mirror in the front hall.

"This is horrible." I brushed my hair back behind my pointy ears and got another shock. I watched my wings change color in the mirror. They changed from flesh-tone into a rainbow of colors before turning bright red and unfurling to their full height.

"Your wings are very beautiful," Ruby said.

"I don't understand what is happening to me."

"Come with me. I'll take you to Los Arboledas. We … your mom can help you." Ruby spoke to me like I was an upset toddler, which seemed more than appropriate.

I sat back down on the floor and Ruby shoved a bottle of water in my hands. I took a few deep gulps and then reached for my phone and called Josie. She answered on the first ring, and then I quickly filled her in on my planned trip to Los Arboledas.

"You're not up for this, Aviana. It's way outside your comfort zone," Josie insisted. "You're hardly brave enough to drive on the streets of Los Angeles."

Josie didn't take a breath. Her words discouraging me from going off to see my mom followed me from room to room while I collected my things and stuffed them into an open suitcase on my bed.

"No one willingly gets on the freeway in Los Angeles at four o'clock in the afternoon unless they've got a good reason. Or a death wish." She made a good point.

"Yes, but Mom said it was a matter of life or death. And I…" How do I explain the dramatic appearance of new appendages on my back to my best friend? "I think I should go see her as soon as possible."

"It better be," Josie said. "If you manage to make it up there in one piece, are you prepared for whatever might happen in Los Arboledas?"

I stopped counting socks into my backpack and looked up at her. "What about Los Arboledas?

"It has a reputation—"

If one more person told me how enchanting Los Arboledas was, I was going to lose it. I cut her off before she could finish her thought. "For sloshy wine-tasting tours."

"Be serious, Aviana. It's not just the wine Los Arboledas is known for. Things happen there. Things that can't be explained by science."

"What are you talking about?" I asked, as if I didn't have a clue.

"C'mon. You've seen the travel ads, haven't you? Los Arboledas is the most romantic spot on earth. Where happily ever after happens every day," she sang the jingle we were both familiar with from late-night TV shows.

"What's wrong with that?" I protested.

"A place devoted to that much happiness must have a much darker and angrier side," Josie explained. "Ying and yang. It's the way of the world."

"I appreciate your concern. I really do. But my family ran away from home on my birthday. I think I get a hall pass to do something completely out of the ordinary." I couldn't tell her about my wings. To be honest, I wasn't sure how I'd ever start that conversation. But there was one person who could help me ... my mom. This was all her fault. I pushed down my fear and anger and simply focused on answers. Wings? Fairy? I needed answers.

"Okay," Josie decided. "You can do this, but you should be prepared and on your guard."

"For what?" I really hoped Josie had an answer.

"I have no idea. But my money's on something completely crazy."

If she only knew. "You're right. I know you're right."

"Text me when you get there," she said. "Or call if you need help."

I ended the call and went to find Ruby in the front hall. She'd gathered some towels, cleaning products from the laundry room, and was on hands and knees in an attempt to clean up the mess I'd made when I'd … feathered? I couldn't remember the exact term she'd used.

"Thank you," I said. "For doing this. You really have gone out of your way."

She smiled, and I felt as if everything I'd ever done was forgiven. "It's no problem she said. I think most of the mess happened here on the marble, but there's a bit of blood on the white carpet in the living room that isn't going to come up easily."

I snorted. That would seriously piss off Madeleine, and right now I couldn't care less. "Please don't worry about it. My stepmom isn't that fussy."

Ruby stood up, blinking at me with her big animated doe eyes. She'd been very nice, and wasn't at all frightened of my current predicament. If I was going to go to Los Arboledas, it wouldn't be bad to have her as my guide.

I'd heard a lot about Los Arboledas, which was nestled into the Santa Ynez Mountains north of Santa Barbara. People ventured north from Los Angeles on weekends to go on sloshy wine-tasting tours. If they were able to afford it, they stayed at the Los Arboledas Inn, where my mom worked. A sprawling luxury resort with a reputation as a popular weekend getaway for people with money to spare, serviced by staff with impeccable discretion.

Sure, my mom hadn't been actively involved in my life since I was five years old. But she was the only member of my immediate family who had remembered my birthday, and she lived in the most beautiful part of California. Plus, I was running out of things to do at home by myself. A trip might be just the thing.

When my anger toward my mother subsided, I had two choices. To stay in my blanket fort or go visit my crazy, albeit absentee, mother in the heart of wine country.

The keyword influencing my final decision to go to Los Arboledas was "wine."

I was currently sporting two extra appendages on my back, and I had questions. A lot of questions. Whatever

Mom had to say to me, I thought I might be able to tolerate it under the influence of a couple of glasses of a nice cabernet. Or Merlot. If nothing else, I would spend the weekend deliriously and deliciously drunk.

CHAPTER 6

Rule #6: A fairy godmother knows she is a one-of-a-kind blend of magic.

Only people who've lived in Los Angeles can truly understand how desperate or crazy you have to be to get on the freeway at rush hour and point the car to the choke point where the 405 Freeway meets the 101. It is an extreme act of defiance. No sane person would risk it unless it was a matter of life and death.

Which is why I was so willing to turn the key fob to Vanessa's car over to Ruby. I wasn't in any condition to drive. Physically I felt like I'd just gone five rounds against an MMA fighter. But Ruby looked bright-eyed and alert. I didn't even ask her if she knew how to drive or had a license. I was done being Vanessa's indentured servant.

Traffic was miserable as we turned onto the 405 and chugged up the Sepulveda Pass. We were moving so slowly; our speed didn't register on the car's electronic dashboard. Once we were West on the 101 Freeway, traffic was moving a little easier. All the lanes opened up when the freeway hit the Pacific Ocean and turned north toward Santa Barbara where the freeway faded into a four-lane road.

I contemplated asking Ruby to make a U-turn near Goleta. I was getting cold feet. Maybe I could simply go back to my old life and pretend I didn't have wings. Nothing good would come of seeing Mom. Dad and Madeleine would be home from Mexico soon with a perfectly good excuse for forgetting my birthday. We could sit down on the forbidden sofa and hash everything out. I would air my grievances, they would share their hopes and dreams for my professional life, and the moment would end in a group hug. Oh, and of course, with tears in his eyes, Dad would get down on bended knee and promise to be the dad I'd always hoped he would be.

Wouldn't he?

My mom was, as my father would be quick to point out, a complete nut job. I knew that. And I wasn't sure I needed to be drawn into her drama right now when I was feeling so fragile.

But I had wings. And pointy ears. I didn't know how Dad would deal with that. So I didn't say a word. And neither did Ruby. We continued north in silence.

The sun was setting over the Pacific Ocean when I first noticed the castle, it looked as if it was levitating above the ground on an ocean mist in the distance. Golden spires rising to the sky created points of light so bright they were almost like a second sun.

I gasped at the sight of an old Spanish-style castle with a red tile roof and white stucco walls.

"What is that?" I asked, pointing into the distance.

"El Encanto," Ruby stated flatly.

"A castle?"

Ruby nodded. "Yes. It's a tourist attraction in Los Arboledas. It's privately owned, so no one can get near it, but people love to take photographs of it from the beach."

"I've seen those photographs," I said.

"It's abandoned. Has been for many years ..." Ruby spoke with an air of mystery in her voice.

"Is that the truth?"

Ruby grinned. "What do you think?"

I rubbed my eyes. "I think everyone in Los Arboledas has a bit of trouble with the truth."

Maybe Ruby was right. It didn't matter if she was telling me the truth or not. "Even if it's nothing but a ghost story, you should definitely keep the wishes-come-true part," I said.

"Los Arboledas will make a believer out of you yet," Ruby said. "Everyone loves a 'once upon a time' story and a happily-ever-after ending."

"You should make a wish," Ruby said.

"Why?"

"In Los Arboledas wishes made when the sky is pink generally come true."

"That is a big bowl of lies," I corrected.

"I'm not kidding," she said with a grin. "The 'pink moment' is actual fact. It's a geographical phenomenon that happens when the fading sunlight is captured and reflected into the valley by the west-facing mountain range."

The clouds around the abandoned castle turned into pink cotton candy before my eyes, and the ever-changing color continued to take my breath away.

I closed my eyes, but I didn't make a wish. For the first time, I was afraid it might come true.

Mom called when we were exiting the freeway into Los Arboledas. "There's been a slight change in plans," she said. "There's an event at the inn tonight I can't get out of. I'm so sorry I can't be home to meet you."

"It's okay, Mom." I tried to keep any emotion out of my voice. Three hours ago, this trip was a matter of life and death. Now that I was almost there, she wasn't home? What is up with that? I probably should've expected nothing less. "Please make yourself at home," she said.

"Fix yourself something to eat and take a bath in the spa tub in my room. I'll be home as soon as I can."

What kind of game was she playing?

Maybe "The Whale" was right. Maybe she was completely insane in the brain. My mom was an unknown commodity. I'd never had to deal with her on my own.

Ruby pointed out her favorite restaurants and coffee shops as we drove through Los Arboledas. Five blocks from the flower-filled park at the center of town, Ruby pulled into the driveway of a little Victorian cottage with a curved thatched roof and delicate gingerbread on the front porch. The house my mom lived in looked like something out of a storybook fairytale.

Suddenly nervous, I straightened my shoulders and gathered my luggage out of the trunk. Ruby lived within walking distance, but she'd offered to stay with me to ease my nervousness. "Are you sure you don't want me to stay with you?"

"I'll be fine. I promise. Go home," I assured her. "I'm going to go right to sleep. Thank you for driving … and for everything else."

As soon as she left I faced the house. The shadows of night turned the quirky little gingerbread cottage into something that more closely resembled a haunted house.

Mom kept a spare key under a pot of flowers on her front porch. And after groping under a dozen moldy pots, I finally found the spare key under some pansies and unlocked the front door.

The living room was filled with dainty furniture. There was an old-fashioned hi-fi console in the corner along with a collection of vintage vinyl and some kind of crazy goddess sculpture on the fireplace mantle.

I deposited my belongings in the tiny guest room and then returned to the kitchen. I opened the doors of the massive stainless-steel side-by-side refrigerator to make myself a snack. I had skipped lunch and I was starving.

"Whoa."

The top two shelves of the fridge contained a dozen gallon jugs of milk. It was just a guess, but Mom was not lactose intolerant. There were a dozen bottles of water on a lower shelf arranged in neat rows as you'd see in a convenience store. A carton of yogurt in the door looked like it was all well past its expiration date. Two bottles of Perrier-Jouet champagne tucked inside one of the door panels caught my eye.

Finally. I've found the one thing my parents have in common: expensive taste in champagne.

Other than the champagne, Mom's fridge was a big disappointment. It was the complete opposite of the fridge at my dad and Madeleine's house. Their fridge was always fully stocked with the basics and frequently also included leftover containers full of yummy delicacies from places like Mr. Chow's and Pizzeria Mozza.

Having had no luck with the fridge, I took a peek into Mom's walk-in pantry. All the shelves were completely bare except for three large tubs of Nutella. Two green apples and a couple of oranges were starting to show their age. They were on the same bare shelf with a geriatric bag of fusilli pasta.

Who needs that much Nutella?

She also had four full shelves of spices and herbs. Martha Stewart, eat your heart out. Lavender, rosemary, fennel, and caraway seeds in oversized mason jars stood next to bottles filled with oils of marjoram and myrrh. I held up one bottle and peered inside its murky depths. Not kidding. Something inside was looking back at me. I quickly put the bottle back on the shelf and shut the door of the pantry.

What is my mother cooking in her kitchen?

There was nothing I wanted to eat in the house. The open doors to the back yard beckoned to me. I wandered out into the garden. As soon as I stepped outside, I was overwhelmed by the sweet and spicy scent of orange blossoms and jasmine vines, while the blooms of a bougainvillea added brilliant color. Beneath the orange tree, a black and white rabbit nibbled on some leafy greens. All of the plants and flowers in Mom's garden were in full bloom, which should've seemed odd because it was so early in the season, but I didn't give it another thought.

Instead, I just stood there enjoying the moment in the serene setting, letting go of a deep sigh. This was nothing like the world I inhabited in Los Angeles. It quickly dawned on me I was very far from home.

A table was arranged on the patio for alfresco dining, and just off the patio in the grass was what looked like a human-sized birdbath carved out of a gorgeous slab of granite in the form of a half shelf. There wasn't any water in the shell tub and there wasn't a spigot anywhere near it. It was all so very peculiar.

Continuing to take everything in, I noticed a chaotic group of lights flashing off and on above the bench in the very back of the garden. I watched them blink on and off in the foliage for a few minutes and concluded they were probably just fireflies. I had never seen a firefly in person, but these seemed so much larger, even larger than a dragonfly. Like small birds, really. Curiosity got the best of me, so I decided to step closer to take a better look.

The big bugs moved across the leaves like a marching band, forming a pattern. Their lighted bodies flickered on and off, spelling out a series of words:

"BEWARE. OF. THE. WITCH."

Fear pinched my stomach. And before I could make my way to safety, the fireflies dispersed, flying off in different directions all at once. When one of the bugs flew past my face, I hit the deck ... hard. I began shrieking with my arms over my head and my eyes closed. I was under attack by a flock of what had to be killer hummingbirds.

I screamed.

It was like a scene out of *The Birds*. Only the birds were much smaller and I was much more frightened. There were flashes of feathers and bone as they dive-bombed me. I covered my head and ducked to avoid the whoosh of their wings as they came so close to my face.

The little bugs weren't insects. I was almost positive they were actually tiny little birds. Still in disbelief, I took a second look at the hummingbird-like creatures. Their wings were beating faster than my heart, which was saying something since my heart was jumping like a jackhammer. There was only one option to get inside, and that was to crawl back in through the doors to the kitchen on my hands and knees, which is exactly what I did.

What kind of little creatures could light up like that?

Shaking, I retreated back to the bathroom. An escape. Mom's bathroom was like a luxury spa. I filled the tub with aromatherapy bubbles, stripped off my clothes, and climbed in for a long soak. Pure bliss.

After what felt like hours, I stepped out and wrapped myself in one of my mom's giant bath sheets before creeping back out into the kitchen.

On the bright side, the killer hummingbirds had disappeared. Feeling a lot safer now, I discovered the kitchen floor covered in dusty glitter. With a broom and dustpan from under the sink, I swept it up and threw it away.

I went back to the guest bedroom, pulled the covers back on the big four-poster, feather bed puffed up high with pillowcases scented with my mom's distinct lavender perfume, and fell asleep.

When I woke up, Mom was seated on a chair across the room in the dark, a light coming from a point near the chair.

"Aviana? Are you awake?" She spoke softly.

"I am now." I rolled over and blinked at her in the dim light.

"How are you feeling? Any better?" She sounded concerned. "I'm sorry I wasn't here when you arrived."

"I'm having a hard time believing any of this is real." I sat up in bed and swung my hands around my head. My wings thumped once against my back. "Wings. I have wings. Why don't you tell me what's going on? What am I some kind of fairy creature?

"You're a fairy by birth. A fairy godmother by trade," she corrected.

I shook my head. "No. It can't be. It's just plain ridiculous, Mom. Fairy godmothers only exist in old-time stories. The kind I don't like to read."

"This is all my fault," she said, sounding very sincere.

"If it was true, wouldn't I have shown some signs of my 'fairy-ness' before now?"

"Fairy godmothers are late bloomers. That's what I told your father. He didn't believe me either."

"This is ridiculous." I was holding on by a thread.

"I must apologize to you. It was my responsibility to tell you the truth a long time ago. When your father sent me away, it was with an added threat. If I ever told you anything about the slight possibility you could be a fairy like your mother, he would make sure I would never have any contact with you again. Ever. I can stand my ground with any foe, but he is an attorney, and a formidable one at that."

"They don't call him 'The Whale' for nothing," I added.

"I wasn't completely sure you would take after me. It wasn't until you told me you were ill on the phone. That's when I knew your wings were fledging and you were emerging from Chrysalis. I knew I had to do something. I couldn't just let you be by yourself. You needed support."

"Dad knows about this?"

"Of course he does. We both knew it was a possibility. I hoped it would be true. He hoped it wouldn't be. Why do you think he kept us apart all of these years? I told him what could happen around your birthday, but he didn't want to believe it. That's why I don't understand why he left you alone on your birthday," she said. "It was almost as if he was frightened to know the truth."

"I've never known him to be scared of anything," I said.

"You're protecting him. I used to do it too. I wanted to think the best of him too. He is worthy. He just doesn't ever end up living up to the trust I've given him. At least not yet."

"He would never approve of this," I affirmed.

"Your father was confident in his ability to protect you from your fate by keeping you far away from me. As your twenty-first birthday approached, I'd told him if you were like me, you'd mature and grow wings. He was unable to admit he wouldn't be able to prevent you from becoming who you really are. Maybe that's why he went to Mexico. He didn't want to face the truth."

"I don't understand any of this," I said. "I just don't get it."

"Just know, Aviana, you and I are descended from an ancient family of fairy godmothers who first started working four centuries ago in the Shetland Islands," she said.

"Okay. Is that phony family history supposed to thrill me?" I asked. "It doesn't sound like it's from Ancestry.com." I yawned.

"But it's true. You must believe me," she persisted.

"Puh-leaze," I said. "I'm not special. I'm average. I've been average all my life."

"You are not average, Aviana. You've been living with people who were trying to keep you from fulfilling your potential. But now you've got wings, and you'll find your powers. You have it all over them. You just didn't know it yet."

My mom came over to the bed, straightened the quilt, and tucked it under my chin. I wasn't used to this kind of TLC from anyone, but just because I didn't ever get it, didn't mean I didn't crave it. When she brushed the hair off my face, I pressed my face into her fingertips like a cat. Her touch was calming. I could feel my body relaxing.

73

I wanted to tell her about the flashing lights in the yard, but I was too exhausted to speak one word.

"Sweet dreams." She kissed me on the forehead and left the room.

I was too close to sleep when I realized my mom had never turned the light on in the room. The only source of light floated out of the door behind her.

Huh. That was odd.

I drifted to sleep in the dark room. I was probably dreaming, but the moving light looked a lot like one of those oversized dragonflies from the garden.

CHAPTER 7

Rule #7: A fairy godmother never falls under the spell of an ersatz prince.

Gray morning light was peeking through the slats in the window blinds in the room. Birds were chirping from the safety of the other side of double-glazed glass. The air was filled with the delicious smell of bacon.

I reached over and grabbed my phone. Josie hadn't texted me. It wasn't like her to go silent. She usually was up for texting twenty-four hours a day, seven days a week.

I called Dr. Bernstein and left word on her voicemail. I stretched the truth and said I wouldn't be in for my early morning appointment on Monday and I'd call to reschedule. Dr. Bernstein had a twenty-four-hour cancellation policy, and I knew Dad would be mad if he was charged her exorbitant fee if I forgot to cancel.

I stretched and yawned but couldn't fall back to sleep with the uncomfortable roll beneath my back. Suddenly my eyes flew open wide. The fold in the sheets under my back wasn't an extra pillow. It was my wings. I sat up straight in bed, and as soon as I did, my wings came to life, flapping and waving above my head.

Before I could fully grasp what was happening, or get my wings under control, my cellphone rang. I didn't recognize the number, but it was a Los Angeles area code. I figured a call from anyone outside of Los Arboledas would be welcome right about now.

"Aviana? It's Dr. Bernstein."

Oh balls!

"Hi," I said. Now was not the time to talk to a mental health professional.

"Is everything all right?"

"Fine. Everything is fine here. How are you, Dr. Bernstein?"

"I was concerned about you after you canceled our next appointment."

"No need for concern. Mmmph ..." I turned too quickly and had to duck to avoid getting smacked in the face by my own wings. "I'm out of town."

"Would you like to reschedule an appointment for your return?" It was a miracle I was able to keep up with what Dr. Bernstein was saying, given the wings had a mind of their own; they were completely freaking me out. I dropped to my knees on the floor, desperate to get out of their way.

"I would, but I don't when exactly I'll be back," I said.

"Has something come up?" she asked.

My wings, I wanted to say.

"I'm visiting my mom," I said. I wanted to be as honest as possible.

"But you said you were estranged from your mom?"

"I was ... I am. She reached out to me on my birthday," I said.

"How did that make you feel?" she asked.

Feelings. Ugh. The last thing I wanted to talk about right now was my "feelings." "Honestly, right now I'm feeling pretty shitty and angry."

"We could schedule some sessions over the phone while you are at your mom's house. Is that something you would like to do, Aviana?"

No. Absolutely not. "Sounds good to me," I said. "But I'll reach out in a few days."

Just then a tapping sound at the window caught my attention. One of those gigantic dragonflies was bouncing off the glass at regular intervals. How had an insect the size of a loaf of bread gotten inside the house unnoticed?

"Shit!" the insect said.

Wait! Was the big bug swearing?

It flew closer to the bed and I took a big swing at it, but sleep had left me without a good grasp on my eye-hand coordination.

"Watch it!" the insect yelped.

A talking dragonfly? Seriously?

I swatted at the flying nuisance a couple times. Just then, the insect buzzed past my face; it was enough for me to notice it was wearing a fedora at a jaunty angle. "Holy crap!"

I heard Mom's heels clicking against the hardwood floors in the hallway just before she opened the door and found me cowering on the floor under the window. "Aviana. What is wrong with you?"

"There's some kind of giant bug in here with me," I said.

"Glenn? Is that you?"

"Who else would it be?" the insect immediately responded.

"I wasn't expecting you so soon."

"Glenn" flew out from behind the curtains. His fedora was tipped at a rakish angle with his tie loosened at the neck. Glenn had a Frank Sinatra-swagger. He looked like he was either coming from or going to a party with the rest of the Rat Pack.

"What is that?" I said, pointing to the talking insect. "What the *hell* is that?"

"That's Glenn," Mom said. "He's a pixie."

"He's really small," I said.

"Hey. I'm seven-and three-quarter inches tall. I'm way above average."

Glenn was flying in a figure-eight pattern near the ceiling. "Besides, I may be small, according to your standards, but you should never underestimate the power of a pixie."

"A pixie? But I thought pixies were …" I stopped myself. What did I know about pixies? Nothing. Up until a few minutes ago I believed "The Pixies" were a punk rock band.

"Chicks?" Glenn asked. "You thought pixies were always chicks? Right? See, I told you, Liliana. Everybody always thinks they're all chicks. I hate that."

"You have to admit, Glenn. There are a lot of female pixies," Mom said. "Female pixies in the wild outnumber males by almost a thousand to one. You can't go getting yourself all worked up over people's misconceptions. It's not worth it."

He smiled. "I like those odds."

"It's not that I thought they were always chicks," I said. "I just believed they were always the figment of someone's overactive imagination."

"That's ridiculous." He laughed off my comment.

Mom nodded at the pixie. "Glenn has been my assistant for ten years. I couldn't do my job without him."

"Stop it," he said. "You're making me blush."

My mom, looking so beautiful, beamed at him. "Go take care of everything. We'll talk later, Glenn." She kept her hair in a sleek bob just brushing the top of her shoulders. In the dim light of the room, her makeup was flawless and her clothes were tasteful and expensive.

I asked my mom about her style once and she said she planned her outfits seven days in advance. Seven days in advance? I prided myself on being über-organized, but she made me feel like a total slacker. It was very possible she needed therapy more than I did.

Once Glenn was out of the room, my mom turned her attention to me and said, "Did you let your father know you arrived safely?"

"I wouldn't be here if he didn't know," I said. If she could lie like a rug, then so could I. "He actually encouraged me to come see you."

"He did?" Mom was taken aback. Maybe I was pushing my luck. But did that stop me? Nope.

"He said it would be nice for me to come here. Just for the weekend. To relax."

"Really?" Mom looked incredulous.

"And what about your birthday? How did your father explain forgetting your birthday?"

"Turns out, it was all on me," I lied. "We made plans, but I forgot I canceled. Madeleine is going to arrange a family celebration next Wednesday at Mr. Chow's. It's not a big deal, Mom."

"It is a big deal. We talked about it last night, maybe you were too tired to remember.

My memories of yesterday were pretty hazy. And I had a lot of questions. Had she spoken about it in detail? "But…"

You're a fairy godmother," Mom said. "It's time to celebrate."

"There must be more to it, isn't there?"

Mom took a deep breath, then she smiled. "The others are out in the garden. They're waiting to meet you and celebrate your Chrysalis. Come join us when you're ready."

Mom's wings unfurled behind her as she walked away. They were magical—able to stretch to great heights and then return to mold themselves to her body as if they were nothing more than a tattoo. Her wings sparkled like precious gemstones, perfectly matching the color of her lilac eyes.

My wings had relaxed back against my body. At first glance they looked like a beautifully drawn tattoo. It would probably be best if they didn't unfurl to their full height again, so I grabbed some tape I found in the nightstand and taped the tips of them to my shoulder blades. Once they were tamed, I got dressed and went out to the kitchen.

Glenn was manning the grill with a pair of tongs twice his size. A covey of pixies was playing hide-and-go-seek in the branches of the tall hedges in the back of the garden, leaving a trail of sparkling fairy dust in the path.

Gathered in Mom's back yard were a group of fairy godmothers, possessed of an otherworldly beauty. They were not at all what I expected. I'd never spent any time thinking about fairies or fairy godmothers before in my life. And I never considered I would be one.

Mom put her arm around my shoulders. "This is my daughter, Aviana."

All eyes turned to me. I felt shy and self-conscious but nodded to the group politely.

"This is my good friend, Sylvie," Mom introduced me to the closest fairy godmother.

Sylvie didn't address me directly when she asked, "She never discovered any of her powers on her own? My daughter had enchanted some clothing by her age."

"She hasn't had time," Mom said. "She had a sheltered upbringing."

"But you are sure she has powers?" Sylvie asked.

"Yes," Mom hissed. "Because she was raised by her father, she doesn't yet fully understand the world is full of limitless possibilities."

In the kitchen we found a small group of fairy godmothers clustered around the rulebook open on my mom's kitchen counter. "Why are they all so excited over that book?" I asked.

"Long, long ago, the Fairy Godmother's Guild created and published twenty-seven rules governing the code of conduct for fairy godmother behavior in *The Fairy Godmother's Rulebook*. Many believe the rulebooks have powers themselves."

"They don't?"

Mom shook her head. "The rulebooks don't have power, the fairies do. Collecting rulebooks in order to amass power is wrong. But that hasn't stopped some fairies from doing it."

"Look at these drawings. Fairy godmothers in tiaras," a petite fairy godmother scoffed. "Puh-leaze. I have a hard enough time pulling off a happily-ever-after ending without trying to balance the family jewels on my head."

The fairy godmothers laughed.

"I'm sure there was a time when that kind of thing was *de rigueur*, but let's face it, if you're not the queen of England, you really don't need a tiara. Although it would be nice just for one night," a dark-haired fairy godmother said.

"Oh, look," Mom said. "Zara's here."

And she was. Zara Wakefield, the Lifestyle Guru. She had attempted to mask her unearthly beauty with dark-framed horn-rimmed glasses. For most women, the glasses would hide their beauty, but the masculine frames only served to emphasize her feline features.

My mouth was hanging open, I couldn't help but stare.

"Zara Wakefield? *She's* a …" I asked.

"Very powerful fairy godmother," Glenn finished my sentence with a tight smile.

"She's one of the new Elders in the Fairy Godmother's Guild," Mom said with a smile pasted on her face.

The woman I'd been stalking on social media was an actual fairy godmother? I couldn't believe it.

And yet I wanted an opportunity to talk to *the* Zara Wakefield, so I made my way into the kitchen. Just as I was about to approach her, I caught her running her fingers over the ancient covers of my family's copy of *The Fairy Godmother's Rulebook*. It was as if she was greeting a long-lost friend ... or making a new one.

"I've never seen a rulebook this old," Zara said. "Your family must've been fairy godmothering forever, Liliana."

"Our family is one of the original six," Mom said. "Our magical powers are ancient."

Zara turned to me. "This must be your daughter."

Mom nodded. "This is my Aviana."

Zara's eyes narrowed. "I feel like I already know you, Aviana. I'm so glad you're exploring your heritage as a fairy godmother," she said with a smirk. "Two fairy godmothers from one family in the Guild. Won't you be jealous, Liliana?"

"Of what?"

"She's young and beautiful. She could challenge your powers as a fairy godmother."

Mom shook her head. "I want only the best for her."

That's when it happened.

A blinding flash of white light. I looked around, I was the only one who could see it. I blinked furiously, and suddenly a vision of Zara appeared. She had the tiny eyes of a fox and a sallow complexion. The vision stopped me in my tracks.

Another flash of white light blinded me, and the image was gone.

Zara stood in front of me, as beautiful as ever, flashing her phony smile.

I attempted to smile back, but she made me nervous. Maybe it was just the light in the kitchen, but her teeth looked as pointy as my ears.

I went back out into the garden to shake off my mixed feelings. The smells of sage and lavender in the warm air created an atmosphere of quiet comfort.

Fairy godmothers reclined under the shade of the orange tree. The secluded garden let them expose their wings to light and air. They looked like a bouquet of late summer flowers, all dressed in silvery tones of purple, lavender, and pink. Outside of this garden, they were oddities in the world they lived in. And now I was one of them.

Suddenly I couldn't catch my breath. My heart thumped in my chest. I was overwhelmed by the feeling of claustrophobia. I had to get out of this garden and away from the fairy godmothers before I spontaneously combusted.

Without pausing for pretense, I ran for the front door. When I opened it, Ruby was standing there, looking just as surprised as I was to see her.

"What are you doing here?" I asked.

She held up a wrapped gift and two bottles of wine. "I'm here to celebrate your Chrysalis with you."

"You're a fairy godmother?"

"Of course I am," she admitted. "I almost spilled the beans in the office the other day. I'm sorry. I didn't know you didn't know."

Ruby handed me the beautifully wrapped present and carried the wine out to the kitchen to greet the other fairy godmothers. I stood by the front door not knowing what to do. Should I stay or should I go?

In the end, I decided to follow Ruby back into the party, where we settled in chairs in the back of my mom's garden. She was the only fairy godmother I'd met since I'd arrived in Los Arboledas who was close to my age. Naturally, I wanted to ask her a few questions.

"You made it through Chrysalis like a champ," Ruby grinned. "I can't imagine how I'd behave if I didn't grow up knowing I was destined to be a fairy godmother, and one day, I'd get my wings."

"You've always known?"

She nodded. "Always. It was a matter of pride in my family. They were thrilled to know one of their kids was going to be a fairy godmother."

"You believed your fate was a blessing?" I asked. "Why do I feel like I've been cursed? This isn't the life I wanted."

"What do you want?" she asked.

"I want to go home. I want to go back to my life. There's got to be some way I can tell the Guild I'm flattered, but no. I don't want my powers."

Ruby didn't answer. A sudden breeze stirred in the garden, and Ruby let her wings unfurl. Fully extended, her ruby-tinted wings stretched from the top of her shoulders down to her ankles, and the feathered tips looked as if they'd been dipped in black paint.

My own wings were giving me fits. I got to my feet and rubbed up against the trunk of the orange tree like a bear, much to Ruby's delight. "What are you doing?"

"My wings itch. Do your wings itch?"

Ruby laughed. "Maybe it's because they're so fresh. You know, a milk bath with some honey really helps with the itch. Every fairy swears by it. "

"Really? I'll have to try that. Maybe if I didn't have pointy ears or emotionally-activated wings, I could deal with all this," I said, gesturing around at the strange tableau of the fairy godmothers gathered in the garden.

"I don't think your fairy features are your biggest obstacle in returning to Los Angeles," Ruby said. "I've seen enough *Real Housewives of Beverly Hills* to know there's at least one surgeon there who would be willing to separate you from any unwanted appendages you might have, for the right price."

"You're right," I said. There was no doubt in my mind Madeleine would know the right plastic surgeon who would agree to the right price. No questions asked.

"But is that what you really want?"

"Yes," I said without hesitation.

"The real problem, I think, is giving up your powers," Ruby said.

"I can't be the first fairy godmother ever to decline her powers, can I?"

"Absolutely not. These days there are more fairy godmothers giving up their powers than ever. Why do you think finding happily ever after is rare in the real world?

There just aren't enough fairy godmothers to go around."

"So, if I give up my powers," I said, "taking that kind of step wouldn't be completely unprecedented."

"No, but …" She stopped herself. She glanced at my mom once or twice with a worried expression on her face. There was something she wasn't saying.

"What's wrong?" I asked.

"If you decide to give up your powers, do you know what will happen?"

I shook my head. "My life will go back to normal?"

Ruby set down her wine glass and turned to look at me. "You are dealing with some very powerful creatures who may not understand why you'd want to throw away your talents."

"What? They're going to kill me?"

"No." She laughed. "Not exactly. I'm not sure what happens, but I do know your powers will be taken away, as well as the powers of every living fairy godmother in your family tree. So, your decision not to be a fairy godmother won't just affect your future. It will affect your mother's and grandmother's as well."

"I've never met her. Is she a fairy godmother too?"

"She's … well, you know they often talk about her in training seminars. She's been in service to the royal family, for, like, ever. Unless you change your mind, she will lose her powers, and you will be the last of a very ancient family of fairy godmothers."

My stomach clenched. I was backed into a corner. If I don't become a fairy godmother, other people will be hurt. They aren't giving me a choice.

I bit down on my lip. "Can I ask you a question? Just between us?"

"Absolutely. Ask me anything." Ruby smiled warmly.

I leaned forward and whispered, "What do you think of Zara?

Ruby hesitated before she spoke. "I try not to."

"Do you trust her?"

"Not even a little," Ruby answered almost before I finished asking the question.

"She acts as if she knows more than any other godmother," I said. "She was surprisingly condescending to my mom."

"She has been remarkably successful as a fairy godmother. And has been given a lot of power." Ruby checked to see if any tiny pests with large ears were buzzing about before she continued, "Not everyone think she's earned her position in the Guild. And I've heard rumors."

"What kind of rumors?"

Ruby slid a few feet further away from me. "I'm not going to answer that question."

"Why not?" Ruby's voice dropped to a whisper. "I'm beyond scared of her. And you should be too. If she knew we were having this conversation, it would be very, very bad."

"Yes, but …" I stopped. The fear in Ruby's eyes was too much.

"Shush," Ruby said. "Most of the pixies are loyal to her. We could get in so much trouble."

"I'm not scared." I wasn't. Which was unusual. I'd been scared for so much of my life.

"Maybe you should be." Ruby shuddered and shook her head.

What wasn't Ruby telling me?

I shuddered. I didn't think my life could get more miserable than working as a legal assistant for my stepsister, but this … this was way worse. I was trapped in a world I was uncertain how to navigate.

I spent the rest of the night helping out in the kitchen. Keeping busy helped me to focus and not worry about everything that had happened to me.

I was beyond exhausted when I crawled into bed. My brain was whirling with thoughts, digesting all the new information about my mom, my grandmother, and my family history. What kind of expectations would they have of me?

I punched my pillow and settled down, trying to block everything out of my mind so I could fall asleep. Just as I was about to turn out the light, my mom stuck her head in the door.

"Would you like to go with me to a yoga class at the inn in the morning? My friend Sylvie is teaching elemental yoga at eight."

"Elemental yoga?" I asked.

Sounds horrible.

"Sure. I'd love to."

I had to try. *Didn't I?*

My pointy ears weren't going away any time soon, I looked like a garden gnome, and I had wings.

Why did it have to be wings?

Ugh.

Double-ugh. With Nutella.

All I wanted was to go back to Los Angeles. And yet I knew instinctively I could never go home again.

CHAPTER 8

Rule #8: A fairy godmother doesn't do favors, nor expects them in return.

I woke up at eight o'clock in the morning to a call from Stern, Fayed, and Lopez. Half-hoping it was my dad, I answered on the first ring.

"Hey. Is everything okay?" Josie asked.

"I'm fine," I said wearily. "What are you doing in Vanessa's office?"

"Don't be mad, but I'm working for her now."

"Working for Vanessa?" Have you lost your mind?"

"Vanessa wanted someone to answer the phone. When my temp agency called about a job, I realized it was yours. And so here I am."

I laughed. "How long do you think you can tolerate her?"

"I dunno," she said. "She's…a lot. How long do you think you'll be gone?"

I blew out a long burst of air. "I have no idea, but it could be awhile."

"I really need the money," Josie said. "So, if you don't mind, I'll keep your chair warm for you until you get back."

"Call me if you have any questions," I said. I was so happy Josie had found a way to solve her money crunch. Knowing I couldn't put off facing my own problems any longer, I threw back the covers, and went out into the kitchen.

Mom was bustling around in the kitchen in a Hard Tail yoga outfit in a shade of purple that one again perfectly matched her eyes. It was as if the color had been created just for her. God, she was so remarkably beautiful. Especially when she smiled. It nearly took my breath away.

"Here, dear. Have a seat." Mom motioned to a place set at the counter.

She walked back to the stove and turned to me. "I didn't have time to do grocery shopping, so I just put a few things together for breakfast from the pantry," she said. She put a plate of blueberry pancakes and bacon in front of me. "I hope you don't mind."

"You had this?" I asked. "In your pantry?"

"Yes," she answered without looking me in the eye. She was lying. I knew it. She knew it. Did I really need to call her on it?

"But I looked for food the other night," I said. "There was nothing in the cupboard but Nutella and pasta."

"I'm sorry, darling. Maybe you just didn't know where to look." She busied herself cleaning up the utensils near the stovetop.

I wasn't going to refuse my favorite breakfast, even if its origins were sketchy. I poured maple syrup on the pancakes and took a big bite.

When I finished breakfast, I changed into my yoga clothes and caught a glimpse of my hair in the bathroom mirror. My wild strawberry-blonde mane would make the lead singer of any '80s hair band jealous.

I pulled my hair all up into a topknot on my head, taped down my wings, worked up a sweat wrestling myself into a sports bra built for women with real breasts, and pulled on a tattered sweatshirt and yoga pants.

I hurried outside where my mom met me in the driveway.

"Are you ready to go?" Mom asked. "I usually ride my bike to work, but I've got an extra bike. A re you game?"

Was she kidding? I hadn't ridden a bike since I was ten years old. No one rides a bike in Los Angeles. We drive everywhere. If we need to go to the next-door neighbor's house, we get in our car and drive down the hill.

"Sounds like fun." I forced a smile. It wasn't anything close to my idea of fun. My idea of fun didn't involve physical exertion of any kind, but I was here in Los Arboledas. And my mom was thrilled I was going with her to yoga class.

Mom got her bike out of her garage. It was green with a big woven basket on the handlebars. The extra bike she had was a baby blue beach cruiser. It had seen better days, but it would get me where I was going. Ready to go, she tucked her yoga mat in the basket on her bike while I slung mine over my back like it was a quiver full of arrows, and we headed off to the inn.

It was a perfect day for a bike ride. The air in Los Arboledas smelled sweet and tangy from the flowers filling every inch of garden space mingling with the salt air in the ocean breezes.

As we made our way, we crossed a little bridge in the middle of town where a group of swans drifted slowly down the river. Mom insisted we stop to watch their progress before turning onto the path leading up to the Los Arboledas Inn. Trees and shrubs had been carefully landscaped and sculpted at great expense on the other side of the driveway leading up to the inn. The grounds surrounding the luxury resort were simply spectacular.

We parked our bikes in a rack in front of the spa building, then I followed Mom into the designated yoga room and found a space for my mat in the back row where I wouldn't be seen.

Mom went right to the front of the room. She greeted Sylvie and then greeted the woman on the mat next to her.

Mom smiled. "How's my bride?"

"I didn't get a wink of sleep last night," the bride wailed. "The dress doesn't zip. I've gained like ten pounds since my last fitting."

"I don't want you to worry about it one more minute," my mom said in a soothing tone. "You'll lose a little water weight in class this morning and be the most beautiful bride ever this afternoon." The bride's shoulders relaxed a little at her words.

"Do you really think everything is going to be all right?" the bride asked.

"Everything has been handled," Mom said.

"Thank you," she said. "You're like the fairy godmother I never knew I needed."

I rolled my eyes. My mother had never been a mother to me, let alone a fairy godmother.

Sylvie clapped her hands to get everyone's attention. "Good morning class, and welcome to Elemental Yoga," she said.

Sylvie's face said she was sixty, but her sculpted body wasn't a day over thirty. She looked amazing.

No more than a few minutes had elapsed before dark rings of perspiration stained my work-out clothes from my armpits to my hips. Sweat puddled under the elastic band of my jog bra. Boob sweat. Was there anything on earth more disgusting?

Why did I agree to do this?

My mom looked perfectly serene as she bent into another pose. As soon as I started the downward-facing dog, I got a little light-headed. To make matters worse, a ribbon of sweat dribbled down from some overheated spot on my torso and dripped off my inverted chin onto the floor.

Sylvie hovered over me as I lay prone on the floor. "How many layers do you have on?"

"Just a few."

"You should take off your sweatshirt," Sylvie suggested.

"I'm trying to lose five or twenty pounds," I said. "And I enjoy sweating."

I wasn't sweating. I was panting like a dog. My cheeks were bright pink, but I didn't want anyone to see my wings. Once the fear of passing took over, I finally acquiesced to Sylvie's instructions and pulled the sweatshirt over my head.

Sylvie continued to lead the class through a variety of poses, moving around the class, adjusting our bodies, and helping us find our balance.

She helped everyone but my mom, who was surgically attached to her constantly buzzing and beeping phone. She stepped out of the yoga room more than once to take a call or to text someone. It was really odd.

"Okay. We're going to clear our minds of any careless thoughts," Sylvie said. "And get ready for Shavasana."

Finally. My entire outlook improved. I had always been an Olympic gold medalist at corpse pose. I closed my eyes and concentrated on keeping perfectly still.

Through almost-closed eyes, I watched Sylvie move quietly around the room, stopping at each mat and spritzing her yoga students with what I guessed was a mixture of distilled water and patchouli oil.

When she stood over my mat, I tried to wave her off.

"It's stress-relieving," Sylvie whispered.

"I'm allergic," I hissed.

Sylvie skipped me and continued around the room until she reached the stressed-out bride in the front row where she spritzed her with something from a bottle my mother had handed her.

By the time class finished Mom was back outside on the phone again. I rolled up both our mats and found her standing just outside the yoga room.

"What did you have Sylvie spray on the bride?" I asked.

"A little elderberry root extract to make her relaxed and happy. Every bride wants to believe she's perfect on her wedding day. Until the scent wears off, she'll believe she's absolutely perfect—as is," she said. "And I have a contingency plan—oh, there she is now."

Mom waved to a woman walking toward us in a housekeeper's uniform.

"Louisa, this is my daughter," she said.

Louisa took my hand and held it. "You look just like your mother."

Why did everyone keep confusing me with the petite ball of fire standing next to me? "We don't look anything alike."

"It's your eyes. I can see it," she said. "I love your mom. She's my fairy job-mother."

"For reals?" I let out. "How interesting."

"Louisa," Mom said, "you are too kind." My mom's cheeks tinted a pinker shade.

It was the second time in under an hour my mother had been referred to as a "fairy godmother."

Was it an open secret in Los Arboledas?

Mom and her friends were running around spraying unsuspecting innocents with herb-scented oils, making them believe all their wishes would come true and that there was such a thing as "happily ever after" endings.

If it weren't for the wings on my back, I'd have a hard time believing everything my mom said was true. And yet, here in Los Arboledas, no one questioned the existence of fairy godmothers. It was no big deal.

"I helped Louisa get her job at the inn, Aviana," Mom said proudly.

"I'm a very good seamstress," Louisa said.

"Were you able to get into the bridal suite without any problems?" Mom asked.

"Yes. I checked the seams on her gown. I released about a half-inch on each side. It should fit her like a glove, and she'll never know a thing."

"Perfect," Mom said.

Mom hugged Louisa good-bye, and we made our way around to the front steps of the main building. That's where my feet stopped moving and my heart skipped a beat.

Nash Nolan, wearing dark aviators, khakis, a navy-blue T-shirt, and a pair of vintage Converse, pulled up to the front of the inn and smoothly exited his Maserati at the valet stand.

What was *he* doing in Los Arboledas?

Mom followed my sightline. "Do you know that young man, Aviana?"

I nodded. "He's my crush."

"Really?" She gave him a thorough looking over.

"Dad can't stop talking about him."

"Your father always had a soft spot for prodigies with money," she said. "I guess some things never change."

I didn't answer. I was too busy watching Nash responding to the valet in front of the hotel. He looked cool and comfortable despite the hot noonday sun.

"He's very attractive," my mom chimed in. "You should ask him out, Aviana. Enjoy yourself."

"Mom. I've hardly dated at all. And so, I can't start with … that."

"Why not?" she asked. "Why not start with the best? There's no rule saying you have to work your way up from the bottom to the top. Why not start with this guy?"

"Okay," I said. "Let's take a time out from fantasyland. He is completely out of my league."

"If that's how you see it, darling, but he looks like a very nice young man. You really should date him."

"Just like that." I was incredulous. "I should just 'date him.'"

"Yes. She was serious. She honestly believed life was that easy. Seriously? When does someone like me actually get the opportunity to date their crush?

"I think you may be overlooking a few minor details." I

crossed my arms over my chest.

"Like what?" She was oblivious.

"Like I don't know him ... and he doesn't know I exist."

As if on cue, Nash took off his sunglasses. And then he waved.

At me. As if my birthday wish had come true.

I turned around to see if someone was standing behind me, but no one was there. Nothing was behind me but a tall ivy-covered, stacked stone wall. I forced myself to close my mouth because it was hanging open like a flytrap.

What is going on? Why is he waving at me?

"C'mon, Mom. This is crazy. He doesn't know me. He must believe I'm someone else."

Nash was still waving. Though to be honest, his waving style had gone from friendly, cool guy to crazy beauty queen on acid.

Just then I was blinded by a flash of bright white light.

He didn't look like Nash, he looked like a thirteen-year-old with thick glasses and a full set of braces. Frustrated and angry as he limped across the finish line last in a race against all the other boys who were twice his size in his seventh-grade class.

Another flash of white light blinded me, and the Nash Nolan 'd been crushing on forever returned.

"Aviana, right?" He moved toward me in a straight line.

"I don't believe this," I muttered under my breath. "What's going on?"

"See," Mom said. "He does know you exist. You guys catch up, and then we can meet at the bike rack."

He glanced in my direction and lowered his sunglasses. "Hi."

"Hi." I checked over my shoulder again.

"What are you doing?"

"Trying to figure out who you're talking to," I said.

"I'm talking to you," he said.

Nash Nolan opened his mouth and more words fell out, but I didn't hear what he was saying. The ground shifted under my feet. It was as if I was on an ocean liner. My world was spinning out of control.

This isn't right. This shouldn't be happening.

And yet when he grinned, I couldn't help smiling back.

He looked at me as if I was somebody. A real somebody.

"Me?" This was crazy. I had to be hallucinating.

He nodded. "I wanted to tell you how brave I think you are."

"You think I'm brave? I think you've got the wrong person."

He nodded. "Throwing yourself a solo birthday party at Mr. Chow's. That takes some kind of courage. I admire your confidence."

"My confidence?" *As if.* I didn't have confidence, but there was no way I was going to point that out to my crush. Not when he had actually noticed that I was alive.

"Yes."

"Thank you."

"It's something I've always struggled with," he said.

"Confidence? You? Seriously?"

He wasn't joking. He was as serious as a heart attack. "We all do, to some extent, don't you think?"

"Yes. I-I think we all do," I repeated his words.

"I could use some lessons." He flashed the most perfect crooked smile again. Then he took off his glasses and wiped the lens clean on the tail of her shirt. "Maybe we should hang out."

"We should 'hang out'?" It wasn't my intention to end my sentence in a question. How was this possible? I'd inhabited a space he frequented for the past four years without him ever glancing in my direction.

Am I being pranked?

This was crazy. Absolutely crazy.

Don't do it. It's a trap.

"Yes," I said. "We should hang out. But right now, I have to go. With my mom."

"Wait," Nathan said. He reached out to touch my arm, but I was already running toward the bike rack.

Why had he noticed me? Was it fairy godmother magic?

He'd never paid attention to me before and now he's suggesting having a date? I'm not going to let my mom's magic hijack Nash's life, or my own.

"Where are you going, Aviana? You should hang out with him." Mom chided me when I caught up to her.

"I don't know what is going on, but I'm not going to be a part of it." I shook my head and grabbed a bike.

"What are you talking about, Aviana?"

"All this magical fairy godmothering and 'happily ever after' nonsense. I don't believe in it, and I'm not going to participate in it. Do you understand?" I confronted her.

Jumping on the bike I rode off.

CHAPTER 9

Rule #9: A fairy godmother knows glass slippers never go out of style.

Mom had some errands to run at the inn, so I rode the bike back to her house alone. Glenn was buzzing around the kitchen, like the annoying little insect I mistook him for the first time we met.

"Where's your mother?" he asked.

"I don't know. She stayed at the inn; she said she had some errands to do." It took every ounce of self-control I had not to bat the little bugger into oblivion.

Glenn looked perplexed. For a brief second, I thought he might dive-bomb me. "She's not answering her phone. Where do you think she could be?"

I hesitated before I spoke. "I-I thought it was your job to keep track of her. Besides, Glenn, honestly, I hardly know her," I said with an edge in my voice. This silenced him but only for a moment.

"Have you tried to call her?"

I picked up my cellphone and dialed my mom. It went directly to her voicemail.

"She's not answering," I said.

"Okay, look," he said. "I'm in a bit of a bind, and I need a favor."

"What's up?"

"We've got a client getting married today. 'Happily ever after' is almost guaranteed, and I don't think there will be any surprises, but I would feel a lot better if there was a fairy godmother there—just to make sure everything runs smoothly."

"I'm not a fairy godmother," I said.

"Technically," Glenn said, "you are. You just don't have any training."

My lips twisted into a grimace. "Technically or otherwise. No."

Glenn pushed the brim of his hat back to an amiable angle. "Your mother and I would really appreciate the help. There's no one else we can ask. Not without alerting Zara. You'd be doing us a sold."

"I haven't had a chance to talk about what the future holds for me with my mom, yet.." I didn't want to air family issues in front of Glenn.

"You're going to love being a fairy godmother," Glenn said. "This will give you a chance to see how cool it can be."

"I'm not going to be a fairy godmother," I protested.

"But…" Glenn looked confused

I crossed my arms over my chest. "I haven't agreed to any of this."

"What else would you do?"

"Currently, I'm a legal assistant," I protested. "That's what I do."

"That's ridiculous," Glenn said. "You need time to adjust to the changes you've been through, that's all."

I nodded. "What do I want me to do?"

"Just go to a wedding."

"That's it?" I asked.

Glenn nodded.

"If anything goes wrong, I can't just snap my fingers

and make things happen," I warned. "If I had magical powers, I would've used them by now."

"You're in the power, you just don't know it. Not yet." Glenn was quick to dismiss my pointless concerns with a wave of his hand. "I don't have the time to argue. I need a fairy godmother, or a reasonable facsimile of one, at this wedding in less than an hour. You're it. See what you can do to fix yourself up. I'll make coffee."

I was still in a defensive posture. "I only brought one good dress."

"Put it on."

Feeling as if I had no other choice but to comply with Glenn's demands, I rummaged through the suitcase I'd dumped on the floor in the guest room. I dug through the pile of rumpled tees, blouses, skirts, and jeans—all of which probably needed to be laundered—and found what I had been looking for: the only dress I'd brought with me. I had jammed it in the bag on the off chance we went out to dinner someplace nice for my birthday.

I gave the dress the sniff test—it passed. Barely. I shook it out a few times—coming dangerously close to knocking over some figurines off a shelf—and checked the bodice for any food embeds someone might mistake for modern jewelry. It passed inspection, so I went in search of the Spanx I needed to wear under the dress.

I took everything with me into the guest bathroom just as Glenn came back from the kitchen.

"Where's the wedding?" I asked through the door.

"The Los Arboledas Inn."

"Something small, tasteful and understated?" I asked.

"Not really."

I pulled the long-sleeved sheath of nude lace over my head and down over the satin slip before making my way to my mom's bedroom to look at myself in her full-length mirror.

Ughhh. The dress emphasized all of the things about my body I hated. I looked like a giant flesh-toned Tootsie

Roll.

Glenn put a thimble-sized cup of coffee down on the dressing table and flew up to hover over my shoulder. I couldn't help notice his wings, which were moving so fast they were almost invisible. He put a finger under his chin, sizing me up in the mirror.

"On the day of her picture-perfect wedding, the bride wore white …" Glenn said as if he was reading the wedding announcement in the *New York Times*. "And fairy godmother wore beige."

"It's not beige," I snapped. "It's blush."

Glenn flew closer to my mirrored reflection and made a face.

"It's beige," he said. "Dead-fish beige."

"I'm new to this, but isn't trying to blend into the background one of the rules of being a fairy godmother?"

"So you have looked at the rulebook," Glenn said with a broad grin.

"Shut up," I deadpanned.

"Blending, yes. Wearing something hideous … not so much. You look … lumpy."

"I am lumpy. Maybe I need another pair of Spanx."

"You are not lumpy. You've got curves."

"I don't have anything else with me wedding-appropriate."

"Let's see what your mom has in her closet, shall we?" Glenn flew into my mother's walk-in closet and turned on the light as I followed closely behind.

"I can't wear my mother's clothes. We're not the same size. She's tiny. Nothing will fit me."

"What about this?" Glenn held up a little black dress on a hanger.

"What is that? My curiosity was aroused. It was the perfect little black cocktail dress. It looked like it had been made for me out of jersey fabric. The mini-dress had a blouson top with crystals sparkling along the boat neckline and open back. "I can't see Mom wearing that."

Glenn shrugged. "Why don't you try it on? Just for giggles."

"I don't think so," I said. "It still has the tags on it."

"Humor me," he said, his face pulled into a dark scowl. "Put it on." His eyes, intense and unblinking, were focused on me. He scared me a little, which prompted me to take the dress out of his hands. The least I could do was go into the bathroom and try it on.

I pulled the Spanx straight down from my body and let it hang in a useless circle around my left ankle. Then I kick-lined it across the room like one of the Radio City Music Hall Rockettes. It landed on top of the shower curtain.

"Touchdown!" I shouted, thrilled to get rid of the Spanx. Just then my wings unfurled over my head in what had to be their own interpretation of a sigh of relief.

"My thoughts exactly," I said to my wings in the mirror as I pulled on the little black dress. "But you guys are going to have to be on your best behavior tonight."

The dress hugged my body, revealing nothing, but hinting at hidden curves. It may have looked simple on the hanger, but it looked like a showstopper on me.

I looked good. Freakin' good. Duchess of Sussex good. It even made my naturally wild mane of hair look planned and perfect, no need for any product. I left the bathroom and went to show Glenn.

"Wow," Glenn said. "Wow, wow, wow."

"I know, right?" I paraded back and forth in front of the mirror like a catwalk model.

Glenn smiled. "You are going to rock this wedding."

"I don't think so." The dress suited me, but … "I am not going out of this house in this dress."

"Shoot me. Shoot me now." Glenn dropped his head into his hands. "Why not?"

"My wings are completely exposed." I turned around and played show-and-tell to make my point. A revealing "V" in the back of the dress showed my wings taped down.

"Your wings!" Glenn looked horrified. "What did you do?"

"Keeping them under control." I shot back. I couldn't help noticing my wings were wilted after being taped for safekeeping.

Glenn's face was grave. "I didn't think you'd go to such lengths."

I twisted myself into a pretzel to take the tape off. The moment they were set free, they stretched and contracted involuntarily. Feathers rained down around me, covering the floor.

"You'll learn to control them," Glenn soothed.

I studied at my reflection in the mirror. "If all that matters is there's something like a fairy godmother at this wedding, just in case, then I'll put the other dress back on and go." I reached for the beige dress, but Glenn got to it first and flew away from me.

"Where are you going?" I spoke sharply.

"Joke's on you. It's a fairy-themed wedding," Glenn shouted over his shoulder. "Every woman in the bridal party is going to be wearing fake wings. You'll blend into the background just like the fairy godmother's rules state."

"Seriously?" I couldn't believe it.

Glenn nodded. "The guests have been invited to wear wings too. They all want to look just like you. If you didn't have wings, you wouldn't blend in. You went through Chrysalis just in the nick of time."

"You've got to be kidding me." My wings were a curse I couldn't get past. I couldn't imagine anyone would actually want a pair.

"Tonight is the perfect time for you to literally stretch your wings and let your inner beauty shine," Glenn said. "Especially in that dress."

"But…" I was speechless. I didn't have any reason not to wear the beautiful little black dress of my dreams to the wedding.

"Any other objections?" Glenn asked, his winning smirk more than I could handle.

"I don't have any shoes to go with this dress," I said triumphantly.

"Shoes?" Glenn seemed surprised. "I've been working for a fairy godmother for ten years. Shoes, I can do."

Glenn flew back inside my mom's closet. I stood in front of the mirror listening to him sorting through boxes.

"If you come back with glass slippers, I'm not putting them on," I insisted. "I'm not Cinderella."

Glenn came back holding a pair of strappy evening sandals covered in Swarovski glass crystals. They were gorgeous. I immediately took them off his hands.

"Stuart Weitzman sandals? In my mom's closet?" I was stunned. "They're my size."

"Put them on," Glenn said through gritted teeth. Why argue with a tiny angry pixie?

The shoes looked amazing. Also, it wasn't lost on me the crystal-studded shoes matched the crystals on the back of the dress. "They're perfect."

"It's a miracle." Off my look, Glenn added, "I'm kidding."

I went into the bathroom to apply some make-up. Pretending to fill my mom's glass slippers for one night might be fun.

"Now that we've nailed the wardrobe," Glenn said. "Let's go over the basics."

"Basics?"

"Fairy Godmother 101," Glenn said. "Now, what is your objective tonight?"

"To make ..." I hesitated. Should I tell the truth? "I haven't read the entire book. Every time I open it, I fall asleep."

"That's the pixie dust. Probably a lot of residue on the pages," he said. "You'll eventually build up an immunity, but for now you'll need to plan on taking a lot of unscheduled naps."

"Hard to argue with that," I said, dabbing watermelon blush onto my cheekbones.

"You say that now, but when you're in a public place or need to be somewhere"—Glenn frowned—"you won't be happy about it. Now, tell me, as a fairy godmother, what is your purpose?"

"A happily-ever-after ending?"

"Close enough." Glenn nodded. "What does a fairy godmother ask herself in any situation that requires her immediate attention?"

"Not a clue." I couldn't focus on Glenn's questions while my reflection in the mirror was glowing.

"A fairy godmother always asks herself 'Who needs my kindness most today?'; being kind is the essence of being a fairy godmother. If all else fails tonight, be kind."

"Like a random act of kindness?" I asked with a barely contained grin.

"Don't. I've seen the bumper sticker. Been there. Done it," he said.

"Right. Okay. Got it. Kindness."

"And what are you supposed to do to make sure 'happily ever after' happens?"

"Whatever ..."

"It takes. That's right." Glenn looked pleased. "Whatever it takes to ensure a 'happily ever after' ending," Glenn said. "Anything, and everything, within your powers, without breaking any of the rules, or else you forfeit all of your powers, got it?"

"But I don't have any powers," I said.

"You don't think you have any powers, but you do. Magic doesn't just happen. It takes years of practice. You can't just snap your fingers and '*voila.*'" Glenn snapped his tiny fingers and suddenly the world was silent. The clock stopped ticking. The fridge stopped humming. The crickets in the garden stopped chirping. It was freakishly quiet.

"Sorry. My bad." Glenn snapped his fingers again. The

whirring sounds of life all around us came back. "Stopped time. You don't need to know how to do that. At least not yet. It's pretty advanced."

"Whoa. Wait. How did you stop time?" My heart was racing. Glenn made it look so easy. Something I had no idea any living creature could do.

"I can't explain it." Glenn shook his head.

"Honestly. I can't do magic."

"Look, some of us have more magical gifts than others, but you shouldn't have to use any of your powers tonight. If anything goes wrong, you can use plain old common sense and a fairy godmother's gentle guiding hand to get it back on track." Glenn waved his tiny hand in the air.

"How will I know if there's a problem I need to address?"

"You'll know. Believe me, you'll know. Here are a couple of fairy godmother wands to keep in the bottom of your purse just in case. They're woven from lavender."

"What do I do with them?" I asked.

"They're used mostly for conjuring and enchantment," Glenn said. "But the scent is also a powerful aphrodisiac. It can stimulate the appetite, and get rid of embarrassing gas and bloating. And I don't need to tell you how often that will come in handy."

"TMI."

"Here's a tin of pixie dust." He floated over a small decorative box on my mom's dresser. I shoved it deep into the bottom of my purse. "Give it a try while you're out tonight. You can cause someone to give an unexpected compliment to a perfect stranger. Which can lead to a heart-warming moment but, honestly, don't go looking for any pro bono work tonight. Keep your focus on the bride and groom getting the happily-ever-after ending they deserve."

I nodded, following Glenn down the hall and out into my mother's garden. He darted underneath an ornamental cabbage, coming back a minute later, frustration furrowing his brow. He shook his head and flew under another shrub. Leaves shook on the tree and bark was dislodged from the trunk. When he returned he looked irked. His hat had been knocked from its original angle, now pushed onto the back of his head. His eyes narrowed as he flew past me into the thick growth of shrubs in the back of the garden.

"What are you doing?" I asked.

"Looking for Joey."

"The bunny?"

"Yep," Glenn said. "He's your date."

"I'm not taking a bunny to a wedding," I said.

"You have to take him. He's your mom's favorite escort, and she promised the groom there would be an extra man at the bridesmaids' table. Chicks dig him."

"But how?" I asked.

"We're going to enchant him."

"Does he speak?" I asked.

"Not a word. But the bridesmaids don't want to have deep conversations with some hot guy they've never met before at a wedding. They just want to dance."

"With a rabbit?"

"Joey is a great dancer," Glenn said. "He's like the Derek Hough of rabbits. You won't be able to get him off the dance floor. He's your secret weapon if anything goes bad."

"What?" I was dressed for a role I wasn't sure I could pull off.

"Not that anything will go bad. It'll all be fine." Glenn spoke in a calm manner. "I promise."

CHAPTER 10

Rule #10: A fairy godmother knows to beware of magical creatures offering favors.

Glenn was right about one thing ...

Joey was a total hottie in human form. By the time we arrived at the wedding venue, he was no longer a sniffing and snuffing; he looked like he'd stepped out of a San Laurent men's cologne commercial in a white dinner jacket and black tuxedo pants.

I turned my keys over the valet and put my arm through Joey's elbow just in time to pull him away from some ornamental cabbage he was beginning to nibble in the landscaping. I was going to have to keep my eyes on him if they served crudities as an appetizer. I pulled him in the direction of the other guests on my way to check in with the wedding planner according to Glenn's instructions.

Jessica Smithson was an heiress. Her mother's family had all the money. Her dad was a hard-working guy who had fallen for a princess. Jessica was marrying a man just like dear old dad.

Jessica and Raphael were being married in the rose

garden with a million-dollar view of the Pacific Ocean. It was like an Instagram feed come to life.

The trees had been strung with miles and miles of fairy lights. Bowers of flowers had been tied to the trunks of trees in the few spots not covered by brightly colored blossoms and vines. The heavenly scent of jasmine, honeysuckle, lavender, and rosemary hung in the deliciously scented warm summer air.

Moroccan lanterns of all different sizes and shapes had been hung above a sea of round tables covered with crisp white linens. Hurricane lamps and glass-covered candles in shades of cream and vanilla added to the garden's bewitching glow.

A harpist was providing background music a few feet from the ceremony. Later her instrument would be rolled away to make room for a dance floor.

Joey hopped out of the car and followed me into the garden. He stared at me intensely but said nothing. He could be an amazing dancer, but his silence was a bit disarming. I was relieved when he followed a waiter with a tray full of crudité in the direction of the dance floor. I snagged a glass of champagne off a cater waiter's tray and took a sip, enjoying the bubbling effervescence on my tongue.

Before I had a chance to take a second sip, Zara appeared next to me. She was dressed in a skin-tight candy-apple red suit dress and four-inch Louboutin heels.

What kind of fairy godmother wears red to a wedding?

"Aviana," she said, her voice a practiced purr. "I understand you're filling in for your mom tonight."

"I'm not sure that's possible," I said.

"Yes. Hers are some mighty big glass slippers to fill."

"So I've heard."

"Oh, I forgot. Your mom doesn't work as a full-time fairy godmother. She has a 'job,'" Zara said, employing the most aggressive air quotes I had ever witnessed for added emphasis.

My dislike of her was rising up in the back of my throat like bile.

"Black is an unusual choice for a wedding," Zara said.

I held my head high in my little black dress and raised my chin to challenge her.

"I was trying to blend. I'm a fairy godmother. It's one of the rules."

"Has blending into the background ever been a 'real' problem for you?" A passive-aggressive smile danced on her lips. She looked mildly stunned as irritation washed over my face. I took a deep calming breath before changing the subject in order to keep from shaking her until her teeth rattled.

"You have an incredible reputation, Zara, but this wedding"—I turned to include the spectacle surrounding us—"*far* exceeds all my expectations of a Wakefield wedding by Wisteria Wholesale."

"I don't like to pat myself on the back," Zara said. "But everyone here is talking about how amazing I am. They're saying this is one of my best efforts. One VIP guest told me it rivals the Governor's Ball at the Academy Awards."

"It is spectacular. It's like a midsummer's night dream come to life," I said.

"Really?" she asked, looking for assurance. She treated my calculated compliment like hand cream, enjoying the pleasure as she soaked it in.

"You know, Aviana…" When she spoke, her lips stuck on her teeth. I could tell she was making an effort to be nice, and it was killing her. "I couldn't have done it all without your mom. She is so good at the 'little things.'"

The little things?

Zara was giving credit to Mom for the "little things?" How dare she?

While I had my own issues with my mom, as a fairy godmother by all accounts, she was a legend. How dare Zara belittle her accomplishments? My wings reacted to my anger and began twitching between my shoulders. I needed to calm down to keep them a secret. I took a calming breath, excused myself to Zara, and walked back to the front of the venue where Jessica's guests were starting to arrive.

The invitations as they had been sent out asked the guests to wear "black ties and gossamer wings," per the bride's request. The guests had thrown themselves into the spirit of the event. Masquerading as fairies, they wore wings of every shape and size. A few carried Swarovski crystal-covered magic wands. And tiaras. Every head had a tiara.

I covered my giggles with my hand. These weren't the kind of people who enjoyed dressing up or believed in fairies. I knew because they were the people I had grown up around in Beverly Hills. These were titans of industry and Hollywood executives. I was surprised Dad and Madeleine hadn't made the guest list. Perhaps they'd had to send their regrets when they planned their trip to Mexico.

A feeling of anticipation hung in the air as I stood near the entrance watching the cars pull up and deposit invited guests near the entrance to the inn. I smiled when I saw an older woman adjusting the elastic bands holding her wings in place after she got out of the car. Her date strolled around to her side and helped her straighten one of the wings. I dug deep in my evening bag and found the little tin of pixie dust Glenn had given me. I had no idea what it would do, but I dumped a few in my palm and blew them toward the older couple.

"You look beautiful tonight," he said, extending his arm to escort her under the flower archway to the backyard party. Her face glowed with the compliment as she smiled up at him.

Smiling at the couple, I was glad to have spread some joy.

After walking around for a bit, I reconnected with Zara at the back of the venue as more guests arrived. "Wow," I said. "It's a sea of tiaras out there."

"It's like being at a fairy godmother family reunion on the island of misfit toys," Zara snapped. She looked annoyed and out of sorts until she noticed someone in the crowd.

"Charmaine," she said with a practiced smile and wave of her hand.

The mother of the bride joined us. She had thrown herself into the spirit of her daughter's wedding and had a pair of wings made to match her custom-made "mother of the bride" dress. Her wings were modest in size but were obviously decorated with real gemstones.

"This is Liliana's daughter, Aviana. She's helping out tonight since Liliana can't be here."

"Ohh. Nice to meet you."

Zara's phone rang and she checked the number. "Excuse me for a moment, I have to take this call."

Zara disappeared, leaving me alone with the mother of the bride.

"You look like your mom. I bet you hear that a lot." Charmaine grinned. "And you have the most beautiful wings ever. Where did you get them?"

I laughed. "They came with the dress."

She took a closer look at my wings, which made me a bit nervous. "How do you get them to stay on?"

"It's magic," I said with a wink.

"Speaking of which, did you know your mom came up with the theme for the wedding?" Charmaine asked. "I know she's just a yoga instructor at the inn, but the manager says she's helped so many brides' wildest dreams come true. I'm certain she's been pulling a lot of strings behind the scenes to make Jessica's fairy tale wedding come true."

"Your happiness is her reward. I'll be sure to tell her," I said.

"Oh, I see someone I need to talk with. Excuse me." Charmaine left to go greet some of her guests moments before Zara returned.

"I've got to coordinate a few things with the caterer. I'll be right back. Don't *do* anything. Got it?"

"No problem." I glanced over my shoulder. My wings were behaving themselves. Despite all of Glenn's reassurances, I was taking a risk being out in public with them on display. I didn't have any control over my wings. Depending on my mood, they would dance to life and flap in a staccato beat over my head.

What if I ran into someone who knew Dad and Madeleine?

Feeling uncomfortable, I stayed near the back of the venue during the processional, just in case, but the ceremony went off without a hitch. The minister was jovial and provided the guests with a chuckle, but when the bride and groom shared their personal vows, there wasn't a dry eye in the garden. They came up the aisle as a married couple for the first time to cheers all around.

And yet I couldn't chase away a sense of impending doom. I pressed my fingers to my temples, hoping to relieve some anxiety, and started making a mental list of my blessings.

I was wearing a gorgeous dress, and Joey, while nothing more than the manifestation of Glenn's creative imagination, did look incredibly handsome. A casual observer would have no doubt I was out on a date with a male model. If ever there was a time in my life for a "selfie," it was now.

I pulled Joey aside and snapped off a duck-faced selfie and posted it on Instagram. A few minutes later, just as I'd hoped, my cellphone rang. I knew Josie would chime in.

"Your date is a total hottie," Josie said. "I'll need all the dirty details.

"I can't talk right now," I joked. "I'm at a very posh event."

"Okay. So, who is this guy?"

"He's one of my mom's neighbors," I said.

"And does your mother have any more neighbors who look like that?"

"She might." I giggled. "I can ask."

"Are you doing okay?" she asked. "Seriously. I worry about you, kid. I always knew you were meant for something better than the legal pool. I just hope you find it." Josie was my longest and best friend. She always worried about me but was my biggest supporter.

"I'm working on it," I said.

"Are you getting any good face?" she asked hopefully.

"If I see anyone famous, you'll be the first person I text."

"Call me if you need me," Josie said.

"Thanks," I said.

I tucked my phone away and looked around at the beautiful scene around me.

Why didn't I want to be a fairy godmother? Why was I fighting so hard?

This was fun. Way better than being a legal assistant. If only I could get the hang of my wings. I glanced at my watch. It was still early, but as far as I could tell, this fairy godmothering business was a piece of cake.

Glenn said I had at least until midnight before I needed to start to worry about Joey's enchantment wearing off. Still, I should keep an eye on him. When I finally found him in the crowd, he was leading three middle-aged women in doing the bunny hop around on the dance floor.

What kind of fairy godmother would I be if I stole their dance partner away while the night was still young and they were still having fun? Maybe I could just relax and enjoy the party for a moment or two.

I'm staying for one more song. Then I'm getting Joey and we're out.

I pulled a tall flute of champagne off a waiter's passing tray and took a sip, savoring the sparkling bubbles dancing on the tip of my tongue. I found my way over to the table with the hors d'oeuvres. Savoring the flavor of the spinach and cheese inside the puff pastry, I nibbled on a spanakopita and bacon-wrapped shrimp. I had just snagged two chicken skewers and a mushroom turnover off a cater waiter's tray and was on my way to check out the seafood tower when *he* walked into my field of vision.

Nash Nolan. My heart skittered.

At first glance, he was taller than all the other men in the room, but he wasn't taller, he was just more vivid. He was wearing an impeccably tailored suit in a dark gray glen plaid fabric with a black shirt underneath. He stole my breath as he made his way toward me with a plate full of appetizers, his eyes targeting the same seafood tower I was coveting.

"Pardon me," he said. "Can I just slip in between here for a couple oysters?"

"Sure," I said. I took a step back to make room for him. It must not have been enough room though, because he brushed close to me as he pushed into the buffet table. He put some oysters on his plate and topped them with fresh horseradish.

He began to walk away before he stopped and looked at me, recognition slowly dawned over his features. "Hello," he said. "I know you."

"Hi," I squeaked.

"Yesterday." He wagged a finger at me.

I nodded. "Yes, but I think you've mistaken me for someone else."

"You weren't at the inn yesterday?"

"No. It was me. I just don't know you.

"I don't know your name, but I know your face."

"You do?"

He nodded. "I've been telling everyone about you.

"Thank you."

He reached out his hand for mine. "Nash Nolan."

"Aviana Willowbrook." His touch sent tingles up my arms and into the tips of my wings. I closed my eyes and willed them to stay quiet.

"Aviana. I knew it would be something beautiful. You're like something out of a dream. My wildest dreams."

I blushed. How could this guy suddenly see me so differently? All the times I'd passed him in the halls of the law firm he'd acted as if I was invisible. This was crazy. Absolutely crazy. I scanned the crowd over his shoulder for Zara, certain she would frown on me for talking to him. After all, she was with him that night at Mr. Chow's. For all I knew, he was her boyfriend.

Nash must've mistaken my distraction for disinterest because he asked, "Are you here with a date?"

I glanced at Joey, who nodded in my direction. He was still dancing with more than one woman at the same time. "Well, I came with someone," I said. "But it's just a set up."

"I understand. I don't want to be a bother." As he started to walk away, he turned back and whispered, "You have beautiful wings." His words made my heart skip a beat.

Like fern heads, my wings unfurled and stretched out to their fullest wingspan. I wanted Nash Nolan. I wanted him bad ... and my wings were certainly aware of my desire.

"Thank you," I whispered, my breath caught in my throat.

You. Have. Beautiful. Wings.

Four little words I never imagined hearing from anyone ever in my life. I kept replaying his words in my head, knowing what they were doing to my wings, but I didn't care ... Nathan thought I had beautiful wings.

"Conceited!" I spat at them. I pushed up against an ivy-covered wall and used my body weight to get them to settle back against my body. I hoped no one was watching.

Just then Zara reappeared.

"Where have you been? I've been looking everywhere for you." Her face was pinched with anger. "I've got to make a couple of calls for the post-wedding brunch tomorrow. I need you to keep an eye on things. Can you do that?" Zara asked.

"No worries. I've got this." I painted a big faux smile on my face and watched Zara disappear into the edges of the party.

I was now officially *the* fairy godmother on duty. The responsibility made me feel jittery, and soon my wings were tapping out a nervous thrum on my shoulders.

"Not now," I whispered, and their beat softened a little.

I looked around the garden, searching the crowd for faces I recognized. Jessica was talking animatedly to a group of well-wishers under the hanging lanterns in the dining area. She looked radiant, smiling and touching each person who reached out for her. Her dress had been designed to fit her strap-on fairy wings, which were a work of art—the curved structure of their skeleton delicately revealed by a layer of shimmering sheer satin.

I watched her step away from the crowd to reach for a glass of water, not realizing one of her silk fairy wings dipped inside one of the candle-filled lanterns hanging low over the dinner tables. It only took a second before the tall white taper had set the tip of her wing on fire. The flammable material making up her gossamer wings went up in flames like dry kindling.

Mayday! Mayday!

There was a lot of party between where I was standing and where Jessica was under the tent. I would have to push my way through an obstacle course of partiers to get to her.

Why would they leave a fairy godmother with no magical skills in charge of a wedding? This was a disaster. If I couldn't get there fast enough to take care of the problem, Jessica was going to be seriously injured.

On the dance floor Joey and the bridesmaids were having a great time. Jessica's mom was with a group of wealthy matrons who were admiring the elegant wedding scene from the terrace up near the house. Jessica's new husband was at the bar, laughing with friends who were hassling him about marrying up. Everyone in my line of sight was having a great time. Even the bartenders and waiters looked like they were having fun.

If only there was a "real" fairy godmother on duty who knew what she was doing. Instead, the only fairy godmother on duty was me. And I was completely useless.

CHAPTER 11

Rule #11: A fairy godmother does whatever it takes to ensure a happily ever after.

The bride was on fire.

Was I the only one of the hundreds of invited guests looking at the bride? Had no one else noticed? Come on, people. The bride is supposed to be the center of attention at her wedding. Why wasn't anyone else in a panic?

Where was this girl's fairy godmother? If ever there was a time when she needed one, now was it. Zara had picked a bad time to go and make some calls.

Shitake mushrooms!

Like it or not, I was the fairy godmother in charge. I had no training, no magical powers, and absolutely no clue, but at least I knew some of the basics. Five hundred wedding guests had no idea the reception was about to go up in smoke. This was going to end in disaster. *Gah!*

Okay. Moving on. Rule number two. Whatever it takes. Whatever it takes to create a happily-ever-after ending.

Jessica's wedding would be talked about for years. Not as it should have been talked about as *the* social event in Southern California, but as the biggest crazy-ass disaster anyone has ever seen. Urban legends would be created about the bride who went up in smoke at her backyard reception.

"Bride BBQed at her own reception. Video at eleven." The newscaster would smirk during a commercial break. Up on YouTube there would be more than one video from a guest's cellphone with a couple of million views. And the whole entire thing would be my fault.

Zara put me in charge. She was depending on me, and I blew it. I had been enjoying a goldfish bowl-sized glass of champagne and gobbling appetizers when I was supposed to be on fairy godmother duty.

It didn't matter. No one moved.

It took less effort for Moses to part the waves on the Red Sea than it did for me to find a clear path to the bride through the partygoers.

"Pardon me's" and "excuse me's" with a tone of complete panic in my voice made no difference at all. The people at this wedding were strategic minglers. They had found their perfect place to party under the giant old live oak trees and they weren't about to budge. They were having too much fun, deliciously pressed against one another as they sipped expensive champagne and nibbled Ahi tuna appetizers. They weren't going anywhere.

To top it off, Jessica was hidden from everyone and didn't seem to have any idea about what was happening.

I wiggled through the crowd and finally made it to the edge of the dance floor, then bolted toward the bride, hidden in the alcove of the hedges.

"Jessica! Your wings are on fire!" I shouted. Between the dance music pumping out of two-story speakers and all of the people talking, my desperate screams of impending disaster were ignored.

Just as I was rushing to the bride's rescue, Joey—who was at the lead of a line of dancers in a conga line— grabbed me around the waist and pushed me into the lead in front of him.

"Joey! Let go!" I admonished, pulling his fingers from around my waist and hauling him from the conga line, pushing toward the bride. He gave me the same dead-eyed look he'd had since he'd undergone his transformation. He was, after all, just a rabbit. If only I had a carrot tucked in my purse.

"Jessica!" I screamed again.

The older woman standing directly in front of me winced and shot me a sour look. She was even less enthusiastic about me when I pushed past her, jostling her plate of hors d'oeuvres.

Flames bounced along the top of her wing, and yet the party continued without anyone noticing the completely freaked-out fairy godmother pushing her way toward the bride. Why hadn't she noticed the heat? Was she under a spell?

Jessica would be scarred for life. My mind flashed forward to the worst-case scenario. The groom keeping vigil at her bedside in the Sherman Oaks burn unit instead of going on a honeymoon. A battalion of news trucks parked in front of the hospital. The news filing reports about how the fairytale wedding had turned into a nightmare.

Not now, Aviana.

I pushed those thoughts out of my mind and kept moving.

I was going to have to do something drastic. I would have to opt for something on a global scale.

"Excuse me!" I pushed past an older woman and man blocking my path and continued to move through conversation groups like a linebacker—apologizing with every step and drawing looks of disdain and ire all along the way.

The fire had already made its way down over the bride's left wing and jumped over to the right. The flames were moving so quickly, completely destroying her wings and getting closer to the back of her dress. The long waves of her beautifully coiffed hair would be the next thing to go up in flames. This was not getting better.

Finally, the groom glanced at his bride and freaked out when he saw the flames licking at the hem of her dress. The best man noticed the fire a moment later and they both went into action, diving toward the bride like a couple of middle linebackers. Together they managed to knock over the cupcake tower next to Jessica. The back of her dress was about to be destroyed by fire, and the front was now covered in the debris of a red velvet cupcake explosion.

Then it hit me. I only had one option.

I snapped my fingers, putting my palm up in the air to make a stop sign.

All motion stopped, besides Joey, of course, who was enchanted and still dancing, busting moves on the dance floor surrounded by a circle of motionless bridesmaids frozen in awkward poses.

Extending the first finger of my left hand straight out from my body, I made a slow-rolling, counter-clockwise motion. Around me all the action that had just happened moved backward as if I'd hit the rewind button on a video. The music made a grating nails-on-chalkboard sound; the vocals distorted.

The red velvet cupcakes jumped off Jessica's dress and settled back onto the display. The frosting on top of the cupcakes showed no signs of having been disturbed. The pink champagne went back into the antique glass no longer lying shattered on the ground.

The bridegroom and the best man were frozen in time, completely horizontal three feet above the ground. It looked as if they were levitating. I slipped between the bride and groom and pulled down the low-hanging lantern that had set off the terrible chain of events and carried it to a rock wall far away from the bride.

The air was still and incredibly quiet, not even a bird was singing. I let out a deep sigh of relief, then somewhere in the stillness, a man cleared his throat. I looked up the stone steps. Nash was standing at the top of the stairs looking down at the party captured in stillness, a look of complete shock plastered on his face.

"What's happening?" He took another step forward.

Why is he still moving?

I snapped my fingers. The party sprang back to life around me—minus the disastrous fire and ruined wedding dress. Jessica was smiling. Raphael and his best man landed on their feet, dancing without missing a beat.

What had he seen?

I glanced around the massive garden party. It had been a huge risk using magic in a public place. Anyone could've seen me, but why did it have to be him?

I studied his face as he came down the stairs. Nothing seemed amiss. Why didn't he freeze like everyone else? I heaved a sigh of relief as I caught his gaze and smiled confidently at him.

He smiled back and sent me a gesture of approval with a tip of his cocktail glass.

I toasted him back with my own champagne. I had done it. I had saved the wedding from complete disaster.

As I took my first sip, I spotted Joey. He was in the middle of the dance floor, dazed and disoriented. I checked the time. It was getting dangerously close to his witching hour. I put the glass of champagne down and went to rescue him.

But Zara found me before I got to him.

"Is everything all right?" she asked.

"Everything is fine?" I said. "I'm going to call it a night; Joey's enchantment is wearing off. I should get him home before anything happens."

"Of course," Zara said.

She looked around at the party as if she was waiting for something to happen.

"Is there anything else you need before I go?" I asked.

"No," she said. "You should go. Take Joey home."

"It was a wonderful party, Zara. You should be very proud."

"I am," she said. "Very, very proud of me."

I was incredulous. Zara believed the wedding was all about her. She was at the center of a universe of her own creation. I wanted to get as far away from her as possible.

I went in search of Joey, finding him in a chair near the dance floor.

"Come on Joey."

I half-carried, half-walked him to a bench near the valet stand. He had lost his groove and was becoming less unaware of his surroundings. He was going to transition back to bunny soon. I had to get him home as soon as possible.

I glanced around, hoping no one would see Joey's strange behavior, when I saw Nash waiting for his car nearby. He had me and Joey under close surveillance. After I'd given my ticket to the valet. Nash moved closer to me and asked, "Is it serious? With you and that guy?"

"No," I said with a giggle. "What about you? You and Zara Wakefield?"

"Strictly business," he said.

"Sharing egg rolls at Mr. Chow's is business?"

"All business," he insisted as if wanting to assure me he was available.

"Joey's a friend of my mom's. The bride wanted an extra man to dance with the bridesmaids."

Nash grinned. "Good. I mean, he was out on the dance floor with every man, woman, and child here, except you. Good thing you're not on a date."

I nodded. "Joey is always the life of the party."

Joey was still in human form, but the way he was sniffing around the ornamental cabbage dotting the border of the flower garden, made me nervous. I pulled him away from a large blossom seconds before he took a bite. Hauling him back up onto his feet, he wobbled a bit, unstable on his hind legs.

"You're leaving?" he asked.

"My job here is done."

"You're not a guest?"

"No. I was working this event."

"You're a wedding planner?"

"No. I'm kind of at a crossroads."

I was saved from elaborating any further when the valet pulled my car up to the stand. "That's my ride. I've got to go."

Nash looked amused, watching me gather up Joey, pushing him into the passenger seat.

"He looks like he's had too much to drink," Nash said. The potion was wearing off, and Joey was starting to act a bit odd.

"Joey? Nah. He doesn't drink. I've seen him take a few sips out of the birdbath, but he doesn't …" I stopped myself before I went any further. "It was nice to meet you …"

"Nash," he said, pointing at himself. As if I needed to be reminded of his name. I had repeated it over and over in my mind every time he was in the office. "Hopefully, I'll see you around the inn … Aviana."

"Hopefully," I said.

"Good night, Aviana." His voice made my stomach turn flip-flops of joy. I smiled before turning to get into the driver's seat so he wouldn't see my wings doing a similar dance of joy.

I drove home slowly, enjoying the peace and quiet. Joey was quiet and I put the top down and let my wings beat in time to the music on the car radio.

When I got back to my mom's house, I put Joey under the orange tree. Then I climbed into the big swing in the back of the garden with an oversized glass of red wine.

I kicked off my glass slippers and did the same thing with my toes. Letting my head fall back on the pillows I watched the intermittent lights of pixies in the back of the garden as they danced through the fruit trees. The world seemed enchanted as I looked at it through fresh eyes.

If you didn't really believe in happy endings, could you make other people's dreams come true?

I wasn't so sure. I did know I'd come from a long line of fairy godmothers. And I was out here working my magic. Like a boss. *Like a freakin' boss.*

CHAPTER 12

Rule #12: A fairy godmother doesn't use her magical powers if a little pixie dust will do.

The Lady Gaga of sparrows woke me the next morning just before dawn. The bird attacked her chirping singsong with such ferocity, no electronic amplification was necessary. I stood at the window for a long time as she and her little winged back-up singers all bopped around on the branches of a cherry tree performing cutting-edge bird dance choreography.

What exactly had my problem been with birds?

I headed for the kitchen where Mom had the doors to the garden open. She was breakfast on the patio in the sunshine. She was, as always, a model of athleisure luxury in a gray metallic Lululemon sweater and gray yoga tights. The color made her eyes sparkle like amethysts. She was as serene as a fairy as I've ever seen, although I sensed a little worry behind her eyes this morning.

"Good morning, darling," she said brightly. "Would you care for some breakfast?"

The table was set for breakfast for two, but I grabbed the bowl set on the table and filled it with cereal to eat over the kitchen sink. "I'm good," I said. "I'll just have some cereal."

Seconds after I poured cereal in a bowl, Glenn appeared on the patio, joining Mom for a cup of morning coffee.

"Hey, kid," Glenn said. "How'd it go last night?"

"Mostly good," I said.

"Mostly?" Glenn asked. He took off his hat and settled next to the sugar bowl, then grabbed a cup of coffee.

"What happened?" Mom asked.

Did they really need the dirty details? It was too much like bragging.

"At one point the bride was on fire." I mimed the flames shooting into the air. Once I had their attention, I couldn't help adding a bit of embellishment. "I mean, fully engulfed, dial 9-1-1, in flames."

My mom gasped. Glenn's coffee cup clattered down into the saucer. That's when I realized I'd gone too far and needed to pull back. "But nothing bad happened …" I stammered my explanation. "I-I stopped time, went back, fixed everything. No one was the wiser."

Mom was stunned speechless. They looked at each other in disbelief. It was Glenn who found his ability to speak first. "You stopped time?"

"Yeah." I went back to chewing my cereal. "Easy peasy."

Mom couldn't hide the growing look of alarm on her face. "That's an advanced fairy godmother skill, Aviana," she murmured. "How would you even know to do that?

I shot a look at Glenn. "I didn't realize."

"Your mother's right. Turning back time involves a lot of moving parts," Glenn said. "You have to make sure you don't miss anyone when you cast the spell."

"Glenn showed me." I wasn't going to let the little pixie lay all the blame at my feet.

Mom turned her laser-like lavender gaze on Glenn, compelling him to admit the truth.

"It happened," he said. "Inadvertently."

"And I'm a quick study," I said.

"Obviously," Mom said flatly. She crossed her arms over her chest, not happy with either one of us.

"Look," I walked out onto the patio to plead my case. "In the end I fixed the trouble and restarted the party. No problem-o."

"Let's hope so." Mom rubbed the back of her neck. "Right now, we don't need to borrow any trouble."

"What about Joey?" Glenn asked.

"His enchantment wore off sooner than I expected, but I got him off the dance floor and brought him home none the worse for wear."

"So, no other problems?" Mom asked.

"No other problems. It went really well." I smiled to cover my lie.

"I'm going up to the inn to teach hot yoga this morning. Do you want to come with me?" Mom asked. "I can show you around my work."

I shook my head. "Thanks, but I need bigger cardio. I'm going to go out for a run. I'll meet you at the inn afterward."

Glad to be outdoors and relieving some of my anxiety. Jogging always helped. The pine trees high up on the nearby mountaintop looked like toothpicks, but the air was so clear I could almost smell their spicy scent. I broke into a disjointed run heading toward El Encanto. I couldn't remember the last time I had exercised of my own free will and volition. Not to mention being in the outdoors, breathing unfiltered air. I ran until I couldn't stand the split in my side any longer, and then I found my way back to my mom's house.

I texted Ruby to let her know I would catch up with her later. She had a riding lesson this morning, so I didn't expect a reply. I took a shower and got dressed. Then headed up to the inn.

Mom was still in her yoga class, so I walked down to a

little organic café near the yoga studio. Moving from the bright light of day into the natural light inside the cool café, I was momentarily blinded.

"Hey, Aviana," a faceless person greeted me as if I was a rock star and they were my biggest fan. I blinked a few times before my sight returned to normal.

Nash was alone in the café, placing his order at the counter. He grinned broadly. "Put whatever she wants on my tab, Oscar," he said to the guy behind the counter.

"Tall dirty chai?" I asked.

Oscar nodded. "Comin' right up."

"What's that?" Nash asked. "It sounds good."

"Chai tea latte with a shot of espresso," I explained.

"Make it two," Nash said. Oscar moved further down the counter to make our drinks. We went outside and sat at a table under the shade of a big striped umbrella while we waited for our coffee order.

"What are you doing at the inn?" he asked.

"I'm meeting my mom."

"That's right. You said your mom is a yoga instructor." Nash thought about it a moment. "Liliana?"

"Yes. How did you know?" I was surprised.

"You look like her."

"Everyone in Los Arboledas keeps telling me how much we look alike." I laughed. "Honestly, I've never seen the resemblance."

"It's there. In the eyes."

"Her eyes are lavender," I protested.

"And yours are green. Forest green." He was staring deeply into mine. "Maybe it's the shape. You can definitely tell you're related."

We chatted for a few minutes until Oscar brought our drinks out on a tray. I took a sip, savoring the flavors, while racking my brain for questions to ask in order to stay with Nash a little longer.

"So … what are you doing in Los Arboledas, Nash Nolan of the Nolan Hotel Group?"

He blushed brightly in the sunlight. "And I thought I was here on the down-low," he said. His smile revealed his dimples. I nearly swooned.

When he took off his dark-framed glasses and rubbed his eyes, I got an unobstructed view of his eyes. His eyes weren't green but in fact a Sherwin-Williams paint sample mix-up of delicious warm browns. I was temporarily lost in them, and I had to give myself a nudge to return to reality and try to form words.

"The … the Nolan Group wouldn't be thinking about buying the inn, would they?" I stammered having recovered from my swoon. "An old-school family-style resort like this doesn't match the Nolan Group business model and neither do its guests."

He pushed his glasses back onto his nose. "You're not a journalist, are you?" he teased.

I shook my head. "The only reason I know way more about your business than I should is that my dad is Hal Stern." I didn't usually name-drop, but I wanted to be honest about where I'd gotten my information. "He worships young guys like you who have a big net worth and even bigger business acumen."

He nodded in agreement. "The inn is old school and run-down. It's been owned by one family for a long time, so it shows it's age, but it provides the Nolan Group with something we've been wanting for a long time: a luxury spa with a worldwide reputation where our high-end business clients can go relax and unwind when they're not working." He paused momentarily.

"And …" he continued, "hipsters love old-school luxury, of which the inn is the epitome."

I could sit and listen to him all day.

"Wow. Your argument is very well-reasoned. Sounds like you have a plan."

"And what about you, Aviana? Last night you mentioned you were at a crossroads."

"I work at Stern, Fayed, and Lopez as a legal assistant

..."

"I hear a 'but' coming." He grinned.

"What do you mean?"

"Like, I'm a legal assistant, but what I really want to do is be an eye doctor."

"An eye doctor?" I giggled like an eighth-grader.

He smiled, revealing his devastating dimples again. "You never know what people's hidden passions are."

"True." A hot flush of color rose up from my neck as my wings strained a bit against the tape holding them down. I had to refocus and think about something other than him. And I needed to give him an honest answer. "I've recently been given a new opportunity. I'm just not sure if I'm cut out for it. And so that's why I'm in Los Arboledas. It seems like a good place to make decisions."

Nash nodded. "You may be right."

I took a sip of my dirty chai to hide my eyes from his intense gaze. Maybe if I didn't look directly at him for a few seconds I could get my attraction to him under control.

I took another sip.

"Do you like what you do?" I asked. "Working for the family business?"

He did a spit-take before a crooked smile split his face and he broke into a deep, loud laugh.

"What?" I asked. "Did I say something funny?"

"No one has ever asked me that before."

"Seriously?"

"I think most people assume if you're born into a family with a successful business that you're on an easy street for the rest of your life. But I was never sure I wanted to go into the hotel business. Most days I'm overscheduled and underwhelmed by what I'm actually able to accomplish. Some days, I think I'd rather work construction."

"You want to build things?"

"Something tangible I could actually hold in my hands

at the end of a day's hard work."

"The inn is a fixer-upper?"

"Maybe."

"Are you handy with a nail and hammer?"

He laughed. "I have bad eyesight and terrible eye-hand coordination. My mom put me in kindergarten when I was three. Shoe-tying was still a problem for me, so she bought me slip-on loafers."

"Cheater," I challenged.

"Yeah, but I could read real books, and I had already memorized the multiplication table. Being advanced sounds like a good thing, but I was always younger and smaller than everyone else in school."

I grinned. "When did you catch up?"

"Not until I was sixteen. And a junior in college."

"Too late," I said. "To help you with bullies."

He nodded. "Way too late."

"I am a late bloomer," I said. "So, I had the opposite problem, but I'm not a stand-out in gym class either."

"I still hate the gym," he said. "Too many memories of being used for target practice during dodge ball."

"If you see me in a gym, shoot me, I've obviously been eaten by zombies," I explained. "How do you feel about camping?"

He grinned. "I can't go. Not without my asthma inhaler. You?"

"I don't mind sitting around a campfire making s'mores and singing 'Kumbaya' at night. But when I wake up in the morning, I want to be wrapped up in a terrycloth robe in a hotel suite."

"I may be able to arrange that," he said.

When I was brave enough to look up into his eyes, he met my gaze without hesitation. Were my feelings written all over my face? I really liked him. He was so much better as a person in reality than he was as my crush in my imagination.

We finished our drinks and started walking on the path

back to the main building. Side by side, I didn't have the distraction of looking directly into his eyes.

"So," he said. "What are you doing in your free time while you're in Los Arboledas?"

"Free time?"

"It's a concept my assistant has been telling me about." He grinned. "She says it's when you don't have any scheduled activities. And I don't have enough of them."

I made a face. "I went for a run this morning."

"A run? Sounds a lot like gym," he said. "Is it possible you might want to spend some of your free time with me? You know ... together? In the same place. At the same time."

My heart skipped a bit. Was he? Wait? Was he asking me out?

"Is this an 'ask out?'"

"A what?"

"Are you 'asking me out' on a date?"

"Yes, but I was trying to handle it a little more, you know, cool. I don't know why. I'm like the most uncool person on the planet." He stopped to consider something for a moment. "So, this is a formal 'ask out.' Tell me, Miss Willowbrook, are you going to need something in writing? Engraved on linen? Should I call your father for permission?"

"No. God, no. Please don't call my dad." And then I added, "It's just. I'm not sure it's a good idea. For me. Right now. I'm just emerging from ... Chrysalis ...

"Chris-a-lis ... What is that?"

"I mentioned it before. I'm in transition. You know, career-wise."

"Maybe I can help. We can talk over your options over dinner?"

"I don't think that's a good idea."

"There are people in the world, like your father, I believe, who would actually seek me out for guidance and counsel."

"Yes, but I'm not like him."

"What if I guarantee no gym and no camping?" he asked.

"On the date? Or for the rest of my life?" I challenged.

"Which one will make you say yes?"

"As long as there's no gym or camping, I have some 'free time' available that I can coordinate with yours," I agreed.

"Dinner? There's this place in Santa Barbara I've wanted to try. You game?"

"All right."

"Just so we're clear," he said. "You've said yes to my 'ask-out' and we're going to go on a 'date.' Provided the activities do not include camping or gym."

I wanted to kiss the teasing smile off his face.

"We're clear." I nodded with enthusiasm.

"Excellent," he said.

We stopped and exchanged cell phone numbers, and he apologized more than once for not being able to make firm plans until he spoke with his assistant.

"She has given me the silent treatment for more than twenty-four hours for double-booking her plans. It's not worth the hassle."

"I understand. It's good you know who's really in charge in the office."

"Thanks for understanding. And Aviana, about the inn …"

"It's your business," I said. "Not mine. I know how to keep a secret."

"Thank you," he said. "I appreciate your discretion."

We separated at the top of the main pathway. Nash waved good-bye, walking toward the administration building for a meeting. I strolled in the opposite direction, forcing myself not to glance over my shoulder to see if he was watching.

I ambled through the garden, stopping to look at the flowers, then found the path to the spa where Mom worked.

I was floating on air, taking the stone steps two at a time, when my phone rang. I answered it without looking at who might be calling.

"Aviana Willowbrook?" I didn't recognize her voice.

"Yes?" I came to a complete halt on the stone stairs down to the yoga studio and spa.

"I have Hal Stern calling for you. Are you available?" It was Glenda, Dad's first assistant. For the past four years, she'd worked at a desk six feet away from mine.

"Hal Stern? For me? Are you sure?" I had to double-check just to be sure.

"Yes."

"The Whale? Seriously?" I was shocked and shook to my core.

Glenda sounded annoyed. "Are you available to take his call … or not?"

I couldn't breathe. My dad hadn't called me before. Not once in my whole life. The only way I figured I'd ever hear from him anytime soon was if he butt-dialed me by accident. "Okay. Sure. I'll take it."

This will be good.

After a brief pause, my dad came on the line. "Aviana? It's your father. We need to talk."

Ya think?

"Really, Dad? You think we need to talk? Now?" I snorted with laughter.

"I had no idea you had run away to Los Arboledas. I was shocked to hear you have completely abandoned your responsibilities as Vanessa's assistant. I hope you've had time to reflect on how badly you're damaging your reputation with your current behavior."

"My reputation? What? As a legal assistant? Seriously? Dad, I have ninety-nine-and-a-half problems right now, and I've got to tell you, my reputation as a legal assistant isn't one of them."

"If you return to Los Angeles immediately, I know I

can be of some assistance to you, Aviana."

"Do you have any idea why I'm in Los Arboledas?"

"I'm assuming your mother told you some kind of crazy mixed-up story about being a fairy," he said. "She's a liar, Aviana. You mustn't believe anything she says."

"You mean I should trust the parent who planned a trip to Mexico on my birthday without me?

"I am a very busy man, Aviana. I didn't call you to discuss my shortcomings."

"Oh, I'll bet you didn't. You called to discuss mine. Unfortunately, at this time I am unwilling to discuss anything with you. Especially what you perceive as *my* shortcomings. I have spent a lifetime being lesser than. To you and Madeleine. To Vanessa and Valerie.

"For the first time in my life, I've got something going on you all don't, and I'm unwilling to give it up in order to live in the shadows again."

"Aviana, you won't be successful when you're carrying around so much anger. You need to let it go."

"You forgot my birthday, Dad."

"I didn't forget it."

"Oh, is that how you're going to play it? So you're saying you knew it was my birthday and went on a family vacation without me?

"I thought you were mature enough to postpone your birthday festivities for a week. You're not a little girl anymore."

"So what you're saying is you didn't forget my birthday, you skipped town."

"You're twisting my words, Aviana."

"You knew what could happen to me on my birthday, and you were too afraid to stick around to be with me when it happened because you knew deep in your heart my mom told you the truth." My voice cracked with emotion. I had never been this confrontational with anyone in my life, least of all my father.

"That's not true. Vanessa told us you would prefer to

139

work," he said.

"Prefer to work? Are you joking? Who prefers work to vacation? Who does that? And why take her word for it? Why not ask me? Why not come straight up and ask me?"

"In hindsight, you're right. I probably should've asked you, but you and I have never had open lines of communication." By his response, I could tell he was going to be as honest with me as I was being with him. This could hurt.

"And whose fault is that? Mine?"

"I will not take the blame for this," he said.

"You were afraid. You were afraid my mom had been telling the truth all these years and one of your kids, granted the underachiever, the one who you'd written off long ago, was going to turn out to be some kind of real-life airy-fairy daydream believer. And you couldn't perish the thought."

"I've spent my life trying to protect you from your mother's delusions. I didn't want her to infect you with her talk of fairies. After all, you could have been totally human. I was wrapped up in her fantasies when we were married but she's a liar and a troublemaker. You have been bamboozled by some of her more seductive ideas."

"You sound like you speak from experience," I said.

"I cannot continue this conversation if you are going to be this hostile. You are going to have to calm down before I can help you. You must listen to me."

"You listen to me." I was a boiling pot finally spilling over. "You had my entire life to help me. Instead you ignored a ticking time bomb you knew was going to explode. You had plenty of time to do something, and yet you did nothing."

"This is my worst nightmare," he said.

"Your worst nightmare? I've got wings. Would've been nice to have a little heads up that there was a chance this could happen. Your daughter is a fairy. With wings." I hissed into the phone. "And I'm stuck here on the central coast of California. I don't know what to do. Got any ideas, big guy? You're 'The Whale.' You always know what to do in every situation. Should I come home and we can troubleshoot?"

"No," he said in a choking voice. "If that's happened to you, don't come here. Don't come home."

Tears rolled down my face. The wet streaks curled under my chin and dripped onto the front of my shirt. I made no attempt to stop or hide them. My tears were a badge of honor. I had earned the right to be this angry.

"I will help you, Aviana. If I can. I just need some time," he said.

"Time's up. Just tell me one thing. Does Madeleine know?" I asked. "Does she know about your first wife? Does she know Mom is a fairy godmother?"

"Of course not," he said. "Who believes in fairies?"

"And what about me? What have you told her about me?"

"You are a late bloomer," he said without any malice.

"A late bloomer?" I was furious. "I am so much more than a late bloomer. I am a fairy by birth and a fairy godmother by trade. Why don't you tell her that?"

"I can't," he said.

"Well, too bad. P.S. I have a feeling being married to Mom was as close as you're ever going to get to a 'happily ever after' ending."

I hit the button to end the call. I'd heard enough.

I took a deep breath and continued down the stairs to the spa. Mom's yoga class had finished by the time I slammed into the studio.

"Are you all right?" Mom asked.

I held up my phone. "Dad."

"Do you want me to talk to him?"

"No. I've got to fight my own battles."

"Let me know if you need help with him. He's a stubborn man, but he isn't heartless," she said.

For the first time, I noticed Sylvie standing close by in

the big open space.

"What's going on with you guys?"

Mom glanced at Sylvie. "Sylvie has news…"

"The inn has been sold," Sylvie said.

I nearly swallowed my tongue. "How did you find out?"

"The yoga room at the inn is a sanctuary of gossip," Mom said. Sylvie's picked up a lot of stories here over the years. Some true. Some crap."

"Yes. Well, this *some* is true," Sylvie said, bending and rolling up the yoga mat at her feet. "The buyer is some upstart. Or kick-start. Or whatever the kids are calling it these days."

"Sounds like she knows what she's talking about," I said.

"That's the thing about Sylvie's gossip," Mom said. "She's usually right."

I couldn't agree more.

CHAPTER 13

*Rule #13: A fairy godmother never lets anyone see
her tugging on the strings of fate.*

When we walked out of the yoga studio, the sunlight
was blinding. I needed shades.

"Mom? Do you know where I can buy a pair of
sunglasses?"

"We can stop by the spa boutique at the inn and put
my employee discount to good use," she said. "I owe you a
birthday present."

It sounded like a good plan, so I agreed and made our
way to the boutique, which was full of high-end resort
wear and yoga clothes. It was not my style, but Mom
picked through the racks—she had a good eye. I left with
clothes to suit my more active lifestyle in Los Arboledas
and a new pair of black square-framed movie star
sunglasses.

We left the spa and took the stone steps up and
through the garden. I crossed my fingers hoping to run
into Nash, but I guess it wasn't meant to be. Just as we
were walking past the administration building, a man called
out Mom's name. A young woman stood next to him.

She turned and waved. "It's Mr. Els, the general manager."

Mom's eyes lit up when she mentioned his name. My mom really liked him. He was the kind of boss who went out of his way to make his employees feel like their contribution mattered, and, in her opinion, he was always impeccably dressed, like a Wall Street banker in a three-piece suit and paisley tie.

"This is my daughter, Aviana." Mom smiled and her violet eyes sparkled with pride. "She's here visiting me from Los Angeles."

"Welcome to Los Arboledas. Have you been enjoying your stay?"

"It's magical," I said with a smile.

He nodded approvingly before turning to address my mom. "I've been looking for you, Liliana," he said. "I wanted to make sure you didn't hear about the sale of the hotel from anyone else."

Too late.

"I must admit, I did hear some rumors, but nothing for sure."

"You should have no worries. You are a valuable member of the staff," he said. "I don't know what kind of voodoo you do down there in the yoga studio, Liliana. I'm just glad you do it here."

"It's not voodoo, Mr. Els, I assure you." Mom was blushing.

"I'm certain you have some kind of supernatural powers, but as long as it's not illegal or could get us in trouble with PETA," Mr. Els said with a wink. "I'm fine with it."

Mr. Els motioned to a woman with the most beautiful dark red hair standing nearby. "Liliana, I want you to meet Harper Thomas," Mr. Els said. "She's a management consultant for the Nolan Group."

Harper's shift dress was classic Grace Kelly. She was wearing a pair of seriously expensive shoes and had the same kind of regal poise as the Duchess of Cambridge.

Harper smiled and put out her hand to shake with my mom. "It's a pleasure to meet you. Mr. Els sings your praises."

Mom blushed. "Thank you, Ms. Thomas."

"I'm leaving this afternoon to go to their corporate headquarters," Mr. Els said. "While I'm in Los Angeles meeting with their executive team, Harper will be here interviewing each member of our staff."

"I'll be making recommendations to the transition team about new assignment capsules for all the inn employees," Harper explained.

"Assignment capsules?" Mom shot a worried glance at Mr. Els.

"No need to worry, Liliana," Mr. Els took the edge off Harper's corporate-speak with his calm manner. "Harper is just going to see where our redundancies are. I can assure you, the inn will always need your services. I was just telling Harper that even though she's here on business, she should find time to try the spa."

"I'd be happy to arrange some spa treatments for you during your stay with us," Mom suggested. "You should really consider finding out what the spa has to offer."

"Oh. No. No. Not for me." Harper shook her head. "I'm sure it's lovely. If you knew me better, you'd understand. I don't relax. Ever. Never have."

"Well, let me know if there is anything I can do for you while you are here, Harper." Mom's face lit up with a warm smile, relieved at the news she would still be needed. "I'm always around." Mom waved to Harper and Mr. Els as we turned to go home.

By the time we had walked home and through the front door of her house, Mom had commuted Mr. Els' suggestion that Harper try a spa treatment into her own personal mission. "I'm going to get that girl in for a one-hour massage and full-body scrub if it's the last thing I do," she said as she reached into the fridge for a pitcher of lemonade.

"Since you're a fairy godmother, shouldn't your mission be finding her Prince Charming rather than a mud facial?" I asked.

Mom gave me her most imperious stare-down. I must've provoked her. She only did it when I said something really stupid. "Not everyone needs romance, Aviana. Harper seems perfectly happy with her job. All she needs is a little balance."

Mom grabbed her glass of lemonade, made her way out to the garden, and sat in the swing. Our conversation wasn't over, so I followed behind her. "But I thought being a fairy godmother was all romance, glitter, and pink champagne."

"Being a fairy godmother isn't all 'bibbidi bobbidi boo.' It's straight-up hard work, twenty-four hours a day, seven days a week." Mom's voice crackled with tension.

"Why are there so many rules for fairy godmothers?"

She shook her head. "Most people have such unrealistic expectations of what their fairy godmother can do for them. We don't handle cash, jewelry, real estate, or revenge, and we can't get you, or anyone's mother, a date with Harry Styles," Mom said.

"Harry Styles?" I asked.

She nodded. "Believe me, I've tried."

I thought for a moment. "What about the guys in BTS?"

"Stop it," she said. Then she burst out laughing. And I joined her. I couldn't help it.

"I'm gonna go get ready to go to the fairy godmothers' governing group." I stood up and spontaneously hugged her, surprising us both.

"Are you talking about the Guild?"

"Yes."

How are you getting there?" she asked. "Do you want me to drive you?"

"Ruby is picking me up."

"Good," Mom said. "No matter what Zara says or does, establishing relationships with other fairy godmothers you can trust should be your focus. You need to know who you can turn to in a pinch."

"You don't think all fairy godmothers can be trusted?" I asked, surprised by her revelation.

"Not as much," she said sadly. "But I'm going to keep my mouth shut. It's important for you to make your own discoveries at El Encanto."

"Thanks, Mom."

"Good luck." I watched as she walked away.

While I was getting dressed, Nash's assistant texted me to confirm our dinner plans. I looked at it again six different times. I couldn't believe I had a date with my crush. I had to tell Josie, but that would have to wait. I tried on three different outfits, uncertain what a fairy godmother should wear. I ended up in my pink Chuck Taylors and a pair of jeans, just as Ruby pulled into the driveway.

We drove toward the ocean and turned off the main road onto a dirt two-track that disappeared into a grove of trees. At a bend in the road, we pulled into the driveway of a small cottage with a blue front door.

"Where are we?" I asked. "Who lives here?" I asked as we got out of the car.

"Sylvie's the gatekeeper for the Guild. Her cottage is at the entrance to the fairy woodlands. She sees everything and everyone coming and going."

Ruby found a path of mossy stones that ran alongside the little house, and we followed the trail through a field of wildflowers in full bloom. Everywhere I looked was like a fairytale had come to life.

"This is beyond my wildest dreams," I said.

"It's amazing, isn't it?" Ruby agreed.

The path continued down into a dark forest where the

sunlight was dappled from the leaves moving in a gentle breeze. They sounded like musical wind chimes and drew my gaze. That's when I glimpsed it for the first time.

A door in the middle of the woods.

"What is that?" I asked.

"I don't know exactly," Ruby said.

"It looks so familiar."

"I think there's a drawing of it in my family's rulebook. I bet there's one in yours too."

Finally, we came to the base of the hill.

The leaves on the trees were so dense, sunlight wasn't able to penetrate. Thankfully, the electric lanterns that hung on the large branches of the tall trees at regular intervals lighted our way through the living tunnel up to the inn on the hill.

It was breathtaking. It was like leaving the real world behind and entering a strange new world of make-believe. I half-expected to see a herd of unicorns grazing under a double-rainbow in the wildflower field as we passed.

The tree-lined path up to the castle was covered in clusters of flowering wisteria vines hung low to the ground creating an intimate archway.

"This is the Tunnel of Love," Ruby said.

"Tunnel of Love?"

She nodded. "It's an important place for fairy godmothers."

Gas lanterns hung on the largest branches at regular intervals lighted our way through the living tunnel to the castle on the hill. At the top we followed a hedge-lined path, turned a corner, and suddenly were in the garden courtyard of El Encanto.

Fairy godmother candidates were gathered in small groups, looking nervously over their shoulders at each other. A covey of pixies was darting in and out of the flowering shrubs. They looked like a cloud of giant mosquitoes as they moved past our faces at close range.

Three of the pixies who'd been playing hide-and-go-seek in a nearby hedge flew over to greet us.

"I'm Briar." Her eyes were blue and her platinum hair floated around her head.

"I'm Heather." Her eyes were blue-violet and her hair was dark blonde.

"I'm Juniper," the third one said. Her eyes were blue and her hair was dark brown. She was plump, and quick to giggle behind her hand.

"We're triplets," they said at the same time.

"Never would've guessed," Ruby said, which made Juniper giggle. Her laughter was so infectious. Soon all five of us were huddled together laughing nervously.

I thought Ruby and I had been the last fairy godmother candidates to arrive until a guy stumbled through the garden hedge from the path.

Tall and lean, with the sleeves of his plaid shirt rolled back to expose his tats, the man exuded an effortless cool factor. He looked uncomfortable, glancing around the room for a friendly face. His eyes kept returning to me and Ruby before he finally joined us.

"Hi, I'm Owen."

I nodded.

Ruby was not subtle as she gave him the full up-and-down look. It was the kind of scrutiny a woman gives a man she finds attractive. I was surprised to see her being so bold about it during our fairy godmother training.

"He's a total hipster hottie," I whispered.

"If you're into that kind of thing," Ruby said. "Do you think he's a fairy?"

"I don't know. You should ask him."

"I'm a fairy," he said. He must have heard us. "A fairy godmother, so it turns out, but I'd prefer it if you called me a fairy god-dude."

"I had no idea guys could be fairy godmothers."

"Me neither," Ruby added.

"I had a hard time believing it myself," Owen said. "I put up a good fight when my mom told me I was the one in our family who'd been chosen to carry on the family trade."

"You didn't know?" I was surprised.

"Not until I grew the wings." He shook his head. "God. I hate those things."

"Aviana didn't know either." Ruby gestured in my direction. "And she's also currently involved in a love-hate relationship with her wings."

Owen smiled. "Knowing you're struggling to show your wings who's boss too makes me feel just a bit better."

I laughed. "I've got a long way to go to catch up."

"Have you read the book?" he asked.

"I glanced at it. There are a lot of rules," I said.

"The pixie dust keeps making me sleepy. I'm probably way behind," he said.

"Seriously? I memorized all of the rules before I started kindergarten," Ruby said.

I knew she meant well, but I don't think it helped us feel any better.

Anxious, I checked the time on my phone. Our welcome session should've started by now. I was about to nudge Ruby and ask her what she thought the reason was for the delay, when a fairy with close-cropped brown hair interrupted us.

"Hey, guys. Mind if I join you?" She was rumpled and a bit disheveled. Her smile was simply dazzling. She looked like something straight out of a toothpaste commercial. Her teeth were so white they were a little blue-ish. "I'm Hazel."

"Aviana," I said. "This is Ruby and Owen." I shifted my purse to my other shoulder so she could join our circle. "Are you a fairy godmother candidate?"

She shook her head. "Tooth fairy. This is my third time in the seminar. I've been having a hard time making a quick getaway. Kids are just so savvy these days."

It took a moment or two before I noticed the garden had grown quiet. The air wasn't moving. The pixies weren't buzzing, and all of the fairies had stopped talking. I glanced at the courtyard entrance to see who had created the hush just in time to see Zara Wakefield appear.

"Okay," Zara said. "We've got a lot of work to do. Come inside and let's get started."

She led us inside of the castle to a small room filled with books. The shelves were two-stories high and had ladders scattered around the room for access to the books near the top. She motioned the fairy godmothers toward the chairs that formed a circle in the center of the room and the covey of pixies among the books on the bookshelves. Once everyone was settled, Zara stood in front of the fireplace and had the full attention of every creature in the room.

"You are here because you were born into a fairy family. But you will have to prove you have the right stuff to be a fairy godmother before you are given training and assignments to fulfill other people's wishes. It's a privilege to be a fairy godmother. And you will all have to prove you're more than worthy." She paused, looking directly at me. I was certain her eyes were boring through my skull. She seemed to be directing all her words at me.

"You will need to memorize all of the rules in the rulebook," she continued. "And be able to recite them when asked. The rules will govern all of the decisions you make and all of the actions you take for the rest of your life."

"Why are the rules so important?" Own whispered.

"Ruby, can you tell us why the rules matter?" Zara prompted. She was standing across the room at least twenty feet away and had still been able to hear him. It's as if she had the hearing of a bird of prey. It totally freaked me out.

"Because witches," Ruby answered.

"I'm sorry. Did you say?" I wasn't sure I'd heard her correctly.

"Ruby is right. We call them witches. There have

always been witches among us. As fairy godmothers, you must be constantly vigilant to make sure other fairy godmothers aren't abusing their power. Using it for their own gain or working against other fairy godmothers or the Guild."

"But witches are witches," I said. "Aren't they easy to identify?"

"Not necessarily," Ruby said.

"Witches often have the same powers," Zara explained. "Many are fairy godmothers who've made it through training, but in the end are tempted to use their powers for evil, not good."

"I'm not sure I completely understand," Owen said.

"Didn't you ever read *Snow White* or *Sleeping Beauty*?" Ruby asked.

"Maybe ..." Owen answered. It had been a long time since I'd read any fairytales too.

"The fairy godmothers in those stories couldn't decide whether to use their powers for good or evil," Ruby explained. "In the end, they went with whatever gave them the most power the fastest."

"And that, boys and girls, is how a fairy godmother turns into a witch," Zara said. She rolled her tongue over her sharp teeth and sent a cold-shiver down my spine.

"It happens just like that." Ruby snapped her fingers.

"A fairy godmother uses her powers only for good of others. She never uses them for herself." Zara smiled, her teeth gleaming in the light. "Witches must be reported to the Guild. Their powers will be extinguished, and their families will be asked to leave the colony."

"Is that why pixies and fairies stick together?" Juniper asked.

"A mutual hate of witches," Briar said.

"I think 'hate' is a strong word," Zara interjected. "Distrust. It's a mutual distrust, but Briar is right. Witches are deceptive and dishonest, and only out for themselves."

I glanced over at Owen, who looked as confused as I

was.

Over the next two hours we went over all the rules. When we finally took a short break, I was exhausted and overwhelmed with knowledge.

Ruby had been asked to help the pixies prepare elderflower and chamomile tea. Alone, Owen and I wandered the garden, watching the pixies buzz between the blossoms in the wildflower field behind the hedges.

When Zara stepped out into the garden, the pixies returned and hovered around her like a cloud of mosquitoes. She glanced in our direction once or twice, her face twisted into a grimace; it made me nervous.

I sipped the tea Ruby had brought out on trays, which did nothing to calm my nerves.

"What do you think they're talking about?" I gestured toward Zara.

"They're pixies," Ruby said. "They're probably trying to make a good impression on her. That's what they do best. Ingratiate themselves."

Every now and then, one of the pixies flew through our conversation. It was annoying, and I wasn't so sure they weren't eavesdropping on us.

As the fifteen-minute break came to an end, Ruby, Owen, and I returned to the library. Slowly, the pixies who'd been playing in the garden ducked inside and took their seats on the bookshelves. Through the open doors, the sun slowly started to sink and the sky started to turn pink around the edges.

When Zara came back to the classroom she was refreshed with a new sense of purpose. She was outwardly calm, but I sensed she had strong emotions lurking just beneath the surface. Her eyes were dark and dangerous. Her fists were balled into anger. And yet she kept her lips tilted upward into a smile. How could she hide her ire so well?

"Has anyone here been practicing magic?" Zara was looking directly at me, her question completely pulling me out of my transfixed state.

I tried to maintain eye contact with her, but I couldn't. Instead, I dropped my gaze, the guilt was too much. My neophyte attempt to stop time kept replaying over and over in my mind like a TikTok video. But there was no way I was going to admit my mistake

"Maybe a love potion," she suggested. "Or a repellent tonic? A sleeping spell? Anybody?"

"Absolutely not," said the tooth fairy. "I play by the rules." She was taking notes and hanging on Zara's every word.

Zara stopped in front of me. "No one at all?"

She waited while we all looked at each other with suspicion. I wondered if this was a trick to keep us from trusting one another and forming bonds of friendship.

I kept my head down and kept my eyes on the paper in front of me. The room was so silent you could hear pixie wings humming in the garden.

When no one said a word, Zara finally returned to the front of the room and moved on to the next topic. "Okay. Let's go back to the basics. Can anyone here tell me what the difference is between a spell and an enchantment?"

No one put a hand in the air. All of the fairies were afraid to go out on a limb.

"You put a spell on a person," Juniper said.

"You enchant an animal, place, or thing," her sister Briar said.

So many rules, so many lessons. My head ached. Would I remember it all?

Two hours later the class was dismissed, and the pixies were gone in a heartbeat, vanishing into the shrubbery nearby. Owen was right behind the pixies, slowing only to hold the door open for Ruby and Hazel.

I was gathering my things when I heard my name called.

"Aviana," Zara said. "Do you have just a moment?"

I nodded and joined her in front of the fireplace. She turned to face me.

"Is there a problem?"

"We encourage our new fairy godmothers to discover their unique skills. But it's come to my attention that you may have used some magic at the wedding, and that might've exposed your magical gifts to a nonbeliever."

I did my best to keep my cool. "You left me in charge. There was a small problem. So, I invoked rule number nine and did whatever it took to ensure the bride's happiness. That was the right thing to do, wasn't it?"

Zara's eyes glittered with coldness. "Just remember what happens to a fairy godmother who breaks the rules. You won't be the only one who feels the consequences of your actions."

"I'm aware," I said, lifting my chin to feign courage.

While I gathered my belongings, Zara kept me under close scrutiny. I didn't dare breathe until I was out in the courtyard garden. I was relieved when I caught up with the others.

"Everything okay?" Ruby asked.

"Fine," I said.

"We were just making plans to meet up with Owen. Are you doing anything tomorrow night?" Ruby asked. "You're welcome to join us."

"I don't know if I can make it. I have … plans."

"You what?"

"I have plans. A date. With a total hottie I've been crushing on for like forever."

"You have got to be kidding me?"

"I know. Who'd a thunk it, right? Me, going out with my crush? He didn't even know I was alive in LA. It could only happen here in Los Arboledas."

"I don't know if that's a good idea," Owen suggested.

Ruby was much clearer in her objection. "Are you out of your mind?"

I was devastated. My sadness was probably written all over my face. "Why? Do you think something bad would happen? Can't I have a love life?"

"Have you talked to your mother about this?" Ruby asked.

"Not yet."

"Maybe you should run it past her," Owen said.

I nodded but didn't understand why I needed my mom's permission. I'd been looking forward to going out with Nash, but now I was afraid I was just boarding another boat steaming its way toward the Ocean of Disaster.

"It's not that it can't happen," Hazel said. "It's more that it shouldn't. Dating normal people isn't for fairy godmothers."

"Never?" I asked. "It's not against the rules. I checked. Twice. It's not on the list. There is no rule against fairy godmothers dating."

"A fairy godmother joyfully embraces the knowledge that happily ever after is her purpose, not her future," Ruby said. "It's the second rule on the list, which doesn't make it any less important."

"Okay. It's implied, but not explicit. Technically, it can be done."

"It's nearly impossible," Hazel said.

"But Mom was with me when I met him for the first time, and she totally encouraged my romantic interest in him."

"I think you're probably taking your mom's actions out of context."

"You can have fun," Ruby said. "Probably even a hookup now and then. We're not angels. You just can't get serious."

"But I don't want a hookup. I want to fall in love." All of their faces fell. It was as if I'd announced I intended to commit murder.

"A fairy godmother's romance? It just isn't done," Hazel said. "I'm a tooth fairy and even I know that."

"Why would you?" Heather asked.

"Not with your schedule," Briar said. "You just won't have time."

"You have so much to do for everyone else. You just …you can't," Juniper added.

"Never?" I glanced at Owen.

He shrugged. "I haven't read the book."

"A fairy godmother doesn't date. Period. End of story," Hazel said. "Fairy godmothers don't have romances of their own. And they never, ever fall in love."

CHAPTER 14

*Rule #14: A fairy godmother never licks toads. It
can be deadly and addictive.*

"This is not a date. I'm not going on a date," I said out
loud in the car on the way to meet Nash. "I'm a fairy
godmother, so it can't be a date. This is nothing. Just a
meal. That's it. Nothing else."

I figured if I said it out loud I might actually
comprehend what I was saying. So it became my mantra as
I drove the winding roads south from Los Arboledas to
Santa Barbara.

If I repeated it over and over. At some point I would
actually start to believe it. Then why did I buy a new dress?

What am I doing?

"This is ridiculous."

Eventually I rationalized what I was doing. Telling
myself technically it wasn't breaking the rules, even though
I knew the reason not dating the love interest of your
protégé wasn't one of the rules explicitly included in *The
Fairy Godmother's Rulebook* was because no other fairy
godmother on earth would consider committing such a
heinous act.

What kind of a fairy godmother was I? Had I completely lost my mind?

I can't do this. I just can't.

But not once did I ever consider turning around. I never called Nash and canceled—even though my cell phone was out in plain sight on the seat next to me. I just kept going. I was like a horse heading back to the stables after a day outside, certain there'd be a rack of hay waiting for me.

I was so caught up in my own thoughts—going over and over the pros and cons of spending time with Nash— I almost didn't notice when the freeway bumped up against the Pacific Ocean and turned sharply south. I had to make the split-second decision to change lanes, cutting off a guy in a Land Rover, which earned me a blast of his car horn and a flash of his middle finger.

I shot him a big toothy smile and waved. "Yeah, thanks, buddy. I've got a magic wand too."

The long rays of the setting sun gave the world a magical golden glow. It was becoming my favorite time of day in the most beautiful part of the world.

Wild sage bushes grew in the strip of grass between the northbound and southbound lanes. The wind tossed their colorful branches and beckoned to me as if enchanted, their movements as if a call of distress.

Mayday, mayday.

Danger. Danger.

Dead ahead.

I ignored their calls for caution and my own common sense, maintaining the posted speed limit on my way to have dinner with my crush.

He'd picked a restaurant in the main shopping district a block from State Street for our meet-up. I gave up my car to the valet and found my way to the main entrance through a set of French doors that opened onto a secluded cobblestone courtyard.

Romantic al fresco dining was illuminated by

candlelight around a Koi fishpond. It was the height of the dinner rush and all the tables were filled with small groups of elegant dinners in quiet conversation in the courtyard.

Uncertain of what to do, I unwittingly stood in the way of the wait staff and busboys until the weight of the stares from the diners made me uncomfortable enough to duck through a wooden arch at the back of the restaurant.

The dark room beyond was wood-paneled and crowded with more people waiting for a table. Others were eating dinner at the huge antique bar that ran the length of the room. In the dim light, I spotted the hostess at a stand near the back of the bar and made my way to her.

"Hi. I'm supposed to be meeting—"

"She's with me," Nash finished my sentence.

I turned to see him stand up from a tall stool at the bar. He was wearing a black shirt and had taken the time to style and comb his hair back over his ears. He smelled of tangy aftershave and hair products. And was even more attractive than I remembered.

I forced myself to think about something other than how Nash made my heart skip a beat, hoping the fluttering of my wings under my cardigan would subside before anyone noticed. I admonished myself for not securing them with duct tape before I left Mom's house.

Why did I keep putting myself in these public situations when I didn't know how to keep my wings under control?

Nash steered me toward an area where other diners were waiting for their table. The touch of his hand in the curve of my lower back almost made me swoon. I took an unsteady step and brushed against his chest.

"Sorry," I said, hoping he wouldn't be able to see what an effect his nearness was having on me.

His gaze swept me from head to toe, not missing any details. I had dressed and redressed six times before leaving my mom's house. Finally, I decided on a floral sundress in soft pastels with a peachy elbow-length cardigan. His eyes drifted back to mine and his crooked geeky smile appeared across his face.

I grinned stupidly back at him. Geeky Nash was my kryptonite.

Just then, the hostess rushed past us with another group in tow, smiling up at Nash. "We're getting the table near the fireplace ready for you. It will be just a moment."

"Thank you," he said, leaning back against the wall next to me. I could feel the heat from his skin. Needing to desperately distract myself, I focused my attention on a man in an un-ironed Hawaiian shirt and khakis at the hostess stand. "Lane, party of two," he said quietly. "I think we have a seven o'clock reservation."

The hostess checked the reservation list on her iPad several times before she spoke. "I'm sorry, sir. I don't see your name listed."

"I made the reservation three weeks ago." His voice rising in panic as he glanced at his wife, who was waiting on a nearby bench. She was wearing a beautiful dress, but her hair was uncombed, and the only makeup she had on was lipstick.

"I'm sorry. I can't find your name in our reservations for tonight." The hostess sounded sincere and sympathetic. "I can try to fit you in, but I don't think we can get you in before nine-thirty. Would you mind waiting?"

The man looked hopefully at his wife for permission to wait. "What do you think, honey?"

"We can't keep the babysitter out that late. It's a school night."

He nodded. "I know, but it's our anniversary."

She shook her head. "Don't blame yourself. I should've called and confirmed. I've just been so …" She yawned.

My fairy godmother instincts were tingling, from the top of my ears to the tip of my wings. I couldn't listen to one more word without taking action.

I touched Nash on the arm to get his attention. His dark eyes immediately searching my face for a reason.

"Can we give those people our table?"

"What?" His brow furrowed in confusion.

"It's their anniversary, and the restaurant can't find their reservation, and she has a baby at home. God only knows when she last had a warm meal cooked by someone other than Chef Boyardee. Or actually been out of the house without a stroller and enough baby stuff to give a seasoned backpacker nightmares. Could we give them our table?"

"Are you serious? People wait months for a table here."

"I know. I Yelped this place this afternoon." I smiled up at him. "Can I ask you a really personal question?"

"Absolutely. I wish you would."

"Did you bring me here to impress me?"

"Maybe ... sorta. Yes." He was squirming in his shoes.

"The gesture is duly noted, and I am suitably impressed," I said. "Now, could we please give our table to that nice couple?"

Nash gave the couple a thorough looking-over. "Her shoes don't match."

"That's what I'm saying. They *need* this. Way more than we do. And I've heard about this taco truck. It's usually parked two streets over. They have the best street tacos ever."

Nash turned to the hostess. "Please let those people— that couple right there—have our table."

"I don't understand." She looked totally confused.

"Seat those people at our table." He pulled a few bills out of his wallet and gave them to her. "Make sure they get the special treatment. Bring them the chocolate lava cake. Make a fuss. It's their anniversary."

The hostess nodded and that was our cue to leave. We returned to the valet.

"Thank you," I said to Nash. "I promise. This will be worth it."

"It better be. " He shot me a look as we were leaving the restaurant. "Okay. Now, where's this incredible taco stand?"

"It's on Third. Do you want to follow me?"

"No. Leave your car here. We'll take mine."

Thankfully, we would not have to wait long to make our way to those tacos. The valet had parked Nash's expensive car in front of the restaurant, so it was easy for them to toss him the keys. He helped me into the passenger side then jogged around to the other, palming the valet a tip before getting into the driver seat.

"Okay," he said, flashing me his crazy geeky smile. It made my stomach throw down a triple flip-triple Salchow combination. "Where to?"

I directed Nash to the part of town that was less touristy with fewer pedestrians and narrower streets. We went through three stoplights before we came to the corner where the taco truck was parked.

"That's it." I pointed to the taco truck parked at the curb.

"There's a line. A really long line. I hate standing in lines." He sounded defeated.

"There is always a line, but a line this size won't be more than fifteen minutes. And the tacos will be totally worth it. Turn right at the next corner. There's an empty lot there where we can park."

Nash turned into the dirt-filled lot full of uneven turf. Turns out, the long line would be the least of his worries because his car had slipped into a pothole. The obscenely expensive car had scraped bottom and made a horrible crunching sound.

"Sorry," I said.

He didn't say anything. I could tell he was beginning to regret handing off our reservation to that couple. I was sure he was seconds away from making a U-turn, but instead he parked at the end of the row and walked around to help me out of the car. He took my hand and held it as we dashed across the street and got into the line.

The daily specials were posted on a chalkboard sign.

The brief wait gave us a chance to discuss and decide what we were going to order. I was hungry. The spicy aroma spilling out of the truck was making my stomach growl.

He nodded at a woman lovingly preparing tortillas with her fingertips. "Look at that," he said. "This is going to be fantastic."

I grinned up at him. So pleased he'd become enthusiastic about the taco truck.

"I'm glad you don't have regrets."

"Not even a little." He grinned. The twinkle in his eyes making me wonder if he was talking about me or the feast we were about to eat. I grinned back at him, hoping he was talking about me.

After we placed our order at the window, we settled at some nearby picnic tables, and within a few minutes, a waitress brought out our food on paper-lined plastic trays. After we thanked her, we dug into the pile of food in front of us. We'd ordered enough to feed a football team.

"Best. Meal. Ever." Nash declared before washing down the last of the chips and guacamole with his beer.

"Worth it?" I asked, popping my last bite of taco into my mouth.

"So worth it," he agreed.

Our conversation was constant and easy. Nash was smart and quick-witted and we had a lot more in common than I expected. Right at that moment there was no place else on earth I'd rather be than with this irresistibly attractive and intriguing man. My wings seemed to agree because they were humming with electricity.

We crossed the street and turned the corner on the way back to the car. That's when the intimacy of being along together hit me. We were on a date. At least, I hadn't said or done anything that would make him believe we weren't on a date. There were certain expectations that went along with acknowledging you were on a date.

Kissing, for example. Kissing was something that could be expected. And any minute now, I would probably want to press my lips to his wide sweet mouth. To feel his soft lips on mine. Feel his breath against my skin.

Yep. I was in big, serious trouble.

I had completely forgotten the speech I had prepared all afternoon. I was supposed to introduce the "topic of dating" over appetizers and suggest to him I knew someone who was more suitable for him than I was over dessert. "She is perfect for you," I would say.

"Sounds great," he would answer. "I can't thank you enough for doing this for me, Aviana. You are so unselfish and giving."

We would agree to be friends. They would live happily ever after, and I would be satisfied to be the kind of model fairy godmother my mother dreamed I could become, who doesn't break rules or gets into trouble.

Instead Nash covered my hand with his as he helped me back into the passenger side of his car. His touch sent tingles through my body. From my fingers, up my arm, and down my spine, ending with fireworks exploding in the tips of my wings.

He didn't say a word and neither did I. Our eyes met briefly before I turned away and closed the door. We both knew exactly what was going to happen next. And as a fairy godmother in good standing with the Guild, I had to be the one to stop any romantic feelings from popping up between us. It was the right thing to do. Anything else would be against the rules.

While Nash walked around the car to the driver's side, I attempted to muster the courage to tell him the truth.

He opened the door, got into the driver's seat, turned to his right, and without any hesitation, swept me up into his arms as his lips searched for mine. I was so hungry for his kiss that I met him halfway across the console, eager for what was about to come. Except, instead of our lips touching, our noses briefly bumped. The misstep was quickly corrected, not long after our lips were brushing together.

His lips were softer than I expected. They covered mine in a warm caress, gently nipping my lips with his teeth. A second kiss was deeper and filled with sweet emotion. Our tongues briefly touched, hinting at deeper explorations to come.

He tasted of cilantro, beer, and a clean fresh flavor best described only as "Nash." He was delicious. My heart was beating fast. My wings lifted away from my shoulders and began to tap lightly on my back in the same cadence as my heart. They couldn't be seen by Nash, but I couldn't ignore their distinct rhythm.

Our lips met again—my mouth opening under his. Our tongues touched and flirted. Sensation after sensation danced through my body. In my wildest dreams I never believed a kiss could make me feel like this.

My heart was aflutter. And unfortunately, so were my wings. They were becoming more and more active. It was incredibly distracting. I tried to concentrate on keeping them under control, but no matter how hard I tried, they wouldn't or couldn't stay still.

"Oh god," I whispered against his lips.

"I know. I feel it too," he whispered, nipping my earlobe. The heat from his breath made all of the hairs on my arms, and all of the feathers on my wings, stand at attention.

My eyes flew wide open. I was in big trouble as my wings were pushing me forward in the seat. Any further, and I was going to end up with my face pressed up against the windshield.

In order to counteract the pressure I was feeling, I pushed back against the seat, pressing them into the dark leather. They were strong and fought against me all the way. I wrapped my arms tighter around his shoulders and drew the full weight of his body down on top of me.

Nash mistook my action as desire, and he pressed his lips to the sensitive skin on my neck. I closed my eyes and let the pleasure wash over me. I could feel the wings pulling away from my body. They would not be ignored. My heart was racing—crazy thoughts filled my passion-drugged mind.

The newly formed bones in the feathered appendages between my shoulder blades were strong and sharp. I worried they would rip the expensive leather upholstery in his car. And there was the fact that I had them. There was no disguising them. No matter what. What was he going to say when he found out the girl he believed he was making out with was a fairy by birth? This was going to be a disaster of epic proportions.

I knew what I had to do; I just hoped Nash would forgive me for it. I pressed my face against his to feel the touch of his skin, and then I breathed deeply so that I would never forget his scent.

Without hesitation, I opened the door, jumped out of the car, and ran toward the darkest part of the parking lot.

Nash shouted after me, but I didn't look back. I crossed my fingers and hoped he didn't get a glimpse of me taking flight, lifting up off the ground within a few steps. It was as if I was on an airport runway. By the time I took my third step, my feet were no longer touching earth. I took off into the night sky in a messy, uncontrolled flight.

CHAPTER 15

***Rule #15: A fairy godmother knows you must give
your dreams the wings to fly.***

Clinging to the branch of an ancient old eucalyptus
tree, I held on for dear life.

Like a bird. Like a freakin' bird.

My heart thudded in my chest. Why hadn't anyone
mentioned there was the possibility I could fly? I bit down
on my lip.

I'd lifted off the ground like a Canada goose, but my
abbreviated flight ended with a hard landing on a branch in
a tree about one hundred feet off the ground. I probably
would've done better if I had opened my eyes just once
while I was in the air.

Too scared to move a muscle, I wrapped my arms and
legs around the trunk of the tree and hung on for dear life.
My sweater was completely shredded. I hoped my wings
wouldn't unfurl and take me on another unplanned and
uncontrolled flight. I tried to regain my control by slowing
my breath, but my wings were still twitchy and nervous. I
held my breath every time they moved.

From my perch, I watched Nash search for me. He

looked everywhere. He was very thorough, looking inside, under, and in between the cars in the lot. He looked high and he looked low. Obviously, he didn't do a great job on the looking high part.

Nash stayed in the parking lot waiting for me to return for over an hour. He walked around the car, walked up and down the street in front of the taco truck. He even called my cell phone a dozen times.

I cursed his perseverance and tenacity every time the intermittent vibration of another incoming phone call pulsed on my hip. He was so kind and so concerned about the well-being of the crazy woman-child-bird who had literally flown away from him.

His compassion made me think of him as a superhero. His willingness to give up a table at a fancy restaurant and eat tacos on the street made my heart go *zing* when he looked at me. And his kiss made me (and my wings) lose control. It didn't have anything to do with him being a millionaire entrepreneur. He was just a boy, and I was a girl falling madly in love with him.

You're not a girl. You're fairy godmother.

Watching from my perch high above the ground, I dealt with the growing realization any further romantic entanglements with him would not be possible. I would have to limit myself to the memories of those stolen kisses in the front seat of his car.

It was a bitter pill to swallow.

It was after midnight when he finally gave up looking for me and reluctantly drove away. I was sad to see him leave, but also grateful. I had no idea how I was ever going to get down from my hiding place in the old eucalyptus tree.

"Able to fly, and I'm scared of heights," I said to no one listening.

Getting up into the tree was the easy part. How would I ever get back onto solid ground again?

My wings had calmed down enough to be tucked back

into their designated space between my shoulder blades. But I had way worse problems. I needed to pee. I shouldn't have had a beer with my tacos.

I wasn't certain my wings were flight-worthy. It didn't matter, since I was still struggling to control them by means other than my emotions. I had to consider my other options. I could call 9-1-1 and ask some hot firefighters to rescue me, but that would require me to loosen my grip on the branch I was clinging to like a barn owl. It would also probably require some sort of realistic explanation of how I had gotten up on the tree. And I didn't have one.

Hello, Mr. Hottie McFirefighter.

I'm a fairy godmother, and I've got brand-new wings and don't how to use them. No, I'm not crazy …

Once the paralysis of fear wore off, I started the slow and deliberate climb out of the tree. At one point I lost my grip and fell, hanging only by my knees. I was upside-down with my dress hanging over my head and my underwear exposed when I took a Scarlett O'Hara "As God is my witness, they're not going to lick me" oath.

I pulled myself up into a sitting position, closed my eyes, and leaped out into the darkness. Without any effort on my part, my wings unfurled and provided enough loft for me to gently tumble to the ground.

Hurrying across the street to the taco truck was still parked and used the restroom in the nearby Quonset hut. One problem solved. Now all I had to do was get my car and go home.

Ugh.

It was a few blocks back to the restaurant where we had started our romantic evening on the posh side of Santa Barbara. The ocean air clung to my skin as I marched along through the darkness.

The upscale restaurant patrons had all gone home. Inside the outdoor dining room, the staff was setting up the tables for the following evening. In the parking lot the valet had brought my car in front of the restaurant—it was the only one left. He seemed both glad and surprised to see me.

"Your boyfriend was looking for you," he said.

"He's not my boyfriend," I replied.

He laughed. "He must've done something pretty bad to make you ghost him in the middle of a date."

"Not really."

"Don't blame yourself. Whatever happened, happened for a reason."

"You think?" I asked.

He nodded, very serious and solemn. "But seriously, how bad can a guy who drives a Maserati be?"

His observation made me laugh, and I gave him all the change I had rolling in the bottom of my purse as a tip. I got into my car and drove toward the closest entrance to the freeway. The street was a dead-end divided into two choices. One freeway on-ramp was marked "South—Los Angeles." The other was marked "North—Los Arboledas."

I had a choice. It was right there in front of me. Go back to Los Angeles and wake up in my room off the kitchen tomorrow morning. Gardenia would be starting the coffee maker. Dad would be in his office shouting into his speakerphone. Madeleine would know of a plastic surgeon who would be happy to remove my wings for a price.

My nightmare would be over. It was that easy.

There was even a slight possibility I'd be able to reconnect with him again. But would he recognize me? He believed I was someone special, filled with confidence and goodness. Nothing could be further from the truth.

Mom would be okay. She'd have her job at the inn to fall back on, unless she was considered "redundant" during the Nolan Group takeover. But what about the grandmother I'd never met? The one who was fairy godmothering all over Europe right at this moment. What would she think?

A shiver went through my body. I didn't realize how much I had to lose.

I had been given magical powers and wings. To whom much is given, much should be expected. I couldn't go back to Los Angeles and hide. I had to go forward.

I pointed the car north.

Being a fairy godmother wasn't going to give me the option to have a relationship with Nash, that was clear. But It would give me the opportunity to help people. I could be there for them at the most dramatic moments in their lives. And that might turn out to be way more exciting than kissing Nash Nolan.

Right?

Yeah. I didn't think I sounded very convincing either. There was no doubt in my mind nothing was going to be as much fun as kissing Nash.

By the time I parked in front of Mom's house, the moon was high overhead. I tiptoed up the front walk and let myself in with the spare key. I was exhausted and practically fell into bed. I'd just put my head on my pillow when a wisp of air tickled my face.

"Glenn? Is that you?" I shouted into the darkness.

He lit up. "I wasn't sure if you were awake."

"I wasn't." Glenn flew closer to me, took a good look at my face, providing his own night light. I had a red welt on my chin where I had been smacked with a branch.

"You look ..." He stopped himself. "Well, you've looked better."

"Thanks," I said. "Tough night. What's going on?"

"We've got an emergency." He was using up nervous energy flying a figure-eight pattern near the ceiling.

"'We?'" I brushed sleep out of my eyes. "Who's this 'we' you're talking about?"

"Your mother and I. We need your help."

I sat up in bed. "You need *my* help? Seriously? What's

up?"

"We've got a runner."

"A what?" I shook my head in confusion.

"A runner," Glenn explained. "Sometimes our clients give up too soon. The level of desperation needed before a fairy godmother is assigned to come to your rescue can be too much to bear. A lot of people give up before we get a chance to turn their dreams into reality."

"Rule number one." I grinned. "A fairy godmother never makes an appearance until she's absolutely and desperately needed." I was actually starting to comprehend a fairy godmother's role.

Glenn seemed pleasantly surprised. "That's right."

"I told you I'd been reading the book," I said.

"I'm impressed." He grinned. "Here's the deal, now and then our clients aren't able to hold out to make it all the way to absolutely and completely desperate before you give up. Chasing your dreams is hard work. Sometimes our clients give up and they run."

"Giving up on your dreams is terrible."

Glenn shook his head. "I think so too, but what do I know? I'm just a pixie. Are you up? I'm going to make some coffee."

I sat up and threw my legs over the edge of the bed. "I'm up."

Glenn left the room, and I stumbled into the bathroom. Under the lights I inspected the cuts and bruises I'd acquired in the tree. Just then Mom stuck her head inside the door. She had a full face of make-up and was dressed for a midnight rendezvous in a chic jumpsuit.

"Are you all right?" she asked.

"I'm fine. I'm still getting the hang of my wings."

Mom was delighted by my confession. "My first assignment nearly killed me."

"Really?" I couldn't imagine Mom getting into trouble, let alone stuck up in a tree.

"I'll go get the car," she said. "You get dressed."

I found an oversized sweatshirt to pull on over my pajamas, grabbed my moccasins, and headed out. Glenn was waiting with a travel mug of coffee.

"Okay. Let's roll," he said.

Mom was behind the wheel in the driveway when we tumbled out of the house. Glenn stood on the passenger seat, forcing me to wedge my full-sized human body into the back seat.

We were the only car moving in Los Arboledas. It was a bit surreal, especially when I thought about all the fairies living in the woodlands nearby. After a short drive, Mom turned onto a side street where Ruby was waiting for us on the corner.

"You looking to join a posse?" I asked.

"I'm here help," Ruby said before scrambling into the back seat. Mom pulled away from the curb a bit before Ruby was completely settled. After a few streets, she stopped on a quiet one in front of the library.

"What happened?" Ruby asked.

"Camille Crush is a local singer-songwriter. She's Internet famous since one of her songs went viral on YouTube," Mom said. "Tonight, her fairy godmother was supposed to help her be discovered by a record guy, but she didn't show up for the gig. And now they're both missing."

Mom and Glenn shared a suspicious look. There was something important they weren't telling us.

"I don't understand. How did you guys lose her?"

By all accounts Mom was a legendary fairy godmother. How had she bobbled this assignment so badly?

"She's Sylvie's client," Glenn said.

"We're looking for one of *Sylvie's* clients?"

"A fairy godmother needs your help," Mom admonished. "Does it really matter which one?"

My annoyance flared. "Sylvie's a little whack-a-doodle, isn't she?"

"You hardly know her," Glenn said sharply. You

haven't given her a chance."

"Now is not the time to judge. Just tell us, what's the plan?" Ruby asked.

"We need to find Sylvie first," Mom said. "And get some details."

Mom made a left back onto Main Street and parked the car near the central shopping district. "If we split up we can cover more ground. You guys go towards the shopping arcade. Glenn and I will go over and check out Central Park."

Ruby and I crossed the street and ducked under the Spanish-style arches of the shopping arcade. The wisteria at the entrance was in full bloom and smelled heavenly. All the stores were dark and quiet.

All at once we heard a sound.

"Did you hear something?" I asked.

Ruby nodded. "Follow me."

We tiptoed to the end of the arcade and noticed all of the lights on inside Wisteria Wholesale, the store owned by Zara Wakefield. The doors were open wide and a classical string quartet cover of *Kings & Queens* was playing over the loudspeakers at decibel levels loud enough to make even the most enthusiastic metalheads voice a few sincere objections.

I peeked inside the store. A fresh flower arrangement on a small wooden table beckoned to customers inside the front door next to stacks of Zara's best-selling coffee table on display. There was a vintage broach bouquet in shades of turquoise. I couldn't resist reaching out to check the price.

"Don't touch it," Ruby hissed. "It's enchanted."

"How can you be so sure?" I asked.

"Recognizing enchanted objects is my superpower."

"Seriously?" I asked. "That is so cool."

"Stay here," Ruby said. Then she moved further into the store, hiding behind furniture and tall stacks of kitchenware. She stopped to take video on her phone between a curved sofa and a semi-circle of floor-to-ceiling mirrors.

That's when I noticed the floor was covered in glitter. Or was it something else? I bent down, picking up some of the silvery dust on my fingertips. It looked like glitter, but there was a chance it was pixie dust, but that couldn't be right.

"Is that what I think it is?" I asked.

"Yep." Ruby stopped taking photos and shoved her phone back into her pocket. "We have to get out of here."

Just then someone shouted from the back of the store. "Hello. Is somebody there?"

"Run," Ruby said. She didn't have to tell me twice.

A split second later she was sprinting at an Olympic record-setting pace down the middle of Main Street. I kept up with her for the first few steps but had to slow down when I got a stitch in my side. We ducked under a low awning near the post office, hiding in the shadows until we caught our breath.

"Do you think she saw us?" I whispered.

"Let's hope not."

"She's using pixie dust—"

Ruby cut me off. "Don't say it. Don't say it. In Los Arboledas even the night has ears."

Glenn was waiting for us when we got back to the car, but Mom was making one last check through Central Park.

"Why is Sylvie so important to my mom?" I asked.

"When your mom came back from Los Angeles without you, she wasn't ... she wasn't herself. She overlooked a few things when she was handling clients. A few assignments got out of hand, but Sylvie was there. Your mom wanted to stay in good standing with the Fairy Godmother's Guild for you," Glenn said. "And now Sylvie is slipping a bit. She's gotten more scatter-brained and forgetful."

"A missing client would certainly cost Sylvie her powers," Ruby added.

"I don't get it," I said.

"Zara wants to consolidate her power in the Guild," Ruby explained. "She doesn't have to answer to more experienced fairy godmothers like your mom. The younger fairy godmothers worship Zara. The older ones are a bit more skeptical of her powers."

"I'm skeptical."

"Me too," Ruby agreed. Ruby pointed to the entrance of Central Park. "There they are."

Mom was crossing the street with her arm around Sylvie. Mom helped Sylvie into the passenger seat, slid behind the steering wheel, then looked at Sylvie. "So now what?" she asked.

"We've got to find Camille before Zara finds her," Sylvie said. "If she finds her, Camille will spill about my mistake. That's all Zara needs to oust me."

"What's up with the record guy? What happened to him?" I asked.

"I put a spell on him," Sylvie said. "Camille was supposed to perform on the outdoor concert at the Old Mill. I turned him into a frog and let him go in the pond near the stage so he'd have a front-row seat. But Camille never showed. And when I went back to the pond to retrieve the frog, he was gone."

I caught a look flash between Mom and Glenn. Sylvie's methods seemed a bit suspect even to them. I was struck by Sylvie's story and started scrolling through my phone for the clue I hoped I'd find as to where exactly the music executive was.

Ruby's head fell back against the seat. "Ugh. He could be anywhere. "

"No. He's not," I said, brandishing my phone. "She took him home."

"How can you be so sure?" Mom asked.

"Her YouTube song that went viral was called 'Frog

Under Glass.'"

"She took him home to make him her pet," Mom said.

"Where does Camille live?" Glenn asked.

"She lives with her parents in 'The Oaks.'" It was neighborhood of small homes built under the sheltering shade of a grove of old oak trees.

"We've got to get this guy back to the inn before the spell wears off," Mom said.

"What about Camille?" Sylvie asked. "She must be desperate by now."

"Let's take this one step at a time," Mom said as she was backing up the car to rescue a frog-shaped music executive from a black-lighted aquarium.

The street Camille lived on was very narrow with no room for parking, so Mom had to park in front of the liquor store at the corner of the street.

Sylvie pointed down the street. "It's the third house on the left."

"Ruby, stay with Sylvie. We'll be right back," Mom said.

Mom, Glenn, and I headed up the dark street. There was a lamp and a television on in the front window of Camille's house. Someone was home. Mom sent Glenn inside on a recon mission.

"Back bedroom. There's a frog in an aquarium under the window," he said when he returned a few minutes later. "You should be able to reach him without actually, you know, doing the entering part of breaking and entering."

"Excellent," I said.

Minutes later I was pressed against the side of the house making my way slowly around to the back bedroom window when my phone rang. The night was so quiet it sounded like a civil disaster alert siren going off. I couldn't grab it fast enough.

"I registered to take the LSATs," Josie sounded jubilant.

"Law school?" I shout-whispered.

"It may be my thing. What do you think?

"Can I call you back?" I pressed back against the side of the house.

"Why? What are you doing?" she asked.

Cupping my hand over the phone, I whispered, "Breaking into someone's house."

"I knew it," Josie shouted in excitement "You're having fun without me."

"Seriously, Josie. Can I call you in a few?"

"Okay, but I'll be expecting all the deets."

I clicked off and positioned myself under the window in the back of the house. It took a few minutes for me to lift the screen and pull it away. After a few moments of struggle, I was finally able to reach into the aquarium and grab the frog. Holding him straight out from my body, I walked down the street to the liquor store.

"What are you doing?" Glenn asked. "Why are you holding him like that?"

"I don't like frogs," I said.

He frowned. "You refuse to make being a fairy godmother easy, don't you?"

Easy? Nothing about being a fairy godmother had been easy so far.

CHAPTER 16

Rule #16: A fairy godmother is responsible for every promise she makes.

Mom called one of the housekeepers at the inn to meet us and let us into the music executive's suite with her passkey. We drove up the main entrance and parked in the employee parking lot. It was a long walk back to the suite, but we made the frog as comfortable as possible in the middle of a king-sized bed.

"I'll check back on him in a little while," Glenn said. "We need to get out of here now."

Back in the parking lot, Ruby said good night.

"Okay," Ruby said. "I think you guys have got this. I'm going to head home. It's an easy from here."

Glenn was also ready to call it a night. "I'm going to make myself scarce." And with a tip of his hat, he flew off into the darkness.

Sylvie was still in distress over her missing client. There was nothing Mom and I could do or say to comfort her.

"Where could she be?" Sylvie wailed.

"Has Camille tried contacting you?" Mom asked.

"No," Sylvie said. "I called her several times. She's not answering."

Suddenly I had an idea. A pretty good idea. "Is there a music store in town?" I asked.

"Yes," Mom answered. "On Mariposa."

"She hung out there in high school," Sylvie said.

"Say no more." Mom started the car and wasted no time getting across town to the music store. There weren't any street lights on this side of town, but as we got closer, there was no doubt a dark-haired girl was seated on the front steps with her guitar case on her lap.

Mom parked in front of the store and turned to Sylvie. "Do you need back up? Or can you handle it from here?"

Sylvie got out of the car and approached the front of the music store. "Camille? Are you all right?"

"I had a bad night," she said, wiping tears on her sleeve.

" Do you need a ride home?"

Camille lifted her head. "Do you have room for my guitar?"

"Sure," Mom said. "Get in."

Sylvie and I made room for the guitar in the back seat and Camille hopped in the front. Within seconds, Camille and Mom were chatting as if they were old friends. It wasn't long before we were pulling up in front of Sylvie's storybook cottage.

Mom tapped me on the knee. "I'm going to drive Camille home. "Can you take Sylvie inside and make her a cup of tea?"

I helped Sylvie out of the car and followed her up the front walk. She looked as if she had the weight of the world on her shoulders. She shuddered as she sat down at the kitchen table.

I put the kettle on for tea and turned to look at Sylvie. She didn't say a word but was obviously still in distress. When I joined her a few minutes later with two cups of tea in hand, she looked a bit calmer, despite the tell-tale dark circles under her eyes. "It's chamomile," I said. "It'll help you sleep."

"Thank you," she said and took a sip of her tea. "You remind me so much of your mother."

"Everyone in Los Arboledas says that, but I really look like my dad."

I reached across the table to put my hand over hers. "You and your mother both have pure hearts," she said.

I gave her a sympathetic smile and glanced down at our entwined hands. Her nails were professionally manicured, but her hands showed her age. Mine were smooth but covered in cuts and abrasions from my adventure in the tree.

"You're going to be a great fairy godmother," Sylvie said.

"Honestly, Sylvie. I'm not sure I'm cut out for this yet."

"None of us are ever sure at first. Just do your best."

"Putting everyone else's needs in front of my own seems like a tall order right now," I hesitated before telling her the truth. "I met someone."

Sylvie laughed, long and loud. "Don't we all."

"But I really like this guy," I said. "He's all I can think about. And I've messed it up so bad."

"It will be okay. You'll figure it out."

Sylvie was such a graceful person, I couldn't say anything that would make her think less of me. No wonder Mom cherished their friendship.

I relaxed into the chair, stretching my legs out in front of me. "Not if I can't control my wings. Is there something … I can do to make them less sensitive?"

Sylvie nodded. "Milk. It's a good source of tryptophan."

"Ruby said it'd help with the itching. It also helps calm them down? Isn't tryptophan the stuff in turkey that makes you sleepy after Thanksgiving dinner?

She nodded. "Think of milk as Xanax for your wings.

No matter what you do, they'll stay against your skin. At first glance, most people will think you have a tattoo."

I was still confused. "So, if I drink a lot of milk, I'll be able to control my wings?"

"You don't drink the milk, Aviana, you bathe in it. My wings don't give me trouble anymore, but I still enjoy a milk bath most nights before bed," Sylvie said. "If you add a little honey and nutmeg, you'll have sweet dreams."

I slept late the next morning and couldn't remember if any of my dreams had been sweet or not. When I checked my phone, I had sixteen new messages. One was Vanessa, which was easy to ignore. The other fifteen were from Nash. He told me to call him back. No matter what had happened. No matter when I got in.

"Aviana, I don't know what happened. I want to know you are okay." His voice cracked. "Just call me and tell me you're safe. I won't ask any other questions. I promise."

I listened to the first five messages. After the first two calls, he sounded worried and upset. By the end of the fifth, he was apoplectic. I erased the next ten messages from him without listening to them.

How could I have been so short-sighted?

I wasn't going to be able to erase the events of last night by wishing it so.

I noticed the door to my mom's room was closed. She was probably still sleeping after a long night chasing wayward clients, so I snuck quietly out of the house and got a bike out of the garage to meet Ruby out at the barn where she took horse-riding lessons.

Ruby, as always, looked bright-eyed for someone who'd been out so late. We sat in the weather-beaten bleachers overlooking an outdoor horse corral to watch her friend Anna put a dressage horse through its paces.

Anna was lost in concentration as she and her horse floated across the ground in a graceful dance synchronized to music blasting out of speakers hung on poles in the outdoor arena. In the mist, the horse and rider looked like they were participating in a choreographed ballet.

"Is Anna …?" I asked.

"Like us? No," Ruby said. "She's human. She was my best friend in high school. She followed her passion and married a cowboy."

"Does she know?" I asked. "About you? About us?"

"Of course not." Ruby laughed. "I mean, I'm sure she's had her suspicions. I think a lot of the locals have, but she'd never asked."

Relaxing while watching Anna warming up her horse, I told Ruby about my disastrous date with Nash, which made her burst into spontaneous giggles.

"It's not funny."

"I'm not laughing at you. I'm laughing near you."

"I really like this guy," I protested.

"Yes, but you're a fairy godmother. It's not like you can ever fall in love and get married. Unless …" Ruby sat up straight. "You're not still considering giving up your powers, are you?"

I shrugged. "I'm not sure all this is worth it. I wish I was as certain as you are."

Ruby shrugged. "Believe me. I've had my moments."

"Would you pursue a relationship with someone who flew away from you while you were kissing?" I boldly told her the truth.

When Ruby recovered from her giggles, she knew exactly what question to ask. "Did he see your wings?"

"Don't know."

"But you took flight in front of him?"

"Kinda. I'm not sure how much he saw, and I'm not sure I want to know."

Ruby took a deep breath and turned to face me. "You're going to have to find out, Aviana. For your sake and the safety of all the other fairy godmothers in the guild."

I shook my head. "It's okay. I'm not going to see him again. Ever. Period. End of story."

Ruby smiled sympathetically. She wasn't going to argue, but we both knew she was right.

"I wish …" I stopped myself.

"You wish what?" Ruby asked. "It's okay. You can tell me what you really want."

"I wish there was a way I could be a fairy godmother at the same time I'm finding my own happily ever after. I don't understand why they have to be mutually exclusive. It's not one of the rules."

"I would think your parents' relationship would be enough to scare you away from romance." Ruby wasn't being snarky, but maybe she had a point.

My heart sank. Nash really was off-limits.

On my way back from the barn, I stopped off at the cafe for a skinny vanilla latte. Hazel was standing near counter where the barista was preparing her coffee drink.

She opened her purse and unloaded a pound of coins into the tip jar. "Hazard of the trade," she said.

I waved goodbye and Hazel hurried off to her next appointment.

With my latte in hand, I walked my bike along the shopping arcade on Main Street then ducked under the flowering vine growing up and over the arbor at the entrance and pressed myself up against the window of Wisteria Wholesale.

"Aviana?"

Nash.

I had been caught red-handed. Looking at wedding dresses. I screamed inside my head but no words come out of my mouth, and I was too stunned to move. He looked rough, with dark circles beneath his eyes. He was dressed

186

in sweats and sneakers.

"What are you doing here?" I asked.

"I've been staking out the cafe for hours. I figured you'd have to get your fix eventually."

He was a computer genius, but it turns out he was pretty smart when it came to human nature too.

"Aviana, talk to me. Are you all right?"

"Yes. I'm fine. I'm fine." My face flushed and the tips of my ears were burning hot. I fluffed my hair to make sure they were covered. "I'm so sorry. It was never my intention ..."

"Please don't apologize ... I was worried when you took off last night," he said.

"I wish ... I wish I had a good excuse, but I don't. All I can say is I'm sorry. I had to go. I hope you'll forgive me. I'll understand if you don't."

"When you disappeared last night, you left me with a lot of unanswered questions."

"But, I ..." I stopped. My face flushed. I was standing on a street corner talking to the guy I'd been crushing on forever. He seemed genuinely concerned about me. He actually cared. Having grown up in a household free of affection or concern, this was a new feeling for me. "I don't ... understand."

"You ghosted me."

I nodded. "Usually guys stop calling and go away when girls do that. I thought wrongly that you would too."

"I can't stop thinking about you," he blurted. Obviously, he wasn't like most guys. Then he added, "I like you."

"I like you too. Very much." But I had...reasons I had to go last night. Reasons I can't tell you. Ever. Reasons we shouldn't ever see each other again. I'm sorry."

His forehead wrinkled. "Don't apologize. It's all my fault. I pushed things too far. I'm a grown-ass man. I should've known better. I hope you'll forgive me."

"But I ditched you."

"Yes. That was a little rude, wasn't it?" he teased.

"You kissed me like you meant it last night."

"I did mean it."

"So, will you let me make it up to you?"

"How?"

"Can I buy you an ice cream cone?

"Okay," I said.

"I'll buy you a double-scoop of whatever you want as long as you promise to say good-bye before you leave me this time."

Seriously? How much trouble could we get into over ice cream cones?

CHAPTER 17

Rule #17: A fairy godmother knows the heart can only whisper what it truly wants.

The little sparrow was at it again. Singing like a diva outside my bedroom window.

Exhausted from sleep deprivation, I slammed the window shut, got back into bed, and put the pillow over my head to drown out the noise. The little bird was singing even louder now. A song that'd been on the radio just last week.

I peered at the obnoxious little bird through the window. She stopped singing and looked back at me, turning her head as if trying to decide if I was friend or foe.

Since the sparrow wasn't going to let me to get any more sleep, I decided to go for a run. In what was quickly becoming my morning routine, I let myself out the front door and headed down the street toward the center of town.

Within a few steps I had broken into a loopy run and my heart was pounding a little harder. The physical exertion was comforting. I cleared my mind of all my worries and concentrated on putting one foot in front of the other.

With each step, I was putting all those years of being the awkward and uncomfortable daughter of "The Whale" and Madeleine behind me. If only I could see through the fog to know where I was going. With each stride, I felt my confidence rise. I promised myself I was going to be even more confident in the future. But I didn't know how yet.

After my run, I showered and dressed in jeans, a pink T-shirt, and my Chucks, shouted a quick good-bye to my mom, and headed out to the garage to get the bike I now considered mine.

I joined Ruby and Owen, and all the other fairy godmother candidates, as we slowly gathered in the garden at El Encanto, chattering nervously amongst ourselves. When Zara arrived, we followed her into the library and she took her place at the front of the room.

I glanced over at Ruby and Owen. I wondered if they were as apprehensive as I was. I knew I had the right instincts to be a fairy godmother. I wanted to help people, but I wasn't so sure about being responsible for other people's happiness. Especially their happily ever after. It seemed like an overwhelming obligation.

What if I couldn't come through in a pinch?

Zara turned off the PowerPoint that had been displayed on the wall and turned back around to us. "So, what do you think would be the best way to administer a love potion?" Zara asked.

Shoot, my mind had been wandering while Zara had been talking.

"In coffee?" one of the pixies hovering near the window suggested.

"Ice cream?" I asked.

"Wine?" Ruby added.

"Wine is a love potion by itself." Ruby and I caught the

giggles, and nothing could make us stop.

Zara closed her eyes as if she couldn't bear to look at us. "For heaven's sake, you guys. It's in the book. Didn't any of you read it?"

My cheeks flushed. I hadn't finished the reading assignment. Some of the older passages in the rulebook was flowery and written in prose that I found difficult to read. Often I had to go back and forth over one sentence five or six times before I got the gist of it.

"That's your assignment for next time. Read. The. Book." Zara sounded exasperated. "Now, back to the question at hand. Thanksgiving dinner is the best way to administer a love potion," she said.

"Thanksgiving dinner? Really?"

"When was the last time you met someone who didn't like Thanksgiving dinner?" she asked.

"Never," Briar squealed while Juniper nodded in solidarity.

"Exactly," Zara said. "That's why the essentials of Thanksgiving dinner should always be your go-to ingredients of any successful fairy potion. Apples, pumpkins, potatoes, or bread."

"Everybody likes apples," I said.

"And they're good for you," the tooth fairy added. "Four out of five dentists recommend eating apples as after-dinner treats."

"If you in a place where you can't find any of the essentials of a Thanksgiving dinner, then what is the next thing on your list?" Zara prompted us.

We looked around the room at each other. We all looked completely clueless.

"Nutella," Zara said.

"Nutella?" I was surprised. "It's like two hundred calories per teaspoon."

"But it's also the food in the world no one dislikes. If you don't have Nutella, try bacon. It's also nearly foolproof, unless you're dealing with someone who's a vegan. Which is why it's always best to start with fruit," Zara added.

At least the mystery of my mom's pantry had been explained.

"Over the next few days, you should also be on the lookout for your familiar," Zara said.

"My familiar?" I asked.

"Your assistant," Ruby said. I must've still looked confused because Ruby added, "Glenn is your mom's familiar."

"Your familiar could take many forms. It might be a cat, an owl, or a guinea pig. You will not choose your familiar; it will choose you. Try to keep an open mind. You don't want to miss this opportunity," Zara announced. "For those of you who haven't already gotten your first assignments, you'll get them tonight. Think of your task as a litmus test to see if you're ready to move forward with the life of a fairy godmother. Your task will not be difficult, and each one was hand-picked for you by a committee of Guild Elders, so you can't trade it with another fairy godmother. This test will decide whether you will become a full member of the Guild."

Suitably horrified murmurs could be heard in the back of the room. Ruby, Owen, and I gave each other worried looks.

"Your tasks must be completed before the last Strawberry Moon of the season. Have no illusions—if you fail to complete your assignments by that deadline, there will be consequences for you and your family." Zara stopped near my chair and fixed me with a long look. I got it. I wasn't stupid. "This could be particularly problematic if you come from a family with a long and illustrious reputation of fairy godmothers."

She wasn't even subtle. As if I didn't know she was talking about me "You cannot share any information about your assignment with other fairy godmothers and magical creatures. It is your responsibility, and yours alone, to make sure whatever has been noted on your personal assignment actually happens. And we will expect frequent updates on your progress. Are there any questions?" she asked.

The room was silent.

"Be careful out there," Zara said. "Take some time to try out some of your new skills. Next time we meet, we'll focus on frog prince and glass slippers. I'll see you all tonight."

There were no fairy godmothers or pixies hanging out in the garden after class. Everyone was too nervous about their first assignments to hang around and chit-chat. So I headed off. As I rode my bike alone through the woodlands, a shiver crawled up my spine. It was very quiet and more than a little spooky, but I couldn't shake the idea that someone was watching me.

Thankfully, I arrived home without incident.

"Have you had lunch?" Mom called when I came through the front door. "I made a salad, and I've got enough for two."

I always had room for lettuce. "Sounds delicious."

"Where's Glenn?" I asked. Usually he was buzzing around Mom's head, bossing her around.

"He's running some errands," Mom said. "I'm enjoying the peace and quiet."

We settled at the table on the patio for lunch. It was nice to have her undivided attention. My cell phone rang, breaking the family-bonding moment. When I saw the name, I knew I had to answer.

"Hey, Aviana, it's Vanessa."

Just in case Vanessa started yelling, I sequestered myself in the guest bedroom.

"How's it going up there?" Vanessa asked. "I understand Los Arboledas is lovely this time of year."

"It's enchanted," I said.

"How long are you planning to stay?" Vanessa asked. "Dad is worried about you."

"Really?" My laugh was brittle.

"Oh, you've always been his favorite." Vanessa's voice was as sweet as sugar, but I didn't trust her an inch. "You're kidding me, right?"

"He asked me to call you," she said. "He's afraid you're going to end up a crazy hippie-dippie, wack-job like your mom."

"That's not an accurate portrait of my mom," I said. "She works hard and she's very good at what she does."

"She's a yoga instructor, isn't she?" she asked. "What kind of career is that?"

"She helps people feel better about themselves. When was the last time you did that?" I asked. "You know what, actually, why didn't you start this conversation with 'I'm sorry'? Until you go there, I've got nothing else to say to you."

Vanessa started to say something else, but I ended the call before she could.

I spent a lot of time that afternoon trying to read the rulebook, but my head wasn't in it. I was too jittery about what was going to happen at El Encanto at midnight. I ended up falling asleep and woke up late for the event. I had to hurry to make it to the woodlands before the witching hour.

Arriving at the Tunnel of Love just before midnight, I was nearly doubled-over with anxiety. Ruby and Owen were already there, standing close together. They waved me over. But we were all too nervous to carry on a conversation.

A covey of pixies had gathered and were hanging out in the trees. I hadn't seen so many of the little creatures in one spot since I'd arrived in Los Arboledas.

Zara stepped forward, dressed in a long flowing gown that I was sure had been designed to make her feel more important. "Welcome to an important night. And good luck to all the candidates. I hope you all do well."

Then she turned and walked back to El Encanto.

"What happens now?" I wondered.

"We run through the Tunnel of Love," Ruby said. "That's where we'll discover our assignments."

"You've got to be kidding me," I said.

"It has to be this way. It's magic," Ruby said with a smile.

Suddenly, it was like the start of a marathon as we all ran into the tunnel at top speed and were immediately hit by cascading showers of pixie dust, as if being glitter-bombed. My skin tingled with every speck that touched me.

I picked up my speed as I ran downhill. I was feeling almost euphoric. Then I started to worry. What if I reached the end of the tunnel and didn't recognize my assignment?

What would happen next?

My worries were beginning to spiral out of control, then Juniper hit me with a tidal wave of sparkling pixie dust and my anxiety disappeared. My heart was filled with optimism as I ran toward the Tunnel of Love's inevitable conclusion without fear.

Ruby was the first fairy godmother to find her assignment. I saw her kick a rolled-up newspaper with the toe of her running shoe, stop sprinting, and circle back. She picked it up and read the headline quietly to herself.

"I got this," she said. Then she wiped some of the pixie dust off her face.

Seeing her so excited gave me a spark of optimism, so I continued on, covered in the glittering dust from my head to my toes. Every color of the rainbow stuck to my skin.

Owen stopped in his tracks and looked up into the night sky. His assignment was written in the stars.

I kept moving inside the dark tunnel, still searching for my assignment. Slowly the number of fairy godmothers dwindled to just a few. I was beginning to worry again that nothing was going to pop up for me when I was a few steps away from the end of the tunnel and the Door in the Woods without any luck. That's when it happened.

A white birch tree was glowing in the dark. It was the only birch tree I had ever seen in the forest.

I walked slowly toward it. I knew in an instant the message was for my eyes only. Carved into the trunk were two sets of initials inside a heart and the symbols for "True Love Always" on either side.

The initials were immediately familiar to me:

V.S. + N.N.

The message was loud and clear in my mind.

My assignment was to spark a romance between Vanessa Stern and Nash Nolan.

My stomach twisted with mixed emotions. Was I really supposed to fix up the guy I've been crushing on with my wicked stepsister? This had to be some kind of cruel joke. He was rich and she was beautiful. That kind of status exchange had been the basis for plenty of Hollywood happily-ever-after endings, why did they need a fairy godmother?

I stayed up late in Mom's garden that night, wondering how I could complete my assignment. I was still recovering from my run through the Tunnel of Love when Nash texted to ask me to meet him for lunch. I couldn't say no. He was now one half of my first assignment.

Nash was waiting for me in the lobby of the inn. His crooked grin made my breath hitch every time I saw it.

We walked down to the gourmet food store on Main Street that he'd heard made good sandwiches.

"This must be the place," he said. "The line is long."

We'd only been in line for a few minutes when I got the urge to play fairy godmother. I couldn't resist.

"Do you see that guy over there? I asked, nudging him to notice a guy at the front of the line.

He nodded. "The one with the pizza and a liter of Dr. Pepper in his basket?"

"Yes." Excitement crept into my voice. I loved matchmaking. "Now look to the left. Do you see her?"

"Where?" Nash asked, scanning the long line in front of us.

"The girl. His girl."

"In the hoodie?" Nash was so bad at this. "No. In the green sweater," I said hopefully.

"Yes." Nash sounded victorious. "I see her."

"She's got a quinoa salad and a slice of triple-tier carrot cake with maple cream cheese frosting," I explained.

Nash looked confused. "Okay. So what?" he asked.

"He's wearing a *Dr. Who* T-shirt. This could really work."

"How do you know?Nash asked.

"She's got a Tardis lunch pail for a purse," I smiled. "They could fall in love and live happily ever after."

"No, no. We're not matchmaking in the express line." Nash said firmly.

"Why not?"

"I hate setups." He shook his head. "They're the worst. It's how you find out how little your friends really think of you."

"You must have bad friends."

"I have great friends with really bad taste." A smile was playing around at the edges of his lips.

"Maybe they don't think as highly of you as you do of yourself," I teased.

He rolled his eyes. "Let's pay for our stuff and get out of here before you do something crazy."

"Where's the fun in that?"

"The fun is we leave people to mind their own business."

"But what if they're soul mates? What if they need our gentle guidance to find their happily ever after?"

"Or not," he said. "If they meet, they meet. We

shouldn't interfere. Let fate be their guide."

But I am fate. I am a fairy godmother.

How could I explain it without revealing too much?

"When given a choice, we should always choose the happily-ever-after ending," I said.

"I don't know if I have time for a full-on happily ever after," he checked his watch. "I've got a meeting at two. So, if we're going to shove these two towards a happily-ever-after ending, we need to put a fire under it."

"No problem," I said. "Watch me."

I had to push a little, but Nathan finally agreed to move out of the express line and let the two Whovians stand next to each other and fall in love.

"I can't believe you're making me do this," he said. We'd gone from being the next in line in the express line to being five people back from the cash register in regular grocery line.

"Don't you feel good about yourself?" I asked.

"No."

He looked over his shoulder. Our targets were in a deep conversation. They both smiling and animated.

"Maybe—" He stopped before he said something worse. "You make me crazy."

"Then why do you keep asking me to hang out with you?"

"Because…" Nash started to answer. Then he stopped. He took a long and admiring look at me. His eyes were warm and a smile played at the corners of his lips.

"Because you like me," I said, returning his admiring gaze. "And as much as you are constantly trying to assure me otherwise, you believe in dreamers. You believe as much as I do that life is about possibilities."

"What I believe is that this line is taking way too long," he protested. He looked over my shoulder at the cash register to see if there was some kind of problem.

"They can take all the time they want. You know you want to spend time with me. Admit it. You like me. Just a little."

"Stop. I admit it. I like you." He grinned. "Way more than a little. But we're not giving cutsies to one more person. I don't care if this is their last day on earth. You can't constantly find a reason to put everyone else before you."

"I beg your pardon?"

He cleared his throat. "You do it all the time. You're always thinking about how to bring other people together. You want to make people happy. All the time. How do you do that?"

"Maybe I was born this way," I said with the confidence of someone who knows their purpose.

Nash suggested a change. "Do you mind if we go back to the inn instead? I have a meeting at two, but there's a beautiful garden I'd love to show you."

"Sounds magical," I said.

Nash and I ate our sandwiches under the sweeping branches of two graceful willow trees nestled in a small, well-tended garden behind the Los Arboledas Inn.

"This spot should be renamed 'The Enchanted Garden,'" I commented.

He nodded in agreement. "I'll call the printers this afternoon and have them change the brochure." He smiled. I couldn't stop grinning. Spending time with him was so sweet.

After lunch, Nash walked me to the front of the hotel where I had left my bike in the rack and patiently waited while I unlocked it.

"I'll text you later," he said. His lips brushed across my mouth for the quickest of seconds, but his touch still managed to make my heart go pitter-pat.

It wasn't the kiss so much as the fact he had kissed me on the front steps of the inn.

I was a little surprised and was a little thrilled by it too.

I kissed him back and waved good-bye as he went back to work, completely unaware we were surrounded by hotel guests, the valets, the concierge…

And my entire family. Well, not my *entire* family, just my father, my stepmother, and my two stepsisters. With their mouths all hanging open, watching me kiss Nash Nolan.

CHAPTER 18

***Rule #18: A fairy godmother makes sure you have
everything you need to believe.***

Madeleine was the first member of my family to
acknowledge me. She stutter-stepped as if she didn't know
whether or not to acknowledge my presence. Finally, she
succumbed to good manners.

"Aviana," Madeleine called. She turned to see if Dad
was watching, and then she threw her arms wide and
enveloped me in a perfume-soaked hug as if we were long-
separated mother and child. "How are you?"

"I'm fine," I said.

"What did you do to your hair?" Vanessa asked. "It
looks fantastic." She gave me her patented air-kisses on
each cheek, thus avoiding any risk of body contact.

"Look at you." Valerie. "You look great." She pushed
me away to take a look at my clothes. "I love this retro-
prepster thing you've got going on. *Tres chic.*"

Valerie's fiancé, Nao, got out of the car, not that he
was paying attention. He was fiddling with his smartphone.
He had dropped his surname so long ago, I couldn't even
remember what it was. He seldom had anything to say to

me, and I was okay with that.

"You remember my sister Aviana, don't you?" Valerie asked. Nao looked up long enough to grunt a greeting in my general direction.

"What are you doing at the inn?" Vanessa asked. "I thought you were staying with your mom."

"I was having lunch. With a friend. What are you guys all doing here?"

I believed they were here for me. They had come to rescue me. They would apologize and make amends. I wouldn't have to make any choices or decisions without their guidance or supervision. My life was back on track. My heart expanded with joy.

"Did you know the Los Arboledas Inn is on the top of the list of the most romantic spots in the world to get married?" Vanessa asked.

"I'm not surprised" In a very short time, I'd fallen in love with Los Arboledas

"Los Arboledas is the headquarters of Wisteria Wholesale," Valerie added. "All of the brides Zara Wakefield features in her magazine get married here. And I have an appointment with Zara tomorrow."

Now I understood. The real reason my family was here was to meet with Zara Wakefield.

"Can you believe it? My daughter is going to have a 'Wakefield Wedding.' I can think of nothing more ..." She was at a loss for words.

"Enchanted," I finished her sentence.

"Yes." Madeleine nodded. "Enchanted."

My father finished supervising the luggage, and walked back over toward us. "Valerie, Vanessa, go with Nao and your mother and check in at the front desk," Dad said. "I want to talk to Aviana for a moment. Alone."

He tapped his toe on the ground waiting for them to go inside the lobby. Then he turned to me. "Are you dating Nash Nolan?"

"I'm not going to discuss my personal life with you," I

said.

"Does he know the truth about you and your mom?"

"It's none of his business ... or yours for that matter," I said.

My ears burned with anger. Dad could say whatever he wanted about me, but my mom was off-limits. My father's inability to believe in her— was at the heart of the problem.

"Don't talk about my mother," I spat. My anger must have surprised him because he backed down immediately.

"Does Nash know about her? Tell him now. Or I will."

"Mom and Nash aren't your concern." I wasn't feeling fierce, but I figured I could fake it for a minute or two. "His family just bought the inn. He doesn't have any day-to-day supervision of her, but technically he is her employer. It would be best if you didn't say anything to put her position at the inn in jeopardy."

Dad's lips thinned. "So then you've already made a decision about your future."

"Don't act like you're here for me. You're here to plan Valerie's wedding. The fact that you ran into me today is a coincidence. Otherwise, I probably never would've known you guys were here."

"That's not true," he said. "Part of the reason I came here was to talk to you about your future."

"I wish I'd learned about mom's side of my ancestry sooner. Did you know fairy godmothers are late bloomers? If I'd known, it would've explained things I didn't understand when I was growing up, Giving me the confidence I so desperately needed."

"I hoped it wasn't true. That you wouldn't be like your mom. That you'd take after me," Dad said. "You don't know how much I hoped."

"And yet, your wishes didn't come true," I said. "Maybe you should've been nicer to your fairy godmother."

"Don't be sarcastic, Aviana." It's not becoming."

"I don't care what you think of me anymore." I had been angry with him for so long, but I had been too frightened to express it. It was good to be able to let go.

"You have choices. I'm sure there is something we can do, Aviana …"

"I thought that at first. I could be surgically altered to fit in with you and Madeleine and the twins. But even if I had surgery, I wouldn't ever fit in with you guys."

"Your mother …"

"Mom is not without her faults, but she is not the crazy air-head you always insisted she was. She's actually quite lovely." It was good to speak the truth. He didn't have the power over me anymore.

"I am sure she has told you some terrible things about me."

"It's funny. She has never said one unkind thing. In fact, I think you broke her heart," I said.

All the blood drained from his face. "That is not true, Aviana. It can't be."

"You only see what you want to see."

Dad took a moment to think about what I'd just said, then added, "You know you can't date Nash, Aviana. He'd never accept your fairy blood. Maybe you should introduce him to your sister. They'd make a really nice couple."

His words cut me to the bone. How did he know that finding a way to spark a romance between Vanessa and Nash was my first assignment?"

"I'm not trying to hurt you, Aviana. I'm trying to protect you. You can't be with him. You know as well as I do that it won't end well.

"Don't tell me what to do," I said. And then I turned and ran. Unable to hear one more word from him.

I was under the shopping arcade on Main Street before I stopped moving. I took a deep breath and looked up at the wisteria blossoms hanging down over the arches.

I was feeling a bit calmer when I noticed a family walk out of Bennett's Ice Cream Parlor a couple of doors down. A mother and father and a school-age boy and girl were all snacking on homemade ice-cream cones as they strolled toward me underneath the arcade.

My ears begin to tingle as they wandered slowly up the sidewalk, doing a little bit of window-shopping along the way.

They stopped now and then to look up and comment on the color of the sky, but their focus was clearly on the pleasure of eating ice cream.

They stopped next to me when a dog came trotting along from the opposite direction. He walked around the corner on his own. A bit scruffy and dirty, but he walked with a sense of purpose as he trotted up the sidewalk.

"Hey! That looks like Hector," the dad said.

"He's the spitting image of Hector," the mom agreed.

The dad got to his knees and tried to call the dog over. The dog was shy at first, but with a little encouragement, eventually went over to the man, his tail wagging along the way. The man put out a hand to pet his fur, and the dog stayed still long enough to enjoy the sensation of touch.

"He's got a tag," he said, grabbing for the dog's collar to take a look.

"What does it say?" she asked.

"Omigosh. Hector." She dropped to her knees next to her husband and buried her face in the dog's matted, dirty fur. "Where have you been?" she cried. "

"Hector!" the kids screamed right before they joined the family pile-on.

I'm not sure what happened next, because my eyes were filling with tears. This was the kind of happily ever after I wanted to spend the rest of my life creating. If only I hadn't been given an impossible task for my first assignment.

"He disappeared six months ago," the mom said. She had joined me on the bench, watching her family's reunion with their beloved pet. "Even though we had him micro-chipped."

"We live six hundred miles from here in northern California," the dad was still dumbfounded. "I don't understand why he turned up here. Of all places the place in the world."

"It's funny"—the mom furrowed her brow—"I'd just been thinking about Hector as the sky was turning pink. I used to walk him at sunset."

"That'll do it," I said.

The owner of the gourmet food store gave them a length of twine to use as a makeshift leash, but Hector wasn't going anywhere. He was with his people.

A lump of emotions filled my throat. Tears formed behind my eyes. I was full-on crying by the time I got back to my mom's house. Then I threw myself across my bed and let go, crying in big gulps. It was so good to let go.

"Is everything okay?" Juniper asked. Her voice startled me. I'd forgotten that Los Arboledas was a place where you were never completely alone.

"I'm fine." I sniffed.

"You can tell me what happened."

"No, thank you," I said. I was not going to pour out my heart to a pixie. Seriously. It was like telling your problems to your teddy bear. What good would it do?

"I'm a good listener." Her voice was calm and steady.

I took a deep breath and the truth poured out.

"My dad showed up in Los Arboledas this afternoon, live and in person, to remind me not to expect too much out of my life. Then I witnessed a bit of magic, and now I'm confused."

Juniper sat down on the nightstand. "Before you shed one more tear over being a disappointment to your father, just remember you are a fairy godmother. You are in the power."

"I don't feel in the power," I said.

"But you are," she insisted. "Being a fairy godmother

isn't about magic. Any witch can do magic. It's about heart. You have a great heart. Don't ever doubt it."

Juniper's words made me feel better.

"I'm here for you," she said. Her eyes bright and warm.

"Here for me?" I was confused. "What do you mean 'here for me'?"

"I'm your familiar," Juniper said.

As soon as Juniper spoke those words, I knew I couldn't ignore my first assignment, even though it was impossible. Even if it broke my heart, getting Nash and Vanessa together would impact both our lives.

I texted Nash and asked him to be my date for dinner at the inn with my family. Then Juniper and I went out to the kitchen. We found a love potion in *The Fairy Godmother's Rulebook* and prepared it with all the crazy ingredients from mom's pantry.

"I hope we're doing this right," I said.

Juniper giggled. "We may be making a poison apple out of a persimmon."

"Only one way to find out." I crossed my fingers and hoped for the best.

Juniper and I finished making our concoction with plenty of time to spare before dinner. So I took my time getting dressed for dinner. I wanted to make sure my wings had a good soaking in a milk bath. It was one thing to lose your temper with your family in public, it was another to let your wings unfurl in anger in the middle of a five-star resort.

I put on a floral sundress I'd found at the inn's boutique a couple of days ago, tucked the love potion into my purse, and headed up to the inn.

Nash met me in the lobby when I arrived. When he smiled I felt like I could do anything. His hair was damp from the shower, and he smelled of soap and peppermint. I hoped he wasn't worried about making a good impression on my family. All he had to do was show up and my father would worship him like a deity.

"You look nervous," he said. "Is everything okay?"

"My relationship with my family isn't stellar," I explained.

"You need me to provide a buffer tonight?"

"I'm afraid I'm putting you in an uncomfortable position," I said. "I'm not the person you think I am. That night at Mr. Chow's, I wasn't there because I had the confidence to throw my own birthday party. I was there alone because my family didn't show up. I thought they were meeting me there, but they went to Mexico instead. On my birthday."

"That's really crappy," Nash said. "And it says a lot more about them than it does about you. Even if you didn't plan to be alone on your birthday, when you were faced with the worst happening to you, you made a party out of it. You're always looking for the happily ever after."

I smiled. "Thank you."

"I also think you have beautiful eyes and are a good kisser, but I'm not going to mention it in front of your father."

"You could say whatever you wanted about me. He wouldn't care," I said. "Trust me. He has already formed his mind about me. You won't be able to change it."

"Yeah, but now that he's revealed who he is, you have the upper hand. And you've got me. And I've got your back."

"You are very nice."

"I am practical. I do what needs to get done. You see the bigger picture and anticipate what will need to be done. It's a special skill, Aviana. One you should remember when you're deciding what you want to do with your life."

"Thank you," I said.

"You look beautiful, by the way." His eyes were warm and kind.

"Thank you," I said again. "But wait until you meet my

sisters."

"What is that supposed to mean?"

"By comparison, I am hardly worthy of note," I said.

"Not possible."

"Wait and see."

As if on cue, Madeleine walked toward me with her arms open wide. And then it happened. After a flash of blinding white light, my fairy godmother's superpower gave me a moment of insight into who she really was. I had always known her to be materialistic and class-conscious, but for the first time in my life, I got a glimpse behind her mask.

A gasp escaped my lips. A sound I attempted to cover by putting my fingers over my mouth. Behind the ever-present smile Madeleine wore on her face, there was nothing there. She was a hollow shell.

I didn't have a moment to digest my newly discovered information about who Madeleine really was before she cut our cursory hug short and reached out to Nash, throwing her arms open wide.

"You must be Nash," she said, pulling him in for an awkward hug. He nodded and greeted her politely.

Valerie and Nao were as self-absorbed as ever. After a neutral greeting, they returned to their phones, but Vanessa smiled when she saw us.

"How are things going at the office?" I asked.

"It's a challenge," she said. "I wish you'd come back. I could make you an offer you couldn't refuse."

"I doubt that very much."

Dad finally appeared and greeted Nash warmly with the same kind of reverence most people reserved for heads of state.

Nash was kind but kept his distance, staying close to me. He kept one hand in the small of my back while he talked with my dad.

I was so caught up in enjoying Nash's company, his touch against my skin, I didn't notice Madeleine was standing next to me until she spoke. Her words were soft, intended for my ears only.

"How did you manage it?" Madeleine was smiling. Her tone was friendly, but when the white light of my insight flashed, her fangs were showing. "How did you manage to catch Nash Nolan?"

"He is not caught. We've been on two dates." I laughed.

"He appears smitten." Her words were delivered with venom. Her daughters were meant to marry well, not her stepdaughter. I had no idea she despised me. At least not until this moment. The mask of mild indifference she wore daily was hiding a lot of anger.

"How did you claim his attention?" Her tone dripped with derision.

"Magic," I said with a broad grin. "I put a spell on him."

"Of course. There could be no other reason for it." Madeleine's eyes were glittering with anger. And in that moment, I knew Dad had been indiscreet. He had told her about my mother's powers. And mine. She knew everything. He had lied to me about not telling her.

I followed the hostess to our table feeling claustrophobic. It was like being thirteen all over again, trapped in a home with an unfeeling father and a stepmother who wrapped up her cruelty in such beautiful packages, there were times when I had thanked her for making me feel helpless and vulnerable.

As if knowing I was in distress, Nash brushed his hand over my shoulder. I looked up and he smiled. For once, I didn't feel alone. Nash had my back.

After dinner, Dad and Madeleine went back to their room and Valerie and Nao took a walk around the inn grounds to see if they could find a location for their vows, leaving Vanessa alone. Now was my chance. I had to at least give it a try.

"It's still early," I said. "Do you want to go to the bar for a drink?"

"Sure," he said.

"Vanessa, why don't you come with us?" I said.

She looked startled. I couldn't remember the last time I had requested to spend time in her company voluntarily. Generally I avoided her like the plague when we weren't in the office.

"I don't know," she said, "Josie has messed up my files so bad, I should probably get back to work."

"I'm buying," he said. "And your files will still be messed up in an hour."

"If you want, I'll help you with them," I offered.

Vanessa flashed a very genuine smile. "You're right. There's no reason why I can't have a little fun."

We strolled into the bar in a quiet area off from the restaurant and took a seat at a high top.

"Let's get appletinis," I said.

"That would be fun," Vanessa agreed.

"I don't think 'tini' anything is really my thing," he said, checking out the beer menu on a chalkboard above the bar.

"Have you had one?"

"No, but ..."

"It'll be fun. I'll be right back," I said.

Under the guise of ordering the drinks at the bar, I took my time checking out the assorted garnishes. They were displayed in individual containers—like a buffet for lovers of olives, lemon twists, maraschino cherries, caper berries, and lychees.

But I had my eye on the apple rings that had been carefully sliced and covered in lemon juice so they wouldn't brown. I had chosen them to be the delivery system for the love potion Juniper and I had cooked up.

I waited until the bartender was looking the other way, and then I pulled one apple ring out of the condiment container and sloshed love potion over the rest of the rings.

I claimed my own cocktail as I slipped the untampered-with garnish into one of the glasses. I let the bartender put the love-potion-covered garnishes in the other two glasses and then carried them back to our table. I set one in front of him and one in front of Vanessa.

I'm not going to lie, I had second, third, and fourth thoughts about leaving Nash and Vanessa alone. I kept thinking about the rules of being a fairy godmother. And I kept getting stuck on the same one over and over.

Who needs my kindness most today?

I was following the instructions of my assignment to the letter, and yet it seemed so wrong. I could feel it in my gut. How could this be right?

I didn't think it would take more than a nudge for Vanessa to see how incredibly charming Nash was. It was the only way I could save my mom from losing her powers, so I excused myself to go to the restroom.

I left them alone at the bar, and I didn't look back.

CHAPTER 19

Rule #19: A fairy godmother never uses a potion without the antidote in her possession.

Juniper was buzzing through the bushes in the garden with the rest of her covey when I got back to my mom's house. It took me a few minutes before I was able to get her attention.

"I've got a job for you," I said.

"No problem," Juniper replied. "What's up?"

"I need you to spy on some people for me."

"That's what I'm here for," she beamed. "You know, I can do things. Things that will make the date go one way or the other, but I can't tell by the way you're talking what I'm supposed to do."

"Don't do anything," I insisted. "There's no need to use magic." Juniper looked as if I'd hurt her feelings. "I'm sorry. I know you're anxious to use your magic, but let's let them interact organically from here on out."

"Got it."

"I already spiked their drinks with love potion. I'm hoping I didn't overdo it. Try to stay out of sight. And promise me, no matter what, no singing or dancing birds tonight, okay?"

"Promise," Juniper said. She raised her wing in a salute before flying off.

After a glass of wine at dinner and two Appletinis at the bar with Nash and Vanessa, I should've been well on my way to tipsy. Instead, I was wired. I was agitated and anxious and my wings were fidgety against my spine.

My mom was out for the evening. She was anticipating some problems at an elopement in Cambria and didn't think she'd be back until morning. Glenn had gone with her, just in case. No creatures were stirring out in the garden. It was unusual. Even when Mom wasn't home, there were usually pixies buzzing in and out of the bushes. I wondered where the rest of the pixies were, but I was grateful for the peace and quiet. I took a deep breath and decided to relax and enjoy the moment.

The tranquility didn't last long. Stress and anxiety caused my wings to be more active—their movements becoming more sharp and jagged as I became increasingly upset and irritated.

I found a bottle of my mom's favorite red wine in the fridge and poured myself a glass hoping to calm my nerves. I put a vintage Sinatra album on the hi-fi and curled up in a corner of the sofa. I was starting to relax when there was a knock at the front door. I made my way to open it and was surprised to find Ruby standing there with a laundry basket in her hands.

"Ugh, Ruby. What is that smell?"

"Pig." She gestured down to the six little piglets in the basket.

I covered my nose and backed away. "The air freshener hasn't been invented that can take on that smell."

"They had piglets at the Farmers Market. I don't think they were going to be taken home as pets."

My face must have shown my fears.

"Please," she said. "Don't judge me. I couldn't leave them at the market to become someone's future Easter dinner."

"You can't keep them," I said.

"I know. You're right. But your mom said I could borrow her car. I can't get them home on my bike."

I gave the keys to Ruby, said our good-byes, and went back in the house. It was a good time for a milk bath. I warmed the milk and honey in the microwave and filled the shallow shell-like tub in the backyard with the warm, rich liquid.

I wrapped my hair up in a towel, got undressed, and slid beneath the surface of the opaque liquid in the shell-shaped tub. It was a wonderful indulgence. I tried not to think about Vanessa being with Nash. I told myself this was how any fairy godmother would celebrate the completion of their first assignment. This should be time for celebration, but I didn't think I had ever been so sad. I took another sip of wine and redoubled my efforts on focusing my thoughts on the pleasure of the bath.

The milk and honey mixture made my skin feel smooth and moisturized. The smell was intoxicating. My wings were excited and active when I first dipped beneath the surface, but after a while, they grew sluggish and relaxed, pressing against my back between my shoulder blades.

I closed my eyes and was enjoying a moment of complete bliss as my whole body relaxed before the doorbell rang once again, shattering my sense of contentment.

I ducked down beneath the surface of the milk and honey mixture. I wasn't expecting anyone. I closed my eyes and took a deep breath. Whoever was at the front door would eventually go away.

The doorbell rang a second time. And then a third. I knew whoever was out there wasn't going to take "no" for an answer. I got out of the tub, quickly dried myself with a towel, and pulled on a white terry cloth robe I had found in my mom's bathroom. I tiptoed through the living room and looked out the peephole at the front porch.

"Open the door." Nash's smooshed-into-the-peephole face was shooting daggers back at me. "Open the door, Aviana. I can see you. I know you're home. You're not fooling anyone."

I took the towel off my head and threw it behind the sofa. I fluffed my hair down over the points of my ears in the reflection of the front hall mirror, forced a smile, and pulled open the front door.

"Hey," I said with exaggerated coolness. "What are you doing here?"

He didn't wait for me to invite him in. He pushed past me and with two long strides was in the center of the living room.

"Are you alone?" I peered into the darkness on the front lawn.

Where was Vanessa?

She was under the influence of a love potion at a four-star resort. Anything could happen.

"Of course, I'm alone," he said.

I needed to get back to the Los Arboledas Inn and check on her as soon as possible.

"How did you know where I live?"

"There's a big sign on the roof. Neon. Bright Lights. Says Aviana sleeps here," he said. His sarcasm registered as a big hint that he wasn't completely happy with me. I closed the door and followed him into the kitchen at the back of the house.

"Is this your mom's house?

"Yes."

"It's nice." He looked completely distracted. And seriously annoyed.

"What are you doing here?" I asked.

"I wanted to tell you a story. You see, something really funny happened to me tonight."

"What was that?" I asked.

"You introduced me to your sister, and then you disappeared."

216

"You looked like you were enjoying each other's company," I suggested.

"We did. I do. Your sister is very smart. We have a lot in common, but I had been led to believe I was out with your family tonight as your date.

"You did? Well, I …"

"Stop lying, Aviana. I like you. And I thought you liked me. I thought we had a thing. And then you … well … I moved too fast. I scared you off."

"No. Nash, it wasn't your fault."

"But I thought we got it back on track, and everything was going okay. I kissed you and you kissed me back. You said you wanted to introduce me to your family. That seemed like a really good sign. I thought you might really like me too."

"I do."

"And then all of a sudden, after dinner, it was as if you were doing what you do."

"What do you mean?"

"I've seen you do it before. You were fixing me up with your sister."

"She's not my sister," I said. "She's my stepsister."

"Good to know, but you're not helping. You were matchmaking me. I'm certain."

"No, I wasn't. I swear." I must admit, at this point I glanced down to see if anything below my waist was on fire because, by all rights, flames should've been shooting out of my pants. I was lying. Seriously lying.

"Don't lie to me, Aviana."

"Lie to you? No. I swear. I haven't. Not really."

"For God's sake, Aviana. Why can't you tell me the truth? What's up with that?"

"Vanessa is lovely," I said. "And she wants it all—full-on career and a full-on family. I want her to have that."

"Your loyalty to your sister is remarkable, but why me?"

"Vanessa may be a more appropriate mate for you than

I am."

"More appropriate mate?" He gave me a long look. "Is this how your commitment-phobia manifests itself?

"I don't have a commitment problem."

"For reals? You do." A grin played at the corners of his mouth as he used my own words against me.

"For reals. Vanessa deserves to meet a nice guy, and you're the nicest guy I know."

"Ah. There it is."

"There what is?"

"The thing you do. When you put everyone else's needs before your own. I get it now."

"I'm not doing that. I'm doing my job."

"You're an unemployed legal assistant; how is finding a mate for your stepsister your job?"

"I am, but I am also ..." I stopped myself right before the truth dribbled out. "I've been helping my mom."

"Your mom? She's a ... yoga instructor," he said. "Isn't she?"

"She ...she does some other stuff on the side." I wasn't completely wrong.

He laughed. It was a dry and brittle sound.

"God, Aviana. I can't believe you're lying to me like this."

"I'm not."

"Then tell me why were you were pimping me out?

"I'm not 'pimpin' you," I said. "Truly. I'm not. It's so hard to explain."

He turned around and walked toward me. His gaze was intense. I'd never seen him like this before.

"What I'm about to tell you is not something I usually have to point out to most people, Aviana," he said. "I'm twenty-five years old. I'm over six feet tall. I have regular features. And I'm a self-made millionaire. With a big "M.""

"Bragging isn't an attractive look for you." Obviously, I couldn't stop lying. Seriously. I would find him attractive if he was speaking in tongues.

"Maybe not, but it is the truth," he said. "And I want to be completely honest with you because I want you to be completely honest with me." He had me backed up against the garden wall and was quickly closing the space between us.

His face was *really close* to mine.

"The size of my bank account is usually a big turn on for women. Of all ages. I don't have any problems getting dates. Ever."

"I know. It's that—" I started.

He cut me off. "So, you don't have to do your matchmaker thing for me. Got it?"

"Got it," I said.

"Promise me you're not going to lie to me anymore?"

"I promise." I would've said anything he wanted me to say at that moment. To please him. To make him happy. I wanted to taste him. To touch him. To feel him. He smelled so good.

"I'm going to say this because I don't want there to be any confusion." He looked me directly in the eyes. "I want you. Not your stepsister, your best friend, or your stepmother. You."

My heart skipped a beat as he used his fingers to brush hair off of my forehead. Then, he lifted my chin, and my heart nearly stopped as he traced a line to my bottom lip with his thumb.

I tried to ignore the electrical spark ignited by his touch, but it was like a fireworks display was going off inside my body.

"You drive me absolutely crazy." His voice dropped to a whisper. He tucked my hair back behind my pointy ears, caressing my cheek with soft whorls. "I've never met anyone like you, and I can't walk away."

He took my hand in his and very gently brushed his lips across the back of my hand, sending a trail of goosebumps up my arm. His touch was electric.

His mouth covered mine. The pleasure of his kiss set

off a chain reaction of delicious sensations all over my body.

"I want to be with you," he said. "Only you. And if I want to date someone other than you, I'll tell you, and then I'll ask them out myself. In that order. Got it?"

I nodded. He took my hand and pulled me out into the swing in the backyard garden.

We sat together looking up at the stars for a long time. Firefly lights blinked in the bushes, and I wondered if some of the lights were pixies.

Were we actually alone? I hoped so. Then he kissed me again, and I didn't give it another thought. I didn't care. All that mattered was that I was having the perfect moment with him.

Even if I knew it wasn't going to last. It couldn't.

Eventually I would have to figure out a way to get Nash to fall in love and live happily ever after with Vanessa, but right now, he was mine and all was right with the world.

That night I had the sweetest dreams. Filled with glass slippers, Prince Charming, and happily-ever-after endings. When I woke in the morning, I knew in my heart my dreams weren't meant to come true.

CHAPTER 20

Rule #20: A fairy godmother never accepts defeat.

Nash stopped by for lunch the next day. He brought take-out and we ate in Mom's kitchen before settling into the chaise lounge chairs in the garden to enjoy the afternoon sun. He reached over and took my hand. Making patterns with his fingertips in the palm of my hand. His touch made me feel as if I was being covered in pixie dust. It was a never-ending euphoric feeling of joy.

I put my head back against the cushion and lifted my chin up to the sun. I couldn't remember being so content in my life. I reached for him and intertwined my fingers with his.

"I have a confession," Nash said.

"What's up?" I asked.

"I had a talk with your dad."

His confession nearly took my breath away.

"I didn't say anything you told me in confidence I didn't confront him. I didn't make him angry. I just wanted him to see you through my eyes if only for a minute or two. I thought it might help."

I kissed him on the cheek. "I doubt you'll ever change

his mind about me. But you're very sweet and I genuinely appreciate the effort."

"What is that sound?" he asked lazily, reclining happily in the chair next to me. He didn't even open his eyes.

"What sound?" I asked, pretending not to hear the sound he was asking about.

"It's like a cat purring." He sat up and looked around. "With a hint of cricket."

"For reals?" I lifted my sunglasses and looked around. "A cat-insect? I can't hear anything." I was lying. I knew what the sound was and where it was coming from. It was clear and distinct. My wings weren't moving, but rather vibrating, as they made a purring sound like a contented cat.

"You can't hear that? Seriously?" he asked.

"Have you had your hearing checked recently?" I insisted.

"No."

"You may want to make an appointment."

"I don't need my hearing checked," he said.

"Let me see about that." I kissed his earlobe, which caused him to draw his breath in a quick intake and reach for me, pulling me closer to him. With the kiss, my wings stilled.

Nash broke our kiss and pulled back, his gaze sliding toward my back.

He traced the lacy outline of my wings with his fingertips. "I didn't know you had a tattoo," he whispered.

He thought my wings were a tattoo.

I held my breath, scared that his touch would send my wings into perpetual motion. But they didn't so much as twitch.

"Yea. A tattoo." I released my breath.

Nash's head tilted and his eyes widened. "Is it me, or are the birds singing a pop song?"

"I beg your pardon?"

"You know the song. It's been on the radio all

summer."

"Stop it," I scoffed. "You know as well as I do that birds don't sing pop songs."

Shielding my eyes from the sun, I looked up into the fruit trees where a dozen birds were lined up like a church choir, singing in perfect harmony. On another branch, a group was clicking their little claws for the clap track. Juniper was sitting in one of the branches directing their voices with a tiny baton. She waved, and I recoiled in fear of the discovery.

"No. I think it's you." I prayed he wouldn't look up then yelped as he suddenly came to life and pulled me down on the chaise lounge next to him.

"I think it's my heart singing because you make me so happy," he said.

"You're such a dork."

He flashed his lopsided grin and my heart jumped as if it was on a trampoline. The effects of the milk bath I had taken the night before were starting to wear off. With each passing minute, they were getting more and more active, and I became increasingly more panicked and uncertain about what to do. I had to get away from him. If only for a few minutes.

I stood up and smiled. "Would you like some of Mom's lavender lemonade? It's delicious. I'll get us a couple of glasses." I didn't give him a moment to voice any objections.

I hid out in the kitchen where I could let my wings do whatever they wanted. When I thought they'd used up a good amount of their extra energy, I came back out into the garden carrying two glasses of lemonade on a tray.

Where I stopped dead in my track. Nash had *The Fairy Godmother's Rulebook* open in his lap. The rules for being a fairy godmother were spelled out very clearly in bold black and gold hand-lettered calligraphy on the pages in front of him.

"What is this?" he asked. "Is it antique? It's beautiful."

I smiled. "It's a birthday gift."

"Do you think the Fairy Godmother's Guild was a kind of ancient secret society?" he asked.

"Maybe." I shrugged.

He thumbed through the pages. "All of these rules. And the stories. I had the same kind of manual for Boy Scouts."

"You were a Boy Scout?"

"Oh, yes," he confirmed. "From Weebelos all the way up."

Then he raised his right hand with three fingers in the air. "A Boy Scout is trustworthy, loyal, helpful, friendly, courteous, kind, obedient, cheerful, thrifty, clean, and reverent."

"When did you memorize the rules?"

"I was probably six or seven."

"I think those qualities are pretty much all you need in a dude," I said.

He nodded. "It's funny. Sometimes I still find myself trying to live by those same rules."

"Rules are very powerful motivation tools," I agreed.

"And so, are the rules in this book the ones that you live by?"

"Why do you ask?"

"The rules in the book remind me of you. Everywhere we go, you're doing something for other people. Making sure they get the good table because it's their anniversary. Getting the hot girl to stand next to the cute-but-geeky guy in line because they have compatible items in their cart. Little scenes of happily ever after follow in your wake," he said. "It makes me want to know more about you."

"I don't know what you're talking about," I said.

He shook his head and grinned. I grinned back. We were ridiculous. I would've been happy to sit and smile at him all afternoon, but twenty minutes later he glanced at his phone and got to his feet.

"I've got to get back to work," he said.

I walked him to the front door, where he kissed me and I kissed him back.

"Text me later."

"Plan on it," he said.

Several kisses later, he got in his car and left.

I hung out in the garden and read the rulebook until mid-afternoon. Then Ruby stopped by to see if I wanted to go to the stables to visit Prince Charming with her. Having nothing else to do for the day, I agreed, but on the condition we'd stop at the inn's little café near the yoga studio to buy pumpkin spice lattes.

The animals in the barn had just been fed when we arrived. The air was perfumed with hay, horse manure, and the leather of the horses' tack. The stomp of animal feet and the soft whicker of horses was comforting. We sat on some hay bales outside of Prince Charming's stall to enjoy the rest of our coffee.

I took a big sip of my latte. "This is delicious."

"I know it's not one of the rules in *The Fairy Godmother's Rulebook*, but I think no fairy godmother should ever underestimate the power of the pumpkin spice," Ruby said.

I giggled and raised my glass. Ruby joined me in tribute. "To the power of pumpkin spice." We both took big slurpy sips of our coffee drinks. "So, what have you been up to?" Ruby asked.

I blurted out the truth. "I kissed Nash."

Ruby snorted coffee. "Okay. I didn't see that one coming. When did this happen?"

"Last night." He came over. Just to talk. Then he came back today for lunch."

"And you …"

"Kissed again." My voice was wistful.

"What are you going to do?" Ruby's question knocked me out of my dream-like state. "You can't stay with him.

Not if you still want to be a fairy godmother."

I let go of a deep breath. "I just needed a moment to bask in the afterglow."

"You shouldn't be basking," Ruby admonished. "I'm serious, Aviana. You've got a problem."

"I know. I do. This would all be a lot easier if my crush wasn't the nicest, most wonderful guy I've ever met."

"What about his feelings? He seems pretty into you. Where do his feelings fit into all of this?"

"He does?" I said hopefully.

"Yes. And PS. What about your first assignment? Have you made any progress?"

I shook my head. "Sometimes I wonder if ..." I searched for a way to tell Ruby my darkest fears without revealing the subject of my first assignment to her.

"Zara has given you an impossible task?" Ruby completed my sentence.

"Yes." I was thrilled that maybe Ruby understood. "But why would she do that?"

"There's only one answer," Ruby said. "And I don't like it."

"Who's going to challenge her authority? Not me."

"That's what worries me the most. She's going to get away with it."

Ruby pressed one finger to her lips. "Shhhhh."

I lowered my voice. "Sometimes when I'm looking at someone, I am momentarily blinded by a flash of white light. And I can see through them ... to their emotional essence. It happened the other day when I was with Nash. And it's happened before. When I was looking at Zara."

Ruby swiveled around and looked at me as if I was a unicorn. "You've got 'inner vision,'" she said. "Not all fairy godmothers have it. Only a very few. It's an amazing gift. Do you know if it runs in your family?"

"I don't know." I made a mental note to ask Mom if she had a similar ability to see people as they really were.

Ruby cleared her throat. "You know ... the deadline to

complete your first assignment isn't until the last Strawberry Moon. Why don't you give it another shot? See if you can do what needs to be done," Ruby suggested.

"What about Owen?" I asked. "Has he completed his first assignment?"

"That guy. He looked like a sleeper the first time he showed up at El Encanto. He hadn't even read the rulebook. Now I think he's trying for some kind of fairy godmother sainthood. He completed his first task in less than twenty-four hours."

"For reals?" I was so frustrated. Owen and Ruby were making fairy godmothering look all so incredibly easy. Would I be the only one to fail?

"Think about it. At least," Ruby suggested. "In the meantime, I need to go see this beauty."

Ruby moved down the hall in the barn to Prince Charming's stall. For Ruby and Prince Charming, it had been love at first sight. The big horse made a gentle snorting sound and nuzzled up against Ruby's neck.

"It's true love," I said with a smile.

Just then Ruby's friend Anna came by. She was leading her horse out to the ring for a riding session. She called to Ruby over her shoulder. "Have the Bryants talked to you about Prince Charming yet?"

"What about him?" Ruby's face fell. Her brows furrowed with worry.

"They've got a new horse that's going to start boarding here next week," Anna said. "They're going to need his stall."

"So? What are they going to do?"

Anna shrugged. "They can't keep him here. He's taking up valuable space and they can't keep shelling out money for his feed. She needs to rent out his stall."

"What will they do with Prince Charming? Where will he go?"

"You don't want to know," Anna said.

Ruby's face fell, pain written all over it. Even though I

hadn't known Ruby very long, I knew she didn't wear her heart on her sleeve. She didn't like anyone to know how vulnerable she was. In truth, Ruby was like an M&M—a hard candy shell over a soft, chocolaty, sweet interior. She was especially soft and gooey for animals, and Prince Charming in particular. The tears falling from her eyes were very real. "How much do they want for him?"

"He's a good horse, Ruby." Anna was brutally honest. "They're going to want fair market value Do you have that kind of cash."

"No." She wiped at her eyes. "But I can get it."

"I got your back, girl. We can knock over a bank and get the money by five." I nodded. "But I'm only in as far as driving the getaway car."

A smile flickered across Ruby's face. "Thanks. You're a good friend. I do have some savings," Ruby said. "I can make a down payment, and I will find a way to get the rest. Don't let them take him before you hear from me."

"Are you sure?" Anna asked.

"Yes. He's mine."

"I'll talk to the Bryants and see if they'll keep him a bit longer," she said.

"Thank you," Ruby said. "I'll make arrangements as soon as I can."

Ruby and I hurried out to the car. I knew she was uneasy leaving Prince Charming behind, and I was worried for her. She was acquiring more animals than she had space to give them homes.

"You're going to have to find a place for your petting zoo," I said.

"I know," Ruby said. "But I can't let anything happen to that horse."

"You can't keep a horse in your condo either. Your HOA is going to have a cow. Figuratively, not literally. Where are we going to find a place for you to keep a horse, a dog, two cats …"

"Three," she corrected me.

"Oh, Ruby, no. A dog, three cats, and, what … how many piglets?"

"Six." Ruby shot me a look. No doubt there were more animals in her condo that she hadn't told me about. "I've got an idea," she said. Then she called Owen and gave him directions to meet us at a place in the country.

Ruby was unusually quiet the rest of the way. She put her feet up on the dash and listened to the radio. When we got closer, she directed me to turn off on Vineyard Lane. The road was the home to a string of wineries in the canyon that soon disappeared around a bend. We turned off on a dirty two-track that took us back to a little farmhouse and ranch buildings tucked under a grove of pepper trees.

Owen was already there, leaning against his car, waiting for us.

The farmhouse was locked up tight. The other buildings looked ramshackle and weather-beaten. Most of the fencing wouldn't keep animals from roaming all over the canyon.

"What is this place?" Owen asked.

"My family's old farm," Ruby answered. "After my dad died, my mom went to live with one of my older sisters. My brother, Beto, attempted to make a go of it here on the farm, but he quickly discovered it wasn't as easy as it looked—he got a better job in Napa and moved away."

Ruby wiped away tears from the corners of her eyes as she looked around at the abandoned buildings and relics of happier and more prosperous times.

"It was a wonderful place to grow up," she said with hopeful magic in her eyes.

"I think it could be again," I said, looking at Owen. "Doesn't look all that far gone. What do you think, Owen?"

Ruby turned to Owen. "Do you think it's possible these buildings could house my animals?"

"Let me take a look around," he said.

Owen took his time wandering around the property. He looked at buildings and checked the fences. "It's well built. I don't think it would take too much to make it into a real home for you and your hopeless little animals, Ruby."

"Really?" she said with a grin so bright it could light up the night.

"Seriously. I could do the construction," Owen said. "But I don't know where we would get the money for the materials."

"I've got a plan," Ruby interjected. "Anna mentioned her son, Jack, did an online fundraiser for the football team's new uniforms last year. He could help you set up a GoFundMe campaign."

"You'd have to be set it up as a non-profit organization," Owen added. "A foundation."

"I can help with that," I said. "Working as a legal assistant all these years will finally pay off."

"Seriously?" Ruby was vibrating with excitement. "We can get it started tonight."

"What about a real-life fundraiser,? Where donors could meet the animals and understand their plight," I suggested. "A party … no, something big and extravagant …like a black-tie gala and silent auction." It was so much fun to help someone make their dreams come true.

"Oh, yes. That's good. A gala," Ruby agreed. "Black Ties and Horse Tails.

"Perfect," I said.

Owen was smiling at Ruby. He was always smiling at her. More and more I was convinced there was a deep and romantic connection forming between the two fairy godmothers.

The little farm was nestled into the woodlands with a glimpse of El Encanto from the barnyard, it was an extraordinary spot in the valley. "A haven for creatures who can't help themselves," I murmured. "The Enchanted Barn."

"That's it. That's what I'll call it," Ruby said. "The Enchanted Barn." Ruby's face glowed. "Animals have always brought me comfort. Now I want to make sure they get all the love and comfort they need."

"You guys get to work on the fundraiser, and I'll start working out here. I'm going to need some help getting the water troughs working again," Owen said. "Do you know a plumber?"

"I can ask around," Ruby said, joining Owen for a closer inspection of the pens.

Just then I was distracted by a text message notification. It was a photo of a six-year-old with a crooked smile in a Boy Scout uniform. Before I had a chance to study it, my phone rang.

"Is this the last time you were in uniform?" I asked.

"Maybe," Nash said. "It was fifth grade."

"Do you think your mom has any other photographs of you as a Boy Scout?"

"I'll ask her. She'll be thrilled to get out all of my old photos." He laughed.

"I thought you were busy until dinner."

"That's why I called." He sounded distracted. I could hear him tapping on a computer keyboard, as if multitasking. "I'm on a flight to Seoul at nine o'clock tonight."

"Tonight?" I tried to cover the disappointment in my voice.

"I thought I had mentioned it to you," Nash said. "Sorry. You make me forget stuff. Like what planet I'm on and what day of the week it is."

"That's a good thing, right?"

"Yes," he said, the warm tones returning to his voice. "I'm not even sure how long I'll be gone. I'll have a better timeframe of things once I get there."

"Sounds good," I said, forcing a smile. "Safe travels."

"I'll call you when I land. I promise."

And just like that, without the use of any kind of any

magic at all, Nash was gone.

CHAPTER 21

Rule #21: A fairy godmother knows true romance cannot be contrived or manipulated.

My ringtone startled me awake. I was back in the little room off the kitchen at Dad and Madeleine's house. *The Fairy Godmother's Rulebook* was open next to me on the bed. Gardenia was moving around in the kitchen, laughing at something someone had said on one of her favorite morning programs.

Beyond the walls of the house I sensed the rush of early morning traffic. It was almost as if nothing in my world had changed and everything that happened to me in Los Arboledas was all a wonderful, hazy, sunshine-dappled dream. I rolled over and my wings crunched underneath me. I smiled. All the evidence I needed that it wasn't all a crazy dream. For the first time ever, my wings gave me comfort.

There was no bird song—no choreographed routine to start my day with a smile. I wondered if Juniper was worried about me. I had forgotten to tell her where I was going.

Truthfully, I hadn't forgotten. I didn't alert Juniper or

233

anyone else I was leaving Los Arboledas. I was afraid they'd try to stop me. After Nash left, I figured if I had any hope of completing my first fairy-godmothering task, I needed to return to Los Angeles and reconnect with Vanessa. I really didn't want to fail, but every morning I was more pessimistic about my chances.

I was conflicted. Uncertain about a future as a fairy godmother, but I also didn't want Mom's fairy godmothering days to be over. I hated the fact that my failure would reflect on her. There had to be some kind of work-around for this crazy mixed-up situation.

Yes, I was falling for Nash. Head over heels.

Yes, I really didn't want him to end up with my sister.

But how was I going to explain all that to my mother when she wanted to know why she had lost all her fairy godmother powers?

I pushed thoughts of Nash out of my mind, got up, and went out into the kitchen just as Dad strolled in to pick up his travel mug full of coffee. He was dressed for the day ahead, checking his emails, ready to head out to the office.

"Aviana." He turned and looked at me. It took me aback. He rarely gave me his full attention. "When did you get in?" His hair was damp, his face pink from the use of strongly-scented aftershave, and his tie hung loosely around his neck.

"Late last night," I stumbled over my words.

"Does Madeleine know you're here?"

Biting my lip, I decided to be honest. "I texted her."

"Huh," he said. "She didn't say anything to me." He looked back toward the master bedroom. Was he deciding if he should go back and risk a confrontation with Madeleine? Had they argued about me?

Something had changed. I could see it in his eyes. "All right," he said. "Well, I'm glad you're here. We can work on a plan to solve your problems together."

I nodded. Dad may've had a change of heart, but I

wasn't ready to bare my soul.

"Is Nash with you? In Los Angeles?" Dad asked. "You should bring him by the house."

I shook my head. "He's not here. He's on a business trip."

He took his coffee mug from Gardenia and moved toward the garage. "Try to have a good day."

He was halfway out the door when he turned around. "If you think of anything I can do for you, anything at all, Aviana," he whispered, "call me direct. On my cell."

"Thank you."

Then he engulfed me in a big bear hug. It was awkward. He had his coffee mug and the *Wall Street Journal* in one hand and an overstuffed briefcase in the other. "I'm sorry for not being here for you. For not being more understanding of your … situation."

He ended up smacking me upside the head with the newspaper as we uncoupled, but I didn't care. It was the first ever tidbit of affection I'd ever gotten from him.

I didn't have spare time to wonder about it. I promised Josie I'd swing by Stern, Fayed, and Lopez and answer a few questions she had. I also figured it was a good place to get Vanessa alone so we could talk candidly.

Gardenia made me a plate of her famous chia seed pancakes before I showered and got dressed. I was on the sidewalk waiting for my Uber when my cell phone rang. It was Ruby. She sounded worried.

"Where are you?" she asked. "Your mom says you left without a word."

"I'm in Los Angeles."

"What about your first assignment? Are you done, or are you giving up?"

"I'm working on it," I said. "It's like a giant jigsaw puzzle. And right now, some of the most important pieces are scattered across the globe."

"Okay. Well, as long as you know what you're doing," she said.

"I haven't a clue. But I've got to try."

"I know you can't ask for help," she said. "But it seems like you should be allowed to strategize with a more experienced fairy godmother. Maybe your mom?"

"Don't I have to do it all on my own?"

"When you get back, you should ask one of the elders for clarity," she said. "Whatever you do, don't ask…"

Ruby didn't finish her sentence. We both knew she meant Zara. Ruby didn't have to worry. Never in a million years would I ask Zara for guidance.

"Thanks," I said as I slid into my Uber driver's car. "Good advice."

Traffic was crazier than usual, by the time I got to the office, Josie was settled at my old desk as if she'd been there for hours when I arrived. "Vanessa's due any minute. Can you grab her some coffee?" she shouted over her shoulder as she ran toward the elevators.

I walked down the hall to the kitchenette, poured coffee in Vanessa's favorite mug, and fixed it the way I knew she liked it. By the time I got back, Vanessa was in her chair looking over her emails. She looked surprised … and relieved to see me.

"Where's Josie?"

"Upstairs in an assistants meeting." Vanessa smiled. "Tell me you're back for good."

I shook my head. "I've got some loose ends to tie up." I didn't know how to start the conversation, so I dove right in. What do you think of Nash?"

"Nash Nolan?" She hedged the question. "Well, I know Dad likes him a lot."

"Do *you* like him?"

She shook her head. "I don't know him very well. I've worked on some contracts for his app. He's pretty much all-business."

"But seriously, would you date him?"

236

"Me? No." She grinned. "You guys make a very cute couple, though."

"We're just friends. I can't … date Nash," I lied. This was it. I had to make one last attempt to complete my first task. "So, hypothetically, would you date him?"

Vanessa raised an eyebrow and laughed. "I don't know where you're going with this, but Nash is not my type."

"Not your type? What's not to like? He's tall. He's super cute and super sweet …" I insisted.

"And a millionaire, I know. Everything Dad has ever wanted for us in a man," she said. "But he's not my type."

I was doomed to fail.

This match wasn't going to work even if I used magic. Who was I kidding? My love potion had been a fizzle, and I didn't see how being able to read people's emotional temperature or turn back time would help me get Nash and Vanessa together.

I needed time to think, so I changed the subject. "How are things working out with Josie? Are things any better?"

"No," she said. "But don't worry. I'm not going to fire her. I'm not mean. At least I'm not as mean as Mom and Dad."

"They're not mean," I protested.

"They're judgy," Vanessa said. "Seriously judgy."

"They may not be as judgy as you think," I said. "Look at me. They don't approve of anything about me, and I'm still living under their roof."

"They've treated you like you're the bad seed your entire life." Vanessa spoke with determined firmness. "They always have. They planned a family vacation without you. And I don't have the strength to be treated as badly by them as you have been."

"Wait? You think I'm strong?" I opened my mouth to respond but quickly closed it again. I needed a moment to let Vanessa's compliment soak in.

Vanessa nodded. "When you wanted your own bedroom, she moved you into the nanny's suite. Mom never took you back-to-school shopping for new clothes, you got hand-me-downs. And my mom always posed you in the upper-left-hand corner of the family Christmas card photo so she could photoshop you out of it."

"Vanessa, I …I choose to live in the room off the kitchen." I wasn't ready to hear her version of the truth.

"No, you didn't," she said. "She convinced you it was what you deserved. And you went along with it because you have always been able to see the best in everyone. You deserve better, Aviana. My mom has been horrible to you, and you never complained."

"She's not that bad, Vanessa."

"Are you kidding me? Do you know how pissed she is that despite her best efforts to make you feel like dirt on the bottom of her shoes, you've thrived? You've glowed up. Even after every evil thing she's done to you. You play by the rules … and you win."

"Please, stop …" I stirred uneasily in the chair.

"No. You need to hear this. You're the best assistant in the office. The partners were constantly threatening to promote you. I had to fight HR every month to keep you on my desk."

"Me?"

"You always act like Madeleine was kind to you. And she wasn't. You know she wasn't. She was wicked. She was oh-so-very wicked," Vanessa said. "I've been tormented with guilt about my part in it for years. I'm not completely sure why she did it—I have a feeling she's always been jealous of your mother—but I'm not going to let it go on any longer."

"Vanessa, seriously," I said. "Stop. This isn't about Madeleine. Or Josie. This is about you."

"Here's what Madeleine wants me to do today while you're in the office. I'm supposed to convince you this job is what you deserve. And it's not. You deserve to follow your heart. Find your passion. Your heart is taking you in a new direction. What about Nash Nolan?"

I shook my head. "He's meant to be with someone else."

"I don't get it. Who says?" Vanessa asked.

Your fairy godmother.

Vanessa was being so honest. I had no other option but to lay all my cards on the table. "He's meant for you, Vanessa. He's *your* Prince Charming."

Vanessa laughed. I'd honestly never seen anyone laugh so hard. Her laughter was so infectious I started giggling too. Pretty soon we were both laughing, though I wasn't sure why.

"You're not kidding, are you?"

I shook my head. "I'm a fairy godmother. Like my mother and grandmother before me."

"Of course, you are." Vanessa laughed. She didn't seem surprised. "You've never been all that subtle."

"About what?" I bit my lip.

"The matchmaking thing you do. It's not new. You've done it all your life. Our au pair married that surfer guy. Keir Bell and Paul Jameson, a match made in the breakroom."

My body stiffened in surprise. "But…"

Vanessa waved off my protest. "Yes. I know. We all know. You have always been kind. Like when Valerie went to Paris to be a runway model, I was so jealous, you tried to make it up to me so I wouldn't feel so bad.

"I did? I don't remember."

"There's always been something magical about you."

I shook my head, unable to believe Vanessa's words. "In my heart of hearts, I've always known you were special.."

"You're special too, Vanessa," I said, hoping to redirect our conversation back to the topic at hand. I needed to get Vanessa together with Nash. "You've always been so smart. And Nash…he's like a brain-iac."

"Aviana," Vanessa insisted. "Nash is not *my* Prince Charming."

"How can you be so certain?"

"Because, Aviana. I am a lesbian," she said. "I mean, it's an open secret, but I haven't told Mom and Dad."

I knew Vanessa hadn't dated a lot, but neither had I. She was always hyper-focused on her career.

Vanessa continued, "I think Mom knows but doesn't want to acknowledge it."

"And Dad?"

Vanessa dismissed my question with a wave. "Dad doesn't have a clue. I know they love me and want the best for me, and they go to all the fundraisers for marriage equality. They act like they are very socially liberal, but I've seen their behavior behind closed doors. I'm afraid they will think I'm making a lifestyle choice."

"It's not a choice, Vanessa," I said.

Vanessa exhaled a long sigh. "I met someone at law school. I thought we were in love, but she broke my heart," she said. "Honestly, the experience was so painful, I'm a little scared to go out with anyone new. I'm not sure I believe in happily-ever-after endings the way you do."

"No Vanessa. You don't understand. When I said I was a fairy godmother, it was more than being a matchmaker." I took a deep breath. "I'm fairy godmother, by trade, but a fairy by birth."

Vanessa looked confused.

I took off my sweater and un-taped the tips of my wings from my shoulders. After being able to move for so long, my wings immediately unfurled over my head.

To her credit, Vanessa didn't hit the deck. She wasn't frightened. She was amazed. She stared at them in awe and wonder as feathers rained down around us.

"Holy crap, Aviana." Vanessa's eyes widened. "That is totally amaze-balls," she said. "They're beautiful. The same as your eyes."

"You should see my mother's," I said. For the first time since they had grown out of my back, I was proud of my wings. Vanessa and I were like giggly thirteen-year-old girls, being honest.

"I can't believe you've been keeping those a secret," she said.

"I can't believe you've been keeping you a secret," I said..

Vanessa smiled. "Aviana? What if Nash is your Prince Charming? Can that happen?"

"No," I said. "Not according to the rules."

"You may be a fairy godmother's daughter, but you are also your father's daughter, and let's face it, Dad doesn't play by the rules, he makes them."

"Dad never had to stare down the Elders of the Fairy Godmother's Guild," I said. "They're formidable."

While Vanessa was in a good mood, I took the opportunity to put in a good word for Josie. "Anyway, you really should give Josie a chance."

"She gets an A for effort, but she's killing me … and the database. It's a slow, violent, and very painful death."

"She will learn it eventually."

She raised the three fingers on her right hand in a scout salute. "I swear on my fairy godmother's honor I will be kind to my assistant."

"Thank you," I said. "I'm going to help Josie with the database."

I smiled at my sister. Today had gone a long way at bridging the pain between us.

Josie had all of my personal items in a box on the floor under her desk. It was official. Whatever the future held for me, it wasn't as Vanessa's assistant.

"I've got so many questions about the filing system," Josie said.

"It's a little confusing at first, but I think you'll get the hang of it."

"And then you have to tell me all about *him*," she said.

"Who?"

"That's Nash Nolan. Do you recognize the hot chick with him?" She handed me her phone with a photo from TMZ of Nash and some hot chick. "TMZ might not recognize you, but I know my BFF when I see her."

I was the hot chick in the photo. We were chatting in between sips of latte. It was obvious we couldn't get enough of each other. Sitting close with our fingertips touching when we talked. It was a disgusting display of public affection I never would've participated in outside of Los Arboledas.

"Crap," I murmured, taking a second look at the photo.

"Did you know you'd become an overnight Internet sensation? You are going to have to give me all the deets. But not until lunch. I can't talk now, I need to focus. There's a fab new raw food bar just up the street. We can talk there."

My jaw fell open. Josie's priorities had always been to goof off first, work later. This new and improved version of my best friend was all-business. If only I could figure out how to be a better fairy godmother.

CHAPTER 22

Rule #22: A fairy godmother makes the world beautiful while everyone else is looking the other way.

Two weeks in Los Angeles went by in a blur.

I helped Josie study for her LSATs, and Vanessa talked me into going to several networking events. I finally committed myself to the idea of being a fairy godmother even though I knew I had no hope of getting past the first assignment. My purpose in life was as much in limbo as ever, but I enjoyed meeting so many different people.

Vanessa was skilled at the chit-chat required at this kind of function, and I almost fell into the pool at the Roosevelt Hotel when she introduced me to one of her work colleagues as her sister.

"Seriously?" I asked her at one of the events. "We've never been family."

"We're stepsisters," she challenged.

"Not in public," I insisted.

Vanessa flashed her cat-who'd-eaten-the-canary grin and pulled me along to the next group of well-dressed and well-connected people. We were both uncertain how we'd tell the world who we really were, but we'd formed a very wicked alliance, and no one, outside of the two of us, was pleased about it.

Meanwhile, Madeleine huffed and puffed around the house like Miss Piggy whenever she saw the two of us bent over a tablet, plotting our next event. Dad was secretly enjoying our adventures, but we drove Josie crazy at the office.

"Between her perfectionism and your compulsion to alphabetize everything in sight, I'm losing my mind." Jose grumbled. She was fast learner and she loved the attention to detail necessary for contract law, which made her an even more valuable assistant to Vanessa than I had ever been.

I didn't miss Nash.

I'm lying. I missed him every minute I was awake. I missed looking into his eyes, but I couldn't miss him too much because he sent text updates every three minutes or so.

He was never off my radar. I don't know what kind of data roaming plan he had, but he texted me at all times of the day and night. He sent photos of the places he went, the people he saw, and the street foods he was eating. Most of which looked outrageously delicious, but there were a few others that neither one of us could identify.

Me: What is it?

Nash: I don't know. I can't pronounce it.

Me: Animal, vegetable, or mineral?

Nash: Yes. I hope so.

He sent several photos of the view of the skyline from his hotel room. I took pictures from my room of the Chateau Marmont against the setting sun. When he asked for selfies, I politely declined, but the longer he was gone, the bolder I became. I had to turn myself into a contortionist in order to take pictures of myself that didn't show off more of my fairy-ness than I wanted to expose. My wings and pointed ears seemed to want a feature in every snap I took. I checked and double-checked each photo before I sent it to him.

I was in a perpetual pink cloud moment of wishful thinking induced by my ever-growing romantic feelings for him.

Vanessa and I went together to the dress fittings for Valerie's wedding. Her wedding dress designer's downtown Los Angeles loft was filled with bolts of white silk, cream-colored tulle, and yards and yards of lace. His work desk was covered with tattered pieces of paper full with pencil sketches.

"I would love an office like this," I said. "It's like being trapped in a daydream."

"About Nash Nolan?" Vanessa teased.

"Stop it." I laughed.

Our giggles were quickly stifled the moment Madeleine and Zara made their appearance. Acting as if they were old and very dear friends, they whispered shared intimacies back and forth. Separately they were formidable. Together, as far as I was concerned, they were an insurmountable obstacle. As long as they were in the room, I made sure to mind my manners.

When the designer swept into the room, it was obvious he'd been informed about who held the purse strings in our group. Madeleine giggled like a little girl while he fussed over her, bowing over her hand, and telling her how beautiful she was. I think I threw up a little in my mouth.

My truce with Vanessa didn't go unnoticed by Zara. I can't say she was too pleased by it. Zara kept her distance as long as Vanessa was next to me. She waited until Vanessa was being fitted for her bridesmaid gown to find her way over to me.

"How are you coming on your first assignment?" Zara asked when we had a moment alone. Malice dripped from every word she spoke.

"It's going great. Better, really, than I could have ever

hoped."

"Really?" She flashed a smile that didn't go all the way up to her eyes. "Then what are you doing in Los Angeles?"

"Nash is out of the country on business," I explained. "We are in constant contact. And he's very anxious to reconnect with Vanessa as soon as he returns."

Zara smirked. "You don't even have a clue, do you? Are you sure it's Vanessa he's so anxious to see again?"

"Absolutely. A fairy godmother knows a true romance can't be contrived or manipulated," I said, quoting *The Fairy Godmother's Rulebook*. I smiled so she could see the teeth I was lying through.

Nash and I were sending text messages back and forth that couldn't be considered business. They were, in fact, becoming more and more romantic, but that was on a need-to-know basis. And Zara definitely didn't need to know. I thanked my lucky stars, and my mom, for having the ability to lie under pressure so gracefully.

"And so, you actually think you'll still pull off your first assignment?" Zara was giddy with laughter.

"Of course," I said. "I come from an ancient line of fairy godmothers. We're not easily defeated."

"All the other fairy godmother candidates have completed their first assignments," Zara said.

"For reals?" I acted as if I didn't have a care in the world, even though every fiber of my being believed she had set me up for failure.

I didn't know how much longer I could stall. I wanted to be able to string Zara along long enough to return to Los Arboledas and warn my mom I'd failed the first assignment. I wanted to be the one who told her our family's long lineage of being fairy godmothers was coming to an end. She would be devastated. Just the thought of how my failure would change her life, broke my heart.

"Aviana! You're next," Valerie said, bringing me out of my daydream and back into harsh reality.

I stood up and started walking toward the fitting room when Madeleine's voice stopped me in my tracks.

"Valerie? I thought you were going to have one of your friends stand up with Vanessa," Madeleine protested. "I thought we agreed to leave Aviana out of this."

"I changed my mind. It should be Aviana," Valerie said. "She is my sister."

"Your *step*sister," she corrected.

"Family," Valerie said with a firmness I had never seen before. Madeleine immediately backed down, but Zara was another matter. She wasn't going away without a fight.

"Are you certain you want Aviana in the bridal party?" Zara asked.

"Yes," Valerie said. "The three of us grew up together. We're sisters. We should be together at this moment in time."

"I will have to make some adjustments," Zara said, which caused Madeleine to give her a supreme bit of side-eye. Her adjustments—whatever they were—were going to cost money. Big money.

I didn't have time to think about it as I was ushered into a small changing room where I was told to undress. I stripped down to a camisole and panties. Vanessa had helped me tape my wings down prior to our visit to the designer. I crossed my fingers and hoped fashion-forward Valerie hadn't selected a backless bridesmaid dress for me to wear on her big day.

What would I do with my wings?

I'd been indulging them in nightly milk baths, hoping it would help me keep them under control while I was in Los Angeles, which had not gone unnoticed. Gardenia asked me more than once if I had any clue why the family's milk consumption had quadrupled since I had returned from Los Arboledas. My helpless shrugs were not the answer she was seeking. I feigned innocence and dismissed her concern. But that didn't stop her from giving me a lot of curious looks.

Fifteen minutes later I was wrapped up in swirls of blush tulle. It was off-the-shoulder, but the back was covered and gave me a rest from hiding my wings.

I caught Vanessa's eyes in the three-way mirror. "What do you think?"

"I never would've picked it out for you," she said. "But it's really not that bad. Makes you look…regal."

"Really?" I spun in place to get a look at my reflection. In fact, I looked a lot like the drawings of my ancient fairy godmother ancestors who'd been captured in pen and ink inside the pages of the rulebook. "All I need is a tiara."

Vanessa's maid of honor dress was more tailored and refined. She dazzled.

"Oh, Vanessa. You look beautiful."

"You don't have to flatter me anymore, she said. "Since you don't work for me."

I shot her a look. "It's the truth."

"This dress does make me feel happy." Vanessa took a couple of delicious twirls in front of the mirror. "It's a beautiful dress."

When Madeleine came over to inspect the dresses with Zara, Vanessa decided it was time to confront her about my forgotten birthday. "Mom, we've got to do something for Aviana's birthday," Vanessa demanded.

"Let it go, Nessa," I pleaded.

"Let's move on to something less controversial," Valerie interjected. "Can we focus on my wedding, people?"

"No," Vanessa insisted. "We need to do a birthday make-good for Aviana. At least we need to have a cake."

"Are you sure, Aviana?" Madeleine shot me her death-ray glance. "It seems awkward now that so much time has passed."

"I smiled brightly for Madeleine's benefit. "Madeleine's right. I don't need any sort of birthday celebration at all."

"Good. That's settled," Madeleine said. She looked extremely satisfied with my answer. She went back to rolling through calls on her phone and I went back into the changing rooms to take off the bridesmaid dress.

I thought my forgotten birthday celebration had been settled, but Vanessa was only too happy to bring it up again in front of Dad when we got back to the house. Dad and Madeleine were getting ready to go out someplace fancy for cocktails.

Dad was in the living room waiting for Madeleine to change when Vanessa made her demands known.

"We still need to have a make-good for Aviana's birthday," Vanessa teased. Dad looked up from whatever he was reading with a smile, looking at me more fondly than he ever had in his life, but Madeleine cut him off before he could answer.

"Aviana told me she wanted to skip her birthday this year," Madeleine interjected.

"No cake?" Dad mock-frowned. I laughed in spite of myself. "There should at least be cake." While he hadn't addressed my missed birthday before, I felt better about our relationship after our conversation the other day.

Vanessa nodded. "Yes. Cake. It's a crime we weren't here to celebrate Aviana's birthday with her."

"Aviana needs a cake, Madeleine," Dad spoke as if he could command a cake to appear. A look passed between Dad and Madeleine I had never seen before. They had always been such a powerful team, nothing ever came between them ... until that moment. I swear I never thought I'd ever live to see the day Dad became #TeamAviana. It put a smile on my face.

"Okay. You guys," I addressed Dad and Vanessa directly. "Enough with the cake campaign. I had two cakes on my birthday this year. I don't need another."

"Is there something you do want?" Dad asked. "You know ... as a present. I noticed you're driving your mom's car around town. Do you need one of your own?"

"All right." Madeleine's smile looked strained as she headed for the door. "We're going to be late. I'm afraid we'll have to finish the discussion at a later date."

Dad looked at me, uncertain of what to do.

"Go," I said. "If you get in trouble with her too, I'll never get my own car."

He grinned sheepishly and followed Madeleine out the front door.

The next day I packed up Mom's car in the afternoon, hoping I'd be there to greet Nash when he arrived. I couldn't put the urban landscape of Los Angeles behind me fast enough. The passing scenery changed from coastal waters to rolling hills. My shoulders pulled away from my ears as I got closer to Los Arboledas and began to relax.

The sun was sinking low in the sky, casting a pinkish glow over the gnarled branches of ancient live oaks and olive trees covering the rolling hills along California's central coast. I took a deep breath and made a wish.

I stumbled to the front door of Mom's small house, dragging my suitcase behind me. Three hours in the car and my clothes were grimy, as if I'd been on a red-eye flight from Los Angeles to New York. I deposited all belongings back in Mom's tiny guest room and started a bath.

Nash texted to say he'd checked into the Los Arboledas Inn. He was on his way out to a meeting, but was anxious to see me and wanted me to come over as soon as I was settled.

Rushing, I quickly tugged my hair into a ponytail and slipped on one of my favorite outfits. *Nash* … It'd been too long since I'd seen him.

On my way to his room, the front desk lady stopped me in my tracks to let me know he was in a meeting.

"You just missed him," she said. "But he left a key for you."

"Thank you," I said.

Nash was staying in the largest suite at the inn, centrally-located in the middle of the property—it was a remodeled ranch-style hacienda house that had been updated and modernized with the finest luxury accommodations.

The suite was decorated in shades of ochre and sapphire blue. The terrace of the suite opened onto a private infinity pool with a view of the entire valley. The pink moment from this suite would be spectacular.

When I walked into the bedroom, his clothes had been neatly put away in the dresser and closet except for one T-shirt tossed over the back of a chair. I picked it up and inhaled his unique scent.

It had been two weeks since I'd seen him. One whiff of Nash and I was drunk. I walked out on the terrace and collapsed into a chaise lounge. I closed my eyes to rest for five minutes. The next thing I knew, Nash was bending over me.

"Aviana?" he whispered.

"I'm awake," I said, yet I snuggled deeper into the pillow.

"No. You're not," he scoffed.

"I am," I insisted sleepily.

"You're snoring."

"I am not." I reached out and touched his face. "Oh, you're not a dream. Hi," I said. My mind was still fogged from sleep. My guard was down. I could only speak the truth. "I missed you."

"I missed you more," he said. And then he kissed me. It was soft and romantic.

We sat on the terrace. I couldn't let go of his hand. I hadn't been aware how much I had been craving his touch.

Nash ordered room service, and we ate hamburgers on the terrace. When I was with him all my problems faded away. I was Aviana. He was Nash. I was a fairy godmother and he was a businessman. He was as much a part of me as my wings. I had no idea what the future held, but I knew as long as his arms were around me, my future was bright.

Yep. For a fairy godmother, I was completely delusional.

The room phone rang and Nash was needed for a meeting with the overnight management.

"I'm sorry to leave you." He bent over and kissed my nose. "I'll hurry back. I promise."

Saddened to watch him leave, I stretched, eyeing the pool. I had it all to myself. Nash wouldn't be back for another hour. No better time for a dip. No one would see me. It was private. I was completely alone.

I stripped down to my underwear and put on a hotel robe. On the terrace, I left the robe on the chaise lounge and slipped beneath the cool water. It was like velvet on my skin. I dove under the water and held my breath, swimming to the deep end. Then I swam back to the shallow end.

I dove deep again. I could feel my wings tuck in between my shoulder blades. Letting my wings unfurl, I allowed them to smack and splash, sending droplets up over the edge and onto the stone of the terrace.

It was heaven on earth. At least I thought it was until I noticed my wings had just splashed water all over Nash's pants.

I screamed. Nash screamed. And then everything went silent.

I stood up in three feet of water, wrapping my arms around my body to cover myself. The toes of Nash's leather shoes were hanging over the edge of the pool. He was staring at me so intensely it was as if it was for the first time. I didn't want to look up. When I did, it was only to discover Nash's face was twisted into a grimace.

My eyes searched his face, attempting to connect with him, but he avoided my gaze. His focus was above my head ... on my wings.

"Aviana. What is going on? Is this some kind of joke?"

I swallowed hard to clear the lump out of my throat. "I wish," I whispered. "I really wish it was, but the truth is I'm a fairy."

"Are you for real?"

I nodded. "Wings and pointy ears, yes. And I can do magic."

"What is wrong with you?"

"Nothing. This is me."

"What kind of creature are you?"

"I'm not a ..." I protested. "I'm a fairy by birth, and I come from a long line of fairy godmothers."

"What?" He kept backing up. Further and further. And I kept moving closer to him.

"Don't come any closer, Aviana," he said. "I don't want to hurt you. But I will if I have to."

"It's me, Nash. I'm still Aviana." If only he looked at me, really looked at me, he'd still see the real me. But every step I took closer to him, he took one back. Until finally he was up against a wall with his hands up to hold me off.

"I'm a fairy. A fairy godmother."

Nash shook his head. "I've never heard of such a thing."

"It's kind of an open secret. Los Arboledas is a fairy woodlands."

"No, it isn't."

"The fairies are the reason why Los Arboledas has a reputation for happily-ever-after endings and wishes that come true."

"I don't know what happened to you. I'm sorry ... I can't."

I reached out to touch him, and he flinched. He'd seen me do magic. Why was he acting this way?"

Don't," he said. "Don't touch me."

"Please, don't be afraid of me. I'm telling the truth. Please."

"I thought … the wedding was just a trick of my eyes. None of it was real." He swallowed. His eyes were dark. "But this … this is too much. No. I can't. I need to go. "

His face was a mask of confusion as he backed toward the door to the suite. He opened the door and left without another word. I knew he wasn't coming back. Not while I was there. Holding myself together with the last wisps of my shredded self-esteem, I gathered my belongings, got dressed, and left.

CHAPTER 23

Rule #23: A fairy godmother uses her powers for good, not evil.

I don't remember how I got from the Los Arboledas Inn to the front steps of my mom's little cottage. I was a quivering mass of feels when I arrived. Thankfully, my mom didn't ask any questions, she just helped me into the house and brought a box of Kleenex into the room and put it on the nightstand while Glenn hovered near the bed lighting up the darkness.

"How much does he know, Aviana?" Mom asked. She kept her voice even and calm. She didn't seem to be upset, even though she had every right to be. In my ill-fated attempt to pass the test to be a fairy godmother, I'd exposed my otherworldly fairy godmother powers to both Nash and Vanessa. I trusted both of them to keep my secret for the time being.

"He knows everything," I said.

"We need to give him a memory charm," Glenn said.

"No," I said. "Please. I want him to remember me."

"Shhh. Just rest right now. We'll talk in the morning," Mom said. "Maybe after a good night's sleep, you'll feel like you can do the right thing."

I closed my eyes and let the tears fall over my lashes onto my cheeks. I willed myself not to hiccup or sob too loudly. I didn't want my mom or Glenn coming back and deciding Nash's memories needed to be erased sooner rather than later. I cried quietly, but it didn't make any difference to my battered and broken heart.

Sleep wouldn't come. I was exhausted, but I couldn't close my eyes. I stared up at the ceiling trying to figure out what had happened. How had my life gotten so far off track? It seemed like yesterday I was juggling everything, and overnight all of my hopes and dreams for my future came crashing down to the ground around me.

What was I was going to do next? Should I stay in Los Arboledas? Should I go back to Los Angeles? When should I break the news to my mom that I had failed the test? Should I wait until after the Gala?

Cradling *The Fairy Godmother's Rulebook* against my body like a comforter, I fell into a fitful sleep.

When I woke up, the sun was streaming in through the window and I could hear my mom and Glenn out in the kitchen.

"Do you think she'll make the right decision?" Glenn asked.

"Shhhhh …" Mom answered in a hush loud enough to wake the dead.

"I don't mean to be insensitive," Glenn said.

"She's going through a rough patch." I heard my mom say. "Just let her be."

Wanting to avoid the conversation, I stayed in bed.

My cell phone vibrated and danced across my nightstand and fell onto the floor. It was Zara. Again. She'd called four times over the past three days. I was going to have to face her and admit my failure sooner or later. It might as well be sooner. The last night of the Strawberry Moon was the night of the gala. I still had time.

"Aviana. I think we need to talk," she said.

"I think you've given me an impossible assignment," I stated flatly.

"A fairy godmother doesn't get to choose their assignments. The Guild assigns you a task and you do it. No questions asked."

Ugh. I wasn't prepared to respond, so I pretended my cellphone had cut out. "Sorry. I can't hear you. I'm going to have to call you back."

I ended the call and decided to go for a run.

When I got back I studied the rulebook from cover to cover. There had to be a clue somewhere between its covers about how I could pass the first test. I learned all of the rules and could recite them out loud by heart, but I still had no idea how I was going to complete my first assignment. I was going to have to tell my mom the truth, but I wasn't ready. Not yet.

Needing a distraction, I threw myself into planning the fundraising gala for Prince Charming and the other homeless animals. The fundraiser was the only part of my life that hadn't imploded.

Ruby and Anna didn't ask any questions. Even though I think they both knew my relationship with Nash was over, and I was completely heartbroken.

I checked my phone every fifteen minutes for a text message or voicemail from him, while simultaneously ignoring phone calls from Valerie and Madeleine. When Juniper arrived with a personal message from Zara telling me to make an immediate appearance at the Guild Hall, I ignored that too.

I didn't want to admit failure. Not to myself. Not to Zara. And most especially not to my mom.

The Fairy Godmother's Rulebook was my greatest comfort. I read it every night when I got into bed. Each rule was accompanied by a little story that began with "Once upon a time ..." and went on to explain the origins of the rule and why it was that the Fairy Godmother's Guild had implemented the rule in the first place. I loved the stories.

But I finally realized nothing in the rulebook was going to help me solve all the problems I was facing. I was on my own.

Instead I focused on helping Ruby with the fundraiser from early in the morning until late at night. Owen put in the same amount of hours out at the farm fixing the fences and repairing door frames. Anna came over and helped us in the office whenever she could get away from her kids.

With the baby bassinette for six little piglets gone, the air quality in Ruby's condo had greatly improved. We pulled the dining room table out into the middle of the room and pushed the sofa and the side chair up against the walls, turning Ruby's living room into our home base for joint operations.

We called it the "war room" and manned our posts all hours of the day. We broke down planning the party into three divisions. Ruby worked on the arrangements for the food and beverages. Anna and Owen helped us organize the vendors and made the arrangements for set-up at the farm, while I organized a team of volunteers to update the invitation list and ask for donations for the silent auction.

We lived on iced skinny lattes and Caesar salads. At night, Ruby and I switched to a modified "Olivia Pope diet," drinking Diet Coke and scarfing microwave popcorn.

Whenever Owen stopped by, he was never without food. We hassled him mercilessly over the bags of greasy french fries he would show up with at all hours of the day and night, complaining about how unhealthy all his snacks were. At the same time we tried to eat as much of his food as possible before he regained control.

Late in the day, when we couldn't concentrate on the gala any longer, we slipped out onto the patio to watch the sunset. I'm not sure if Ruby or Owen were making any wishes on pink clouds, but I sure was. I was full of wishes.

And regrets.

On the rays of more than one cotton candy-hued sunset, I wished I had never left Los Angeles. I wished I'd never met Nash. I wished I didn't have wings. I wished for a way to leave the Fairy Godmother's Guild without damaging my mother and her powers. The only thing I didn't wish for was to discover a way to finish my first assignment. It didn't seem to matter anymore. I'd lost all hope. And I was fairly certain none of my wishes were going to come true.

On Sunday afternoon Mom put a whole chicken with carrots and baby potatoes in the oven to roast. The center island counter was soon filled with bottles and bowls. Sylvie brought her famous salted caramel cheesecake and put it in the fridge. Hazel had been to the Farmers Market and brought sugar snap peas just picked from the garden.

As if by magic, the garden filled with fairy godmothers, and the bushes and shrubs sparkled with the lights from dozens of pixies who'd come to share in the fun. The fairies all had stories to tell about their adventures with their protégés. Some made me laugh and some made me cry.

I was thankful Zara didn't make an appearance, so I could block out all of my worries and focused only on enjoying the fairy godmothers in the Guild. I took comfort in their joys and their heartaches. I made lavender wands and sipped lemonade while they gave me tips for creating love potions and other magical medicinal cocktails.

Never did I let on that there was little chance that I would ever get to put any enchantment or spell into use. They didn't need to know. And I wouldn't have missed out on giving them the pleasure of sharing their hard-earned knowledge with me. It was like being wrapped up in a warm cocoon of happiness. It was no wonder my mom never wanted to leave the safety of this sisterhood again.

If my mind was ever idle, my thoughts were about Nash. Or I fretted over what Zara had planned for me. I needed to tell Mom I wasn't going to make it past the first task. I had a lot of questions and not a lot of answers. So I refocused all my energy on the gala fundraiser. Providing a safe haven for homeless animals might be my last act as a fairy godmother, and I wanted to savor every second of it.

Two days before the gala Ruby and I were sorting the silent auction items when I came across an envelope with the Los Arboledas Inn return address in the upper left-hand corner.

"You got a donation from the Los Arboledas Inn? Who authorized this?"

"Nash."

"You're kidding?"

"No," she said. "They were on the list to call for a donation. I left a message and he called me back right away."

I studied the envelope. "Three-night stay at the Los Arboledas Inn," had been written on the outside—it wasn't his handwriting.

"How long do you think there have been fairies living in the woodlands of Los Arboledas?" I asked.

"Over a hundred years," Ruby said. "At least that's how far my family goes back in the woodland.

"So that means there were fairies here at the turn of the twentieth century when they originally built the inn?"

"Absolutely." Ruby nodded. "No doubt some of them worked at the inn. Creatures. That's what they called us then."

"They still do," I whispered. The ugly words Nash had used that night were stuck in my head. And nothing would ever make me forget the look on his face.

"Everything okay with you?" she asked. "How is your

heart?" Ruby must've sensed I was feeling fragile.

"Healing." I said. "Thank you for asking."

"Have you given any thought to what you're going to wear?"

"For what?" I was stumped. Why was Ruby asking about my wardrobe?

"To the gala that we've been planning every day and night?" she asked.

"Ack. I keep forgetting all of this is going to end up in a party," I said. It was the truth. I was too caught up in the logistics of getting a couple hundred people together in one place to spend any time on myself. "What about you? Did you get a new dress?"

"Absolutely," Ruby said. "My reward for working so hard. You should too."

"I'll order something online tonight."

"Do not let me catch you in that vanilla tootsie roll lace," Ruby demanded. "I won't let you come in the gates in that horrible excuse for a dress."

"I promise." I raised my right hand and swore an oath, but within fifteen minutes any thoughts I'd had about buying a party dress had been forgotten.

Ruby and I spent the day of the gala at the farm setting up and making sure nothing was overlooked. I stayed late so Ruby could leave early and get dressed. When I got back to Mom's house, she had Dean Martin on the hi-fi in the living room and was keeping a bit of dinner warm for me on the stove.

"I'm not really hungry." It was true. Food didn't really interest me.

"You have to eat," she said. "You can't keep going on lettuce and Diet Coke."

I was surprised and a little taken aback that she knew how Ruby and I had been living. "You've been working very hard, Aviana. Do you need any help getting ready?"

"No. I'm going to figure out what to wear," I said. "And then I'll take a shower."

Most of my clothes were still scattered on the floor, or half-in and half-out of the suitcase I had never unpacked, once again. My mom must have sensed my dilemma because she appeared at my door soon after I entered.

"What are you wearing tonight?" I asked.

"I bought a new dress," she said. "It's lavender."

"That'll be nice. I'm sure it'll do amazing things to your eyes."

"What about you? What are you going to wear?" Mom asked.

"I should've bought something new, but…"

I pulled a couple of the most likely candidates out of the piles of clothes on the floor and spread them out on the bed. Wrapped in a light blue silk robe, my mom looked over my choices. "Pretty slim pickings," she said as she left my room.

"I've been so focused on the gala, I just forgot that I'd actually have to attend the event," I said. "Woulda. Coulda. Shoulda planned better."

I picked up the long-sleeved sheath of nude lace Glenn had taken away from me before Jessica and Raphael's wedding.

"Vanilla Tootsie Roll it is," I said. I held the dress up in front of me looked at myself in her full-length mirror. It was dreadful, but I didn't care.

I took a shower. Thankfully, it gave me the little spark of energy I so desperately needed. I wrapped myself in a towel and padded back into the guest bedroom.

My breath caught in my throat.

The dress on my bed had changed. In place of my old beige lace dress was a powdery pink evening gown. Layers of chiffon were decorated with all-over silver beading. It was styled with a plunging V-neckline and sheer sleeves that gave it a vintage delicacy. It was the most beautiful dress I'd ever seen.

"It's beautiful, " I breathed the words, not wanting to break the spell.

"I hoped you'd think so," Mom said.

"But this gown is enchanted," I said.

"I don't know what you're talking about," Mom protested.

"It's against the rules," I said, letting my fingers trail over the beading on the bodice.

"I've been living with the rules a lot longer than you, Aviana. But just in case, you should know I set a six-hour timer on the enchantment for the dress. If you aren't home by then—you should be. You don't want to be caught dead in that beige dress. When you get home tonight, you should burn it."

I giggled. I held the dress up in front of a full-length mirror. I could tell it would be a perfect fit. "You really shouldn't be enchanting objects on my behalf."

"Enchanted objects? I don't know what you're talking about," Mom said. She attempted to look innocent, but she missed by a mile. "Can I help it if I want my daughter to be the most beautiful one at the ball?"

"It's not a royal ball, Mom," I said. "And the only Prince Charming there will be a horse.

"I know. But you and Ruby have been working so hard," she said. "I want you to celebrate all you've accomplished. I'm so proud of you. I wanted you to feel beautiful inside and out."

Tears sparkled in her eyes. It took me aback. My mom never got emotional. I wasn't sure I was ready for it and quickly changed the subject. "You look fantastic," I said. "But you always do."

"Glenn will be here shortly We're going to go and help Sylvie get ready." She held my face in her hands. "No matter what happens tonight. I want you to know I believe in you. Whatever choices you make, they are the right ones for you. Do you understand?"

I nodded. Now would be a good time to tell her the

truth, but I couldn't speak. My failure would mark the end of her days as a fairy godmother.

I waited for her to leave before I threw myself across the bed and cried until the tears stopped. I was wrapped up in a robe putting on my make up when Vanessa appeared without a knock. Her hair was pulled back in a messy bun and her glasses were crooked on her face.

"What are you doing here?" I asked.

"I heard you were having a bad day." She reached out and hugged me. It was awkward as hell, but it was backed up by honest emotion, so it gave me some comfort.

"Do you need help getting ready?" she asked.

"It's just a fundraiser," I said.

"Dad bought tickets for everyone. He insisted Madeleine leave work early in order to support you on your big night." Vanessa continued, "Dad is very proud of you and how you've been handling yourself with all the changes. He knows you're struggling, but he believes you're going to find your way. "

Vanessa sat down on the bed, smiling up at me. "How's Nash?" she asked.

"Nash dumped me," I said with a quiver in my voice.

"He wasn't worthy." She said without missing a beat.

I bit down on my lip. "I love him."

"Then don't give up hope."

"I'm glad you're here." I hugged her again.

The beautiful pink dress I'd put on a hanger on the closet door caught Vanessa's eye. "Oh, Aviana. Is this what you're going to wear? It's beautiful. I'm not sure I brought anything appropriate. Josie didn't tell me it was black tie." Vanessa put her hands on her hips. "You know, this kind of thing never would've happened when you were my assistant."

"Thank you." I laughed. "For making me feel normal."

"Normal, ha." She laughed. "For a chick with wings.

I smiled. "You're never going to let that go, are you?"

"That's what older sisters are for," she said. "I tease

264

because I love."

I would cherish this moment forever. Even if I never became a full-fledged fairy godmother, for as long as I had them, I was going to use my powers for good

"I know exactly what you should wear to the gala," I said.

CHAPTER 24

*Rule #24: A fairy godmother knows not everyone
can be Prince Charming.*

Ruby and Prince Charming were greeting "Black Tie &
Tails" gala attendees at the front gate of "The Enchanted
Barn" when I arrived—late as usual—for the party. As the
guest of honor, Prince Charming looked good—and he
knew it, begging for peppermint candies from the gala
attendees. Acting as the big horse's own personal glam
squad, Ruby had brushed his mane and tail to get out all of
the tangles.

Ruby was radiant in a dark red gown that showed off
her slender shoulders and petite figure. Owen would barely
be able to contain his admiration for her, and Ruby would
act like she didn't notice. Or if she did, she didn't let on.

When they were together, Ruby and Owen had an easy
camaraderie that was punctuated by long wistful gazes. I
wondered if it was possible for two fairy godmothers to
find romance together. Maybe I just had "happily ever
after" on the brain, but right now I needed to focus. All
hands on deck were needed for the party.

One of Ruby's sisters had taken on the tall task of

decorating the farm for the party. Wildflowers in bursts of color filled aluminum buckets that had been placed at regular intervals along the fencing. Picnic tables, covered with crisp white linen, and set with silverware and crystal glassware carried off the rustic-chic theme of an enchanted barnyard.

Owen scored a big win by getting several local food trucks to provide catering for our invited guests. Parked in a horseshoe circle in the middle of the farmyard, the trucks were serving delicious street food to people dressed in evening gowns and tuxes.

It was Ruby's genius idea to have the gala at the farm. It was the perfect way to show off what would soon be a new shelter for homeless animals. The gala gave us the opportunity to show the donors and gala attendees how their generous donations had already been spent, and how much help we still needed to bring the abandoned farm back into working order.

The staff would use the main floor of old farmhouse as the office of "The Enchanted Barn." Rooms upstairs would be available for vets and animal trainers to spend the night. Ruby would eventually give up her condo and become a permanent fixture. I was amazed at the way her love of animals was guiding her career decisions.

"Do you think you'll be able to juggle being a fairy godmother with being a horse whisperer?" I asked once I got the chance to catch up with her.

"I like to think of myself as a fairy godmother … for animals," she said with a dazzling smile. "I'll handle people on the side."

"That sounds perfect," I said with a smile.

"Are you still uncertain of your future?" Ruby asked.

I nodded.

"Here's a news flash for you," Ruby said. "Being a fairy godmother is a little like being pregnant. You either are, or you aren't. There's no in-between. You've come this far, don't you dare let Zara win."

"I promise I will not go down without a fight."

"Do you need my help?" Ruby asked, placing her small hand on my arm. Her touch made me feel calm.

"I appreciate the offer, but I have to face what's ahead on my own." I hoped I'd be brave enough to face Zara and end it once and for all.

"We've been through too much together for you to go back to LA and hide from who you really are again," Ruby said. Her support brought tears to my eyes.

"That's not what I'm planning to do."

"Isn't it?" She knew me too well.

"Ruby, it's complicated. It's not what you think."

"I know more than you think I do," she said. I was always surprised when she revealed the steely side of her personality. "I may not be yours, but I am, after all, a fairy godmother."

"I know you and Owen both completed your first assignments," I said. I had a feeling dealing was going to get messy, and I didn't want anyone else hurt. "I'm thrilled you're moving on to the next steps."

Ruby nodded gently. "Thank you."

"I'm going to go and check in with Jack on the set-up for the games," I said. "I'll see you later."

Crossing the farmyard, I noticed my mom walking up the dirt driveway in her shimmering lavender dress. She looked just as glamorous as always surrounded by Sylvie and her other fairy friends. They were all dressed in shades of silver and lilac, they sparkled like in the moonlight. I watched them laughing and talking as if they didn't have a care in the world. No one would know they were the ones who stepped in when someone was feeling absolutely desperate. Their beauty was so unearthly, more than one guest turned to stare at them.

If they only knew the truth.

Mom stopped dead in her tracks when she saw me. "What happened?" she asked. "Where is your beautiful dress?"

I pointed across the yard to where Vanessa and Valerie were waiting in line for tacos at the Mexican food truck. Valerie looked like the supermodel she once was in a short shift dress, but Vanessa was giving her competition. Wrapped up in the pink tulle dress, she looked like a sweet confection.

"It went for a good cause," I said.

Mom crossed her arms over her chest and shook her head. "That dress was for you."

"But I didn't need the enchantment. Not tonight. And Vanessa did."

I was perfectly happy wearing the little black dress Glenn had found for me to wear to Jessica and Raphael's wedding. I loved this dress. It made me feel comfortable in my own skin. Plus, I got to wear the glass crystal-covered shoes again.

"You are my daughter. I'm proud of you. No matter what." Mom smiled. I needed to come clean, but I couldn't do it with a big lump of emotion stuck in my throat. Instead, I gave her a big smile.

"Your friends are waiting for you," I said. "Have fun tonight. We can talk tomorrow."

Within a half-hour the farmyard was filled with people all in black-tie and elegant gowns. Anna's son Jack had organized a group of his high school friends to set up and work the carnival games—each one was in charge of a different booth—which had caused a small knot of teenage girls to mingle near games of ring toss, whack-a-mole, and basketball shooter.

In the middle of all those girls, I spotted my dad handing the jacket of his tux to Madeleine while he got down to the serious business of throwing baseballs at glass bottles.

"She wants the big yellow monkey," he said, nodding toward my stepmother. "And I'm not going to let her down." He was turning into a big goofball.

I waved to him. "I have to do the silent auction. I'll be

back."

There was so much to do. I was running all night. In between tasks, I stopped off at the cheeseburger truck and asked them to make me a double-double with cheese. I had just taken a big gooey bite when I looked up to see Dr. Bernstein in line at the taco truck.

"Dr. Bernstein? What are you doing here?" I nearly choked on my burger.

"I bought a ticket for the gala," she said. "I wanted to see if Los Arboledas lived up to its reputation as the place where 'happily ever after' happens every day."

I laughed. "What do you think so far?"

"Better than I ever expected," she said.

"Are you staying at the inn? I asked, but before she had a chance to say another word, Owen appeared next to me. He had washed and combed his hair and beard. He was wearing a dark suit and a crisp white shirt. He looked … seriously hot.

"Owen, have you met Dr. Bernstein?" I asked.

He nodded a greeting and offered her a tall flute of champagne. "Would you care for a drink?"

"Thank you," she said, taking the glass from his hands and melting under his dark gaze.

"What brings you to Los Arboledas?" he asked as he led her away. I was standing there with my mouth hanging open when Owen looked back over his shoulder and gave me a wink.

I knew he'd finished his first fairy godmother assignment in record time. For a guy who wasn't certain he was meant to be in this business, he was starting to look like a superstar taking on the task of finding a happily-ever-after ending for my therapist.

Later in the evening I was drawn to a makeshift stage in the middle of a small corral, where Camille was singing a dead-slow version of "Moon River" backed by a bluegrass band. She had the voice of an angel, making the classic song so incredibly mournful and sad.

"Who is she?" Valerie's fiancé said in my ear. His voice startled me out of my reverie.

"I didn't know you'd come up for the gala, Nao," I said.

"Since Val and I are getting married up here, she'll use any excuse to get to Los Arboledas and check in with Zara," he said.

"Zara. Of course. Everyone needs to check in with Zara."

Camille hit a beautiful note, and Nao and I returned to staring at her. We were both mesmerized.

"Do you know her?" he prompted again.

"Camille. She's a local musician," I said. "She writes her own stuff too."

"She's amazing," he said. "The label's been looking for someone like her."

"My mom's friend Sylvie knows her really well. She's right over there." I pointed to Sylvie, who was lurking in the trees beyond the bandstand. "She can introduce you to her."

Nao introduce himself to Sylvie, and my heart filled with joy. Camille's musical dreams would be coming true, and my sister's fiancé wouldn't be turned into a frog. More importantly, Sylvie would be saved from the wrath of Zara.

Satisfied with this turn of events, I was on my way to find Ruby to announce the winners of the silent auction when Nash arrived. He was in a midnight blue tux talking to Harper. She was in a classic gown, and I could see my mother's influence in the color choice. A pale blue that would highlight the striking color of her eyes. The structured shape perfectly suited Harper's straightforward personality.

Nash and Harper were the perfect pair. Of course. They were like supermodels in shades of cool blue. He was my dream come true when he was in a T-shirt, jeans, and sneakers, but I had to admit that he looked pretty fabulous in his tux.

Nash eyeballed the crowd with his familiar hooded gaze. It was an old habit from growing up shy and geeky, making him come across aloof and elitist to anyone who didn't know him. Or love him.

He smiled when he spotted me. Or grimaced. I wasn't sure which it was, but I was grateful for his acknowledgment of my existence. I closed the distance between us.

"Nash." I smiled up at him and briefly looked into his eyes, but I couldn't hold his gaze. If I looked him in the eyes, I was afraid my broken heart would be on full display. Just then Ruby appeared by my side as if I had sent up an SOS beacon for help.

"Hey Nash," she said. "Thank you for coming. We appreciate your generous donation."

"Ruby," Nash greeted her warmly. "You should be very proud. Tonight looks like an unbelievable success."

"Thank you," she said. "I thought you were going to be out of town."

"I'm leaving first thing in the morning for Bahrain," he said. "So I can't stay late."

Before I had a chance to speak, Mom appeared on the other side of me.

"Mom," I said. "This is my friend Nash."

Nash grinned nervously. "Liliana. Your reputation proceeds you."

Mom ignored his compliment, instead her eyes traveled from his head to his feet and then back down again. She had no shame. It was a little embarrassing. But as soon as she did it, his magical hold over me went away.

I looked at Nash with fresh eyes. He was just a guy. And I was Liliana's daughter—as far as my mom was concerned, one was much more important than the other. That's all I needed to feel like I was standing on my own two feet.

"I'm glad we got the chance to meet," she said. " Please give my best to your father."

"My father?" Nash was surprised. "You know my dad."

"Tell him Liliana sends her regards," she said with a wink. Then she turned and walked away, leaving Nash speechless. I had no idea if she knew his dad or if she was just trying to freak him out. Either way, I couldn't help smile.

A look of alarm crossed Nash's face. I covered my giggles with my hand.

"It was nice to see you again. Really. Nice," I said, pausing when I realized I was making word salad rather than sense. I took a deep breath and tried again. "It's time to reveal the winners of the silent auction, so I have to run. Thank you for coming tonight. Ruby and I—we really appreciate your support."

I grabbed Ruby and we turned and walked away, I forced myself not to look back until I was out of sight, hidden in the darkness near the barn.

Nash took a drink off a silver tray. The waiter said something that made him laugh. I stood in the semi-darkness and made one last wish in the fading glow light of a Los Arboledas sunset.

If only I was the one making him laugh.

I looked up at the moon rising in the dusky sky. In a few more hours my failure to complete my first assignment would be official.

On the other side of the farmyard, Mom introduced Harper to Vanessa. I couldn't see Harper's face, but Vanessa looked like Cinderella in the dress my mother had enchanted for me. I could see the electricity snap in the air between them.

Harper and Vanessa?

Watching them connect so easily made me wonder if getting Harper and Vanessa together was the work of a fairy godmother somewhere.

Mom? Was it possible she was Vanessa's fairy godmother? I suppose I'd been in Los Arboledas long enough to realize almost anything was possible.

I walked toward the barn with so many thoughts racing through my mind, I almost didn't see Anna seated at a picnic table sharing cotton candy with her little girl.

"Have you seen Ruby?" I asked.

"I think she's giving tours through the barn," Anna said.

"When she talks about the goats, money just seems to appear out of thin air," I said.

"I know. It's almost like magic."

"Almost," I said.

After parting ways with Anna, I went out to the stables to find Ruby.

Prince Charming was settled in for the night. He was chomping loudly on his oats, having flirted with everyone who paid him a visit that night. As soon as he saw me, he put his nose out for treats.

I was feeding Prince Charming peppermints from my purse when I heard voices coming from deep in the barn. In the hall, I glimpsed Jack sitting on a hay bale in the tack room. Thinking he might know where Ruby was, I took off my shoes to avoid tripping over the uneven floor and tiptoed closer. That's when I realized Jack wasn't alone.

Someone with him. I didn't recognize the deep rumble of the other person's voice at first, so I took a couple more steps. Soon, recognition kicked in.

It was Nash. He was talking to Jack. I froze in my tracks and made a quick retreat to Prince Charming's stall. The horse whickered in greeting to me.

"Shhh," I soothed, rubbing the white mark on his long equine nose, hoping to keep him quiet long enough to eavesdrop on their conversation. Prince Charming decided my undivided attention was an invitation to check out my purse for more treats.

I unwrapped peppermints to keep him quiet while he crunched loudly on the sweets, taking one after another out of my palm with his big slobbery tongue. Leaning toward the hall, I could barely hear Jack and Nash's conversation over the sounds of Prince Charming's loud bites.

"She's so out of my league," Jack said. "And so into this geek."

"I find that hard to believe," Nash answered.

"My mom told me back when she was in high school, the quarterback dated the head cheerleader. But those were the olden days. These days the head cheerleader dates the head of the AV club or the guy who's starring in his own Disney TV show."

"Do you think she really likes him? Or is she just dating him for his money?"

"I dunno," Jack said. "But I don't blame her either way. He sold his first app for like two million. I don't have a chance. He's not even all that nice to her. She's always complaining to me about him."

"Why do you think she's going out with him?" Nash asked.

"Did you hear the part about how he sold his first dot com for two million? He's working on setting up his next IPO. It's going to be huge." Jack sounded dejected.

"If she's going out with this guy for his money, clearly she isn't all that."

"You think so?" Jack sounded a bit more hopeful.

"I know so," Nash said. "I am that guy, and I wouldn't want to go out with that girl. If it makes you feel any better, the geek doesn't always end up with the girl."

"It does make me feel maybe a little better."

"You're sixteen. I'm not sure it's time for you to be looking for your one true love. Maybe you should find a girl to hang out with that likes to do the same things you do."

"What? Like snowboarding?" Jack asked.

"Exactly. No pressure. Be her friend."

"I don't want to get stuck in the 'friend zone.'"

"Nobody wants to be stuck in the 'friend zone,' but in reality, life is all about possibilities. The things we can't know for sure. The ways that we can make things happen if we simply believe they are possible."

"That's nice," Jack said.

"I didn't learn that until it was too late." Nash sounded remorseful. "Make sure you listen to her. Keep your mind open and your mouth shut. That's a big one. Validate her beliefs in herself—no matter what she says, no matter what kind of crazy you think she's talking. If you love her, you have to give her a chance and let her be her very best."

"How will I know when I find her?" Jack asked.

"You'll know. You'll just know," Nash said. "You hungry?"

"Always," Jack said.

"Let's hit the taco truck? Their tortillas are homemade. Best I've ever had."

I listened to their footsteps as they made their way out of the barn. Once they were gone, I pressed my face into Prince Charming's side and let my tears fall down my face. Fortunately, my sobs didn't interrupt Prince Charming from enjoying his evening oats. He was the perfect date. If you liked the strong, silent type who occasionally stands on your strappy evening sandals.

I don't know how long I stayed with Prince Charming. I was a soggy mess when Ruby and Juniper found me stumbling out of the barn a bit later on.

"Where are your shoes?" Juniper asked.

"I kicked them off behind the hay bales."

"Can you go see if you can find them, Juniper?" Ruby asked. She had already gone into repair mood, dabbing at my eyeliner and makeup that was running down my face.

"Thank you!" I shouted as Juniper disappeared into the stables.

"Come and sit down," Ruby said. "I'm afraid you're going to pick up a splinter out here in your bare feet." She led me to a nearby picnic table.

"What did you do to your Fendi bag?"

"I let Prince Charming use it as a feedbag."

"It's completely destroyed," Ruby said.

Juniper flew back into view, levitating near my shoulder. "I couldn't find your shoes. Are you sure you had them on when you went into the barn?"

"I'm sure," I said. "They couldn't just disappear. But It's okay. I've got my Asics in my bag in the office. I'll put those on."

"I'll go look again," Juniper offered. Once she was out of sight, I crumpled on the picnic table bench.

Ruby turned to me. "Do you want to explain to me why your sister was wearing an enchanted dress?"

I shook my head. "He's the one, Ruby," I said softly. "He's the one."

"Oh, I don't know. If he were really Prince Charming, he'd be here right now eating peppermints out of your purse," she said with a rueful smile.

"I appreciated your sense of humor right now, I really do. I know it doesn't look like it because I'm crying." I sniffed. "Do you think he ever really liked me? For reals?"

"No. He's in love with the pony two stalls down," she said. "Wait? Are we talking about my Prince Charming or yours?"

"Mine," I said.

Ruby grinned with a glint in her eyes. "He liked you. He liked you just fine."

Ruby held my hand. Her friendship had helped me through some of the darkest hours of my life. The fairy godmothers in Los Arboledas gave me the sense of belonging I had ached for all of my life. I couldn't think of any better reasons to put up a fight when the time came.

CHAPTER 25

Rule #25: A fairy godmother knows change is inevitable but can't be forced.

I didn't notice until the gala was over that the stars were out in full force in the night sky, and the moon—the last Strawberry Moon of the year—was setting over the ocean. It was official. I had failed the test and would never become a member of the Fairy Godmother's Guild.

Owen and I stayed after the gala to help Ruby and an army of volunteers take away most of the wreckage from the party.

I made one last pass through the stables in search of my glass shoes. They were definitely gone. I retrieved my purse from the office and noticed I had one new voicemail message on my phone.

"Aviana. It's Zara. Your time is up. You have failed to complete your first assignment. I hope you've discussed your failure with your mother. I'd hate for it to come as a surprise to her when she wakes up tomorrow morning and her powers are yanked away from her grasp." Her laugh was dark and dirty. "Bring your family's rulebook to the fairy woodland. If you return it to me at the Guild tonight,

279

there's a chance we can negotiate you being allowed to return to your life in Los Angeles. If you hold out, it's all over for the Willowbrook fairy godmothers."

I listened to Zara's voicemail twice. It chilled my blood. I was about to listen to it a third time, but Vanessa interrupted me.

"Do you need a ride back to Los Arboledas? We're headed back to the inn."

Stunned. Surprised. Frightened. All the air left my lungs. I didn't think I'd be able to take another breath. It was a moment before I was able to comprehend what Vanessa was saying to me.

"What?"

Vanessa reached out and put her hand on my arm. "Are you all right?"

"I'm fine."

We're headed back to the inn. Will you be okay on your own?"

I nodded. "I'll be fine. Can I borrow your car?"

"Sure," Vanessa said without a beat. "Where are you going?"

"I can't tell you, but it's an errand I have to run tonight. Something I forgot to do. Not a big deal. I just have to get it done."

Vanessa dug the key fob to her most precious possession out of her purse. "Are you sure you don't need backup?"

I shook my head. "I'm fine. I'll be fine."

"Text me when you get back to your mom's house," Vanessa said. "So I know you're safe." She hugged me as if it was something we'd been doing all of our lives. Just as she was about to let go, I pulled her back and hugged her again.

"Be happy," I said.

She nodded. "You too."

"Thanks." I smiled.

I stumbled back toward the barn where Ruby was making one last check on the animals before she left.

"Everything okay?" she asked.

"Have you seen my mom?"

"She left about an hour ago." Then she added the kicker. "With Zara."

My stomach dropped. Zara was going to inflict punishment on my mom before she took me out. She was going to take away her powers.

Without another word, I turned around and ran out of the barn. Ruby shouted after me, but I couldn't hear anything she was saying.

I found my way down the long driveway. Bouncing off objects in the dark as if I was trapped in a pinball machine, I finally found Vanessa's car parked alongside the main road and got in.

Speeding along the twisting and turning canyon roads as fast as I could, I made my way back to my mom's house. There weren't any lights on inside the little storybook cottage when I pulled up. I ran up the front walk, dug the spare key out from under the pots, and burst through the front door.

"Mom!" I yelled.

Silence. She wasn't there. The garden was quiet too. No Glenn, Juniper, or other pixies in the bushes. It was unusual.

I was half-surprised Zara wasn't in the house waiting for me. For some reason, I thought not passing the first test would result in benign ending. Zara would ask for my family's rulebook. Then she'd give me a memory charm to erase any thoughts of my mother and the rest of the Fairy Godmother's Guild. Then I'd be sent back to Los Angeles, without any memories of everything and everyone in Los Arboledas I'd grown to care for so much.

It wasn't until I was standing alone in the eerie silence of Mom's garden that I realized giving up my fairy godmother powers was a much bigger deal. I was going to lose a great deal more than just my memories of Los Arboledas. And Zara had taken Mom as insurance to make sure I showed up at the Guild with The Fairy Godmother's Rulebook to face my fate.

I went into the guest bedroom and picked the book up off of the nightstand. Running my fingers over its ancient covers, I marveled at how much just the sight and feel of it gave me comfort and made me feel powerful. The book had come into my possession under mysterious circumstances but, now, it was like a hug from a long-lost friend.

Just as my ancestors had before me, I'd left notes in the margins. They were like love letters being passed down from one generation to the next generation. Every time I read them I laughed and I cried. Now, I was going to be the last fairy godmother in my family to touch its pages.

I didn't know what was going to happen to me tonight, but I did know who I was facing. Zara Wakefield would be a formidable opponent, and despite the fact that I knew this confrontation had been coming for weeks, I still hadn't formulated a workable plan to defeat her.

I got back in Vanessa's car and drove back through town. I turned onto the highway leading toward El Encanto. My heart was heavy. I was so disappointed in myself. Mostly I was sorry I hadn't prepared Mom for this night.

I pulled over by the side of the road twice to text Ruby and Owen. I typed out messages asking them for help. But I never sent them. It would be selfish. They'd passed the test and were moving on as full-fledged members of the Guild. If they got involved in my mess, they might jeopardize their own futures as fairy godmothers. I couldn't live with that.

This wasn't their fight. It was mine. I squared my shoulders as I turned onto the coastal road before the turn-off to Sylvie's cottage.

It had become very windy and the water was breaking up and over the rocks, leaving droplets on the windshield of my car. Atop the mountain the distance of the golden spires of El Encanto glowed in the dark as if they were lit from the inside out.

My anxiety spiked when the fence that I used as the landmark for the turn-off onto the dirt road back to Sylvie's cottage came into view.

I wasn't surprised the cottage was dark and it didn't look like anyone was home. I parked the car in the driveway, and though it wasn't easy, I found the footpath leading into the fairy woodlands and El Encanto.

I stopped at the bottom of the Tunnel of Love and looked up the path to El Encanto. I had never been in the tunnel when the lanterns lighting the path weren't lit.

Maybe Zara wasn't in the castle. Maybe she had taken my mom to the most spine-chilling place I had visited since arriving in Los Arboledas.

The door in the middle of the woods.

I ran through the woods as fast as I could. Falling and tripping over branches. I didn't have any idea what I was going to find when I got there, but I hoped Mom wasn't already on the other side of the door.

I would turn the book over to Zara and make sure my mom was okay. Then I would beg Zara. I would do whatever she wanted. Give up everything if she would spare my mother's fairy godmother powers. I was more than happy to relinquish all of mine.

Zara was waiting by the door in the middle of the woods when I arrived. I had a stitch in my side from running through the woods. I had stop and catch my breath.

Floating candle sconces lit up the dense grove of trees around the wooden door. Built from wide wooden planks and finished with rusty hinges, the door was much larger than I remembered.

"Did you bring The Fairy Godmother's Rulebook?" Zara asked.

"Where's my mom?" I demanded, trying to maintain the illusion of bravery.

"I have no idea. As far as I know she's working on an assignment."

"You're lying," I laughed. "Tell me where she is."

"Give me the Willowbrook rulebook first," she snarled.

I gave up the book without a fight. Zara took it from me eagerly. All I really wanted was to see my mom, but watching Zara's greedy fingers touch the pages of my family's rulebook was like being stabbed in the heart.

Her eyes glowed with rapacious glee. "I've grown to have quite a collection. I'd have more, but your mother seems to be determined to save Sylvie from her own mistakes," she said with a sour twist on her face. "I must admit, your family's rulebook is one of the most beautiful I've ever seen. I've been looking forward to claiming it as my own ever since the day we met. It's been in your family for such a long time. It's so sad to see a good thing end, but I knew you didn't have what it takes to be a fairy godmother the moment I laid eyes on you."

I bit my tongue and refrained from any sharp retort. I wanted her to be sympathetic to letting my mom be. "What happens now?" I asked.

"You'll go away."

"That's fine. I'll go. But I want to know where my mom is. I want to talk to her first. Get her here, right now."

"Do you really think you're in a position to make any kind of requests? You've failed, Aviana. And now your mom, and your infamous grandmother, will have to figure out a life without their powers, or the fellowship of the other fairy godmothers who've they grown to count on during their lifetime service to the Guild. They'll be given a memory charm and expected to earn a living without the use of any kind of magic."

I swallowed hard. "You said if I gave you the book, we could negotiate."

"I lied." An wicked smile crossed her face. "Yes. It's terrible. Your mom will have to suffer because you're no good at fairy godmothering. "

I didn't take the bait. I wasn't going to trade insults with Zara. My own fate was settled. But the longer we stood next to the door in the middle of the woods, I couldn't help but wonder if Zara was bluffing. Maybe she really didn't know where my mom was.

"Where is my mom?"

"What makes you think your mother hasn't already surrendered and forgotten all about you?"

"I know here. She wouldn't do anything without speaking with me first. This is all just ... so sad, Zara," I said, trying to reason with her. "Why does it have to be this way?"

"I don't make the rules, Aviana. It is what it is. It seems only poetic that your demise will lead to your mother's as well. Your grandmother in Europe will, I'm sure, be very disappointed. She'll end up a crazy old woman in a crumbling old house on the North Sea."

"Stop it," I said. "Being a bitter winner isn't a good look on anyone. Especially not you."

"You really don't get how big of a deal this is, do you?" Zara sneered. "That you failed so spectacularly."

"How could I succeed when I was set up to fail?"

She laughed. "Do you really think so?"

"You gave me an impossible task."

"Was it really impossible, Aviana? Or were you just a fairy godmother who wanted the handsome prince and the ability to create happily-ever-after endings too? What a very greedy girl you are."

"I'm not greedy. I fell in love."

"Spare me," she snarled. "You're almost as bad at love as you are at magic.

"I beg your pardon," I protested.

"You almost killed the groom when you stopped time at the wedding. Your love potion you slipped into your sister's cocktail didn't work. And that's just the stuff I know about. How many rules did you break? How many other times did you attempt magic that wouldn't work? The Guild is better off without you, Aviana."

I shook my head. "This isn't about my magical skills. A fairy godmother candidate's first assignment isn't even supposed to involve magic. You said that yourself. It didn't matter if I played by the rules, the outcome was always going to be the same. Admit it."

Zara considered me for a long time. "If there were more than one generation of Willowbrook fairy godmothers in the Guild, would the rest of us be safe? It was too much of a risk. I did it for the good of the colony. Don't you see?"

"You're the one who's gone crazy with power. How long have you been using your magic to enhance your success?

Zara looked at me through narrowed eyes. "Do you have any idea what you're saying?"

I nodded. "I'm saying you're a witch."

Zara's laugh was dry and bitter. "A fairy godmother and a witch are very different creatures, but I guess to a novice it can be hard to tell the difference."

I wasn't going to back down. Not now. I stood my ground. "I'm not afraid any more You've been using your fairy godmother powers for financial gain. And you and I both know that's against the rules."

"You don't have any idea what you're talking about," Zara hissed.

"I can't imagine what else you've been doing," I said. "Without a moral compass for guidance."

"No one will believe you," Zara snapped. "Not that it matters. Once you're behind the door in the woods, no one will hear your excuses."

I glanced at the door. Her words had me a bit shook.

"Get going." Zara waved her hands. "Step through the door in the woods and face your fate."

I took a step closer to the door. The fog trickling out had a metallic odor. It smelled like danger. I wasn't sure I would be able to force myself to go through the door. "What is on the other side?"

"No one knows. But for your sake, I hope it's truly terrifying," Zara said.

I held my ground. The muscles in my body tensed, preparing for a fight. Wings aloft. Arms akimbo.

I stuttered stepping forward just as Mom appeared out of the trees. Juniper and Glenn appeared right behind her.

"What are you doing here?" Zara asked.

"I didn't find out about this little meeting until almost too late. The full membership of the Guild has to vote on an expulsion through the door in the woods. You can't just drag someone out here and force her to go through the door against her will like this." She shook her head. "You are so ridiculous."

"You're bitter over losing your powers," Zara hissed. "Because your daughter failed her first assignment."

"It was an impossible task," I insisted.

Mom was implacable, circling Zara without any fear at all. "Why is it, Zara, that my daughter seems to think that her first assignment was to create a romance for the young man she's had a crush on for years and her stepsister? That's a bit cruel, isn't it? Even for you."

"It doesn't matter what her assignment was. What's important is that she thought she couldn't complete it," Zara insisted.

"Oh, please." Mom challenged Zara's version of the truth. "I was on the committee, and I distinctly remember that her first assignment was making sure Jessica Smithson's wedding went off without a hitch. You even insisted going along to watch and make sure she didn't get any assistance from me. By all accounts, Jessica and

Raphael are living happily ever after. Aviana was done before any of the other fairy godmother candidates got their first tasks. So why have you been leading her astray for so long?"

Mom reached out and touched me. "I'm so sorry, my darling girl. I wasn't allowed to discuss anything about your assignment with you. I didn't want Zara to have a reason to disqualify you."

"I don't know what you're accusing me of, Liliana. I'm sure if well take a moment to discuss, we can find a solution." Zara sounded shrill.

Mom shook her head. "You are a witch," she said. "And what's worse, it's getting harder and harder for you to hide it."

"Do you have any proof?" Zara asked.

Ruby stepped out from behind the shadows of the trees, standing next to me in solidarity. "I believe in Aviana."

Zara tossed her head back and laughed. "You think I'm scared of the two of you—a failed fairy godmother and an animal hoarder?"

"You're using pixie dust in your store to enhance your sales and success. I've got the proof right here," she said, holding out her phone.

Sylvie stepped forward and took her place next to Ruby.

"Oh, Sylvie, you pathetic creature, what are you doing here?" Zara asked.

"I know you tampered with the frog charm I put on the music executive. I have proof on my phone." Sylvie held it aloft.

Zara laughed. "Stop it. You don't even know how to use a smartphone."

Then Owen stepped forward. "I believe all the stories these fairy godmothers have told tonight. Zara Wakefield is a witch. She needs to go. We can't wait another minute."

"No," Zara snapped. "I'm not going anywhere."

The other members of the Guild came forward from the darkness. The number of fairies who appeared to back me up surprised me. I had no idea there were so many members of the Guild.

It must've surprised Zara too. Too see all the fairy godmothers join together to get rid of her. She looked nervous and genuinely frightened as the group gathered and grew in size and numbers.

Glenn was orbiting like an annoying little gnat around Mom's head. "Get the Willowbrook rulebook from her, Glenn."

Glenn buzzed forward and reached out to grab the rulebook from Zara's hands, just as a flash of light illuminated the trees in the grove. Glenn tumbled to the ground in a shower of sparkling electricity, followed by his hat and the rulebook.

Almost immediately a covey of pixies swooped down around Glenn's inert form. Mom rushed over, kneeling on the ground to check on her loyal assistant.

"What happened," Glenn sat up in a daze. His voice sounded groggy.

"There was an accident," Mom cooed. Then she turned to the pixies. "Take him back to my garden. I'll be along shortly."

Mom stood up. Her rage simmering just beneath the surface. She faced the semi-circle of fairy godmothers.

"Do I have the votes to expel Zara Wakefield from the Guild?" she asked.

The chorus of 'ayes' from the assembled members was unanimous.

Mom turned to face Zara. "If you had behaved any better, you would have been given time," my mom said, "to turn your Fairy Godmother's Rulebook over to the Guild, get your things together, close your store, and get out of town. But you have no respect for the powers given to you or the fairies that have grown to trust you."

The members of the Guild gathered in a circle around

Zara and the door. Slowly, the circle tightened and grew smaller, forcing Zara to back up, taking steps closer and closer to the danger leaking out of the door.

Zara's face was a mask of fear. Her lips twisted into an ugly sneer. "This is all far from over," she said.

"Maybe or maybe not. The Guild will go on without you," Mom said. "But you're done. Get on with it."

"Where will I go? What will I do" Zara asked. Her eyes were now clearly filled with fear.

"I, for one, don't care anymore," Mom said.

"None of us do," Sylvie added. Her tone was sharper than I'd ever heard her speak before. "Just get out."

"Get out," Owen said forcefully.

Zara took a step forward. The mist wrapped around her ankles, pulling her forward through the door in the woods. Just like that she disappeared. The door slammed shut, but fingers of the mist lingered in the wildflowers growing on the forest floor.

I collapsed on the ground. The cool moss cradled my head. Mom rushed over. The others in the Guild gathered around us. Knowing I would have their support for the rest of my life gave me comfort.

"Juniper?" Mom called, and the little pixie flew out of the darkness and hovered over us. "Keep track of Zara on the other side of the door for a bit, will you? I don't trust her not to find some way to return."

"I'm on it." She opened the door in the woods, flying straight into its hidden depths without any hesitation. The door slammed shut behind her. A few wisps from the other side hung in the air.

But Zara Wakefield was gone.

CHAPTER 26

Rule #26: A fairy godmother commits to her assignments with her mind, body, and soul.

A fog had crept in overnight and blanketed Los Arboledas and the surrounding valley. It would burn off in a few short hours, but for now, just the sharp tips of El Encanto were visible through the wisps of the smoky clouds on the nearby mountaintop.

I would never see Nash again. That was my first thought. His goofy imperfect grin was my second.

Gah!

I was not going to start another day with a pity party. I needed to focus on what I had instead of what I didn't have. I forced myself to focus on all of the good things that had happened to me and let go of the bad.

It was my mantra as I threw back the covers and put my feet on the floor. I just needed time. Eventually I would stop thinking about him every moment of every day.

Wouldn't I?

I kept moving, hoping that perpetual motion would keep the pain away. I pulled on my leggings and sweatshirt before heading out of the house.

A few cars were parked near the shopping arcade, but downtown Los Arboledas was mostly deserted. I hung a left at Central Park and crossed into the residential neighborhood. Engulfed by the ocean mist, I broke into my stride. I didn't know what the future held for me, but I knew for certain I wanted to live in Los Arboledas. It was home.

I jogged out of town, following the shady lane back into the forest where Sylvie lived. Birds and other woodland critters were scuttling about in the trees. I couldn't see El Encanto through the mist, but I knew it was there. I smiled thinking about it. I was no longer living in fear of its secrets.

As I turned to head back to my mom's house, my strides grew longer. It was as if I was walking on air and didn't need my wings to fly.

With each step I took, I counted my many blessings. The gala had been a huge success. We had raised one hundred thousand dollars for Prince Charming and the other homeless animals to begin their lives at The Enchanted Barn. But at the top of my list of things I was grateful for was that I had passed the test. I was a fairy godmother.

I needed to complete my training, and the Guild Elders had plans for a new class of fairy godmothers, but they wanted to clean the slate after Zara's untimely departure. Our formal training had been delayed, but I could learn so much from my mom. If I kept busy, I wouldn't have time to dwell on my broken heart.

The sun broke through the fog while I was on the pine-needle covered path in front of Sylvie's cottage. I was re-energized and almost happy enjoying the dappled sunlight on my face. I walked back into town, forcing myself not to think about Nash. Not once.

Not gonna lie. I managed to do it for at least ninety seconds.

I called it a win.

When I got back to her house, Mom was in the kitchen, humming along with one of her favorite Johnny Mathis songs. "Chances are ..." she sang. I didn't need to point it out to her, she had to know the irony of a fairy godmother singing that song.

My place was set at the table with a placemat and a glass for my orange juice. A platter of bacon was set out on the counter, and Mom was just starting to make pancakes when I walked in.

"Darling." She spoke with a warm smile in her voice. "How was your run?" I still had no idea where my mother had picked up her phony European accent, but now that I knew her better, everything about it was absolutely charming.

"Okay." The doors in the kitchen were open to the garden. A flurry of activity in the foliage was being created by a covey of pixies. "Have you seen Juniper?"

"She's been hanging out in the jasmine vine with her sisters all morning." Mom lit the stove under the griddle. "Are you feeling better?"

"I think so," I said. "I finally caught up on some sleep."

"How do you want your pancakes? With blueberries or without?"

"With," I said.

"Excellent." She grinned. "You are your mother's daughter."

A minute later Juniper flew into the room with a thimble-sized iced-blended coffee in her hands. She took off her messenger bag and sprawled across my placemat like it was a beach towel with her feet propped up on the sugar bowl.

"How's Glenn?" I asked. "Do you know if he's feeling better?"

"Word in the hibiscus bushes says he's going to be fine," Juniper answered.

"He saved my life," Mom said.

Juniper dismissed Mom's concerns with a toss of her hand. "He got his wings singed a little, and is playing the sympathy card. He's got a battalion of Tinkerbells taking numbers and waiting in line to nurse him back to health."

"Some things never change," Mom agreed. She poured a cup of coffee and sat down next to me.

"How's it going?" Juniper asked.

"Better," I said. "How 'bout you?

"Good. I'm glad. I was really looking forward to being your sidekick."

"Really?"

"Yeah. You're not as cotton candy ridiculous as the others. You're a bit edgy," she said with a grin. "And this is for you." She pulled a giant dahlia from her bag and offered it to me.

"It's beautiful," I said. "It's my favorite flower."

"I know." Juniper grinned. She had all the makings of a loyal and true familiar.

"I think I'm going to be okay," I said. "I was anxious and uncertain when I first got up this morning, but I feel good—now that I know my purpose is being a fairy godmother."

"Really?" Mom seemed surprised. "Truth?"

"I wish I knew what the future will bring."

"Don't we all," Mom said. "I'm certain your future will be much like many others. Lots of highs and lows. As your mom, I'm hoping for mostly highs."

"Now?" Juniper asked. "Can I do it now?"

"Yes," Mom said.

Juniper put her hand under the flap of her messenger bag and withdrew a thick creamy envelope with gilt corners, shoving it into my hands.

I took it with shaking fingers. I couldn't speak. My throat had completely closed up. I couldn't believe I was holding it in my hands. Beautiful and engraved.

"What do you think?" Mom asked.

"I'm thrilled beyond my wildest dreams."

"I'm so glad. If you don't want to live at the castle. You can stay with me, but your father made me promise you'll visit him at least once a month. If you don't, he'll come up here. And then God help us all."

"It's nice." I smiled. "To have a place where I belong."

"It's a gift not everyone gets, Aviana. Especially not at your age," Mom said. "Just promise you'll make time for a life of your own, Aviana."

"The *Fairy Godmother's Rulebook* says …"

"Screw the rulebook, Aviana. That thing was written in the sixteenth century. We have to adapt to a new world."

I couldn't stop giggling.

"How did you ever get the idea Nash was supposed to be Vanessa's happily ever after?" Mom asked.

"On the night we were supposed to get our first assignments, there was a tree at the end of the Tunnel of Love. It had their initials carved on it."

Mom shrugged. "I don't know about the tree, but I know that was not the task the Elders had decided on for you. First assignments are always easy. Not something as involved and difficult as sparking a romance, and creating a happily-ever-after ending for two random people."

"That's hard?" I asked.

"It's really difficult," Mom said, laughing. "Who knows? Maybe Zara knew you had a crush on Nash, so she thought you'd have a hard time choosing to do the right thing.

"I did use advanced magic at the wedding," I admitted.

Mom shook her head. "Even so Zara couldn't deny the fact that you had passed your first assignment. The wedding was, by all accounts, absolute perfection. Gaslighting you into believe you had a different assignment, was all the proof I needed that she was, as we'd expected for some time, a witch."

"Mom, I have to ask you a question. When you called me on my birthday. I was having a terrible day…

"You sounded dreadful," she added. "But I don't know

any fairy who would say the day she grows her wings is her favorite. It makes me nauseated just to think about it again."

"So you didn't call me that day because I was absolutely desperate?

"No." Mom looked confused.

"You mean…You're not my fairy godmother?"

"Oh, for heaven's sake, Aviana. No. I'm your mom. I want you to be happy, Aviana. That's all."

"Rule number two," I said, "'A fairy godmother embraces the knowledge happily ever after is her purpose, not her future.' I'm excited to be able to create happiness for other people." It was the truth. For the first time I had direction and purpose.

Mom took a deep breath. "That was the hardest rule for me. I knew from the day I was born that I was destined to be a fairy godmother, but it was the last thing I wanted. Your father was a friend of the manager of the inn. One of a group of men who used to drive up to Los Arboledas on the weekend to play golf. He was so handsome. And charming."

"It was a different time back then. If you were a fairy godmother, you were a fairy godmother. No one worked outside of the Guild. And I wasn't clever enough to invent a job to showcase my skills. I burnt some bridges when I started hanging out with your father and his friends at the inn. I didn't hesitate when he asked me to marry him."

"He didn't know I was a fairy godmother." She shook her head from the memories. "The day you were born I sat up all night looking at your face so I wouldn't ever forget what you looked like, just in case. I've never seen such a beautiful child. You were like an angel. When your father realized the truth. He told me I had to get out. I was devastated, returning to Los Arboledas without you."

"But Sunday came and the guild members showed up at my house like nothing was out of the ordinary. I was so grateful. I focused on my work and didn't let anyone see my pain. I should've fought harder for you. To see you more often, but I loved you so much, and I was so afraid your father wouldn't let me see you at all if I did anything to make him angry."

I squeezed her hand and held it tight.

"Anyway, enough talk of days gone by and promises broken. She smiled. "I hope you enjoy being a fairy godmother there ever was."

"I'll never be able to fill your shoes."

"Magic takes time, Aviana. No one just snaps their fingers and performs a spell. For heaven's sake, real magic isn't just smoke and mirrors. This isn't Las Vegas. Your magical powers aren't like the windshield wipers of your car—you can't just turn them on and off with a voice command. It will take time."

My mind was racing. I still had so many questions. "What about Vanessa? She deserves a happily ever after."

"You're going to have to trust me," she said. "Vanessa is my number one priority right now. I'm pretty good at my job, so you can rest assured I'm doing everything in my power to guide her to happiness."

I swallowed hard. "And Nash?" I wasn't sure I wanted to know her answer, but I had to ask.

"Nash?" Mom looked confused. "He wasn't ever on my radar. But happily ever after is the destination at the end of a fairy's story. If he's not there yet, maybe his story is to be continued…"

"…Or maybe his story isn't a fairy tale," I suggested.

Mom smiled. 'The possibilities are endless."

After breakfast, I took a shower and got dressed in my favorite polka-dot sundress. I walked past the wall-long mirror in the master bathroom.

"Would you let this chick handle your happily ever after?" I asked my own reflection out loud. "Yes. Yes, I think I would." I was pleased and surprised by my positive and confident response to my own question.

It was the beginning of a brand-new day.

CHAPTER 27

Rule #27: A fairy godmother never underestimates another fairy godmother's power.

I grabbed my purse, locked the front door, and shoved the key to Mom's house back under the pot on the front porch where I had found it originally. I practically skipped down the front walk and out the picket gate to my car. My spirits were starting to lift along with the mist.

My new car had been a birthday gift from Mom and Dad. She picked it out but he'd paid for it. The car suited my personality and always made me smile.

I took the long way into town, past the long and elegant arcade, slowing when I turned into the inn's long elegant driveway. I parked the "pumpkin-mobile" in the guest parking lot and walked down the path to the administration building. Harper was busy on a conference call when I arrived, so the receptionist had me wait in the lobby. I spent a few fretful minutes waiting to see her, worrying that our conversation was going to be less than pleasant. It wasn't until she walked out and smiled broadly that I started to relax.

"Oh good. You're here," Harper said. "Great party last

night. We were all impressed."

"Thank you," I said. "It was a team effort."

"I called you here because we'd like to offer you a contract. I think you will find our salary and executive compensation package very competitive."

She must've sensed my hesitation.

"Are you considering other offers?"

"No. No. I haven't found another position. I'm just not sure I'll be able to do any full-time work," I said. "I want to continue to help Ruby with the horse sanctuary. And I'm also working on several projects with my mother."

I didn't know when the Fairy Godmother's Guild would be giving me a new assignment, but I knew that when it happened, I would have to drop everything else and give my new protégé my full attention.

"Would you consider working at the inn on a consultant basis?" Harper asked.

"Yes, but I feel like I might've missed a conversation. Does Nash know about this?"

Harper looked surprised. "Oh, yes. I wouldn't have consider talking to you unless Nash was fully on board."

"Oh." I was surprised.

"Have you talked to him?" she asked.

"No. Not since ..." I stopped. We had exchanged pleasantries at the gala, but we hadn't really talked since he found out I was a fairy and had been lying to him since the day we first met. "No, we haven't talked since…well, for a bit."

"I know he wants to talk to you. I'll call him and let him know you're here."

Harper picked up the phone and dialed a few numbers. "I'm in the human resources department. Aviana is here. Will you tell him? I know he's anxious to see her," Harper said. "I'll tell her." She hung up the phone. "He wants you to wait in the 'Enchanted Garden.' Do you know where that is?"

"Yes."

"He'll be down to speak with you shortly."

Why did I think I'd get away without ever speaking to Nash again. Of course we had to speak. Especially if we were both going to be spending large amounts of time in Los Arboledas. Inevitably our paths would cross in such a small town.

In a matter of seconds, the Band-Aid holding my heart together had been ripped off and blood was pumping out of a fresh wound.

I was light-headed as I walked outside and followed the path down to the garden to wait for Nash. It had once been my happy place, the place where I first learned magic. It was where we fell in love.

I took off my cardigan and placed it next to me on the seat. I figured it was best to face him with my wings exposed. I needed all the strength they gave me.

My breath caught in my throat as he walked toward me. He was wearing my favorite purple cashmere sweater with dark jeans. His stride was long and confident. He had something wrapped up in brown paper under his arm. His dark curls were longer than I remembered. His skin was paler. He was still the most beautiful man I had ever met in my life.

What was he going to say? And what was I going to do? I had a terrible feeling all I was going to do was cry. A lump was already forming in my throat, and tears were welling up behind my eyes.

"Hello." His voice cracked. He sounded vulnerable. His intense gaze went right through me. He must know I am still madly in love with him. He must know that I can't stop thinking about him.

"Hello." I stood up and struggled to maintain eye contact. He was so close. I smelled the clean and spicy scent of his cologne.

"Thank you for agreeing to meet me here. I want to apologize for my behavior the last time we were alone together," he said.

"Under the circumstances, I think your behavior was exemplary," I said. "If I had been in your shoes, I'm not sure I would've acted any differently."

"I don't think so," Nash said. "Don't forget. I've read the rules. A fairy godmother always asks herself 'Who needs my kindness most today?' It's one of the most important rules. One of the basics. I know you. You would've acted with the grace you've always shown anyone you've ever met. I've always admired that quality in you."

"Thank you," I said. I could feel my cheeks flush.

"I don't believe in fairy tales," he said. "Never have. Not sure I ever will."

"No surprise," I said.

"No," he said. "I guess not. And you can imagine how I feel about fairies. They are creatures inhabiting children's fantasies and nothing more. I really don't want any fairy wings in my life."

"I know," I said. "I understand. I really do. Better than …"

"Unless they're a part of a naughty Halloween costume," he added with a gleam in his eyes.

"What?" I said.

"You heard me," he said with a wicked grin.

I laughed. He always made me laugh when I wanted to cry.

He looked relieved. He reached for my hand and I welcomed his touch.

"Before I met you, I only believed in facts and figures represented in Venn diagrams, balance sheets, and profit and loss statements," he said. "Everything I needed to know about the world could be detailed on a spreadsheet. But now, I wonder if maybe there's more to the world than anyone can see at first glance. Someone recently told me fairies make the world beautiful while the rest of us are too busy to notice. And I want to believe, if you'll help me."

I nodded, but I was confused.

Did he want a fairy godmother to look after his guests at the Los Arboledas Inn, or did he want me?

"Most kids believe in magic," he said. "I drew pictures of dragons to decorate my room when I was little. I'm embarrassed to say I had forgotten that fact. I guess it's adults who learn to question the power of imagination."

"I understand," I said. "I was a skeptic too, but I've discovered that there's more magic in the world than most of us care to admit."

"We'd have to take it slow," he said. "Very slow."

He was using the plural "we." Was he talking about us? *Together?*

My heart did a flip-flop. And then another.

"I'm sorry I freaked out before. It was a big surprise, but I've done a lot of thinking. There are still a lot of things I don't understand. But I want to try. I've missed you."

I didn't know what to say. There was so much I wanted to share with him, but could I? I wasn't sure. What if he failed me the same way my father had failed Mom?

"You'd have to talk to me," he said. "You'd have to be willing to explain and make me understand."

"Yes. But some of it, though, is against the rules," I said. "I am a fairy godmother. That is a fact. Telling you all of my secrets is against the rules. You'd have to be okay with that."

"I'm not sure I can live with being kept in the dark by someone I'm in love with," he said. "But I will try."

I opened my mouth to speak and then closed it.

What did he say? Did he mean it?

His "I love you" had been carelessly tossed into our conversation as if it didn't have any value attached to it at all.

"Be honest with me, Aviana," he said. "What were you just going to say?"

"Honestly, I was just going to tell you I love you too."

"I love you," he said again without any hesitation. "Did

I forget to start this conversation with 'I love you'? Because that was how I planned it in my head. I would open with I love you, and I can't imagine a life without you. And then I was going to beg. After that I was hoping we would kiss, and one thing would lead to another and everything would just fall into place."

I laughed. He flashed his crooked smile at me and I wondered why I didn't just stop this conversation right there, but I couldn't. There was more that he'd have to understand.

"It's just that it's more complicated than that, Nash. Our love, our story, should we choose to continue, will always be more complicated than others."

"Complicated but not impossible?" he asked.

"Complicated, but not impossible," I agreed.

"So, are you willing to find a way for us to be together?" he asked. It seemed like such a solemn and reverential moment.

Am I willing? Was he kidding?

"Yes," I said. "With my whole heart, yes."

"I almost forgot. These are for you." He shoved the lumpy mess of brown paper toward me.

I unwrapped and peeked inside only to find my missing crystal sandals.

"I took them last night," he said. "I figured that if you wouldn't see me today, you'd have to meet me somewhere, some place, some time so I could return them."

"I'm not Cinderella," I said.

"That's good." He grinned. "Because this time Prince Charming fell for the fairy godmother."

Nash drew me into his embrace. I leaned against him and pressed my face against his bare neck. It was so sweet to be back in his arms.

My wings stirred on my back. He moved his hands down to my waist so that he wouldn't impede their natural movements.

"So, how do these work, exactly?" he asked.

"I don't know. Truth is, I can't always control my wings," I said. "I do know they are always more active when I'm excited."

"Seriously?" Nash had a gleam in his eye. "That's good to know."

I closed my eyes. His warm mouth covered mine. For the first time ever, I concentrated on just being next to him instead of worrying about keeping my wings hidden and under control. He pulled me closer. Tears fell down my face. I knew this was exactly where I belonged. Nash and I were a perfect fit.

***

What happens next?

I don't know. I can't see into the future. It's not one of my superpowers. All that matters to me is that I'm with a guy who's crazy about me and I'm going to get to do what I love for a living.

I'm a fairy godmother.

I couldn't dream of a better life.

Or could I?

Nah.

It wasn't so long ago that I didn't believe in fairy tales and had no hope of ever having my own happily-ever-after ending. I'm starting a new journey, but this time I know the ending.

Fairy tales really do come true.

You just have to believe.

THE END

ACKNOWLEDGEMENTS

First, thank you to every reader for taking Aviana Willowbrook into your heart and imagination. She has lived in mine for a very long time. I wrote her for everyone who ever wondered if they were living the life of Cinderella or one of her wicked stepsisters. Or even worse, the fairy godmother, who was always captured during her less photogenic middle age years in classic fairy tales. This never seemed right to me, which is how Aviana was born.

Thank you to Melissa Keir, for falling in love with an idea and trusting that I could make it into something special. I am so grateful to Yezanira Venecia took on the challenge of reshaping this script. I am most grateful for her patience. And Najla Qamber and her team of superstars who always make the most delicious book covers.

Sam Tschida (pronounced "cheetah"), and my classmates at Smut U, inspire me to be a better writer. I want to thank the regulars to the morning writing sessions: Jennifer K., Jeannine, Sarah K., Cristina P., Dara, and the amazing cast of writers who stop by and write with us when their time permits. You've taught me how important it is to write every day.

My dearest and most darling romance writing mentors, Chandra and Barbara. You are been the best thing that ever happened to me and my writing. I am grateful and I have grown to depend on your friendship and kindness. I will never be able to say thank you often enough.

Thank you to Katie McCoach, and Julie Ganis for your bravery in looking at this book when it was a bumpy manuscript and giving professional notes and most-needed guidance. Thank you to Maggie Marr for listening and representing my best interests. I am always to grateful to you.

Finally, I'd like to quote Canadian singer-songwriter Bryan Adams to honor *The Handsomest Man Alive*, "Everything I do, I do it for you." You are my north, south, east and west. My immediate family isn't big, but I love them dearly. I get my sense of humor from my mom, and I love her more than anything in the world.

OTHER BOOKS BY SARAH VANCE-TOMPKINS

Drama student Hannah Evans isn't kissing any frogs on her path to find Prince Charming. She's determined to share the perfect first kiss -- with the perfect boy -- in the perfect place -- or she's not kissing at all. When Hannah meets a cute ginger-haired boy in first class lounge in the London airport, she knows he's 'The One.'

Pop star Theo Callahan is on the road to get as far away as possible from his back-stabbing best friend, and his supermodel girlfriend who broke his heart. Until one shy smile from Hannah has him rethinking all of his travel plans.

Theo is smitten, but he's worried she's just a groupie in search of the ultimate selfie. Can Theo learn to trust Hannah in time to share one perfect first kiss, or will Hannah be forced to kiss a frog?

Beaches, boyfriends and danger...summer is certainly hot! Grab a hold tight as these eight authors wow you with stories from sweet to sizzling! After all, every day can have some summer fun!

Breaking Girl Code by Brooke Moss

Aubrey is having the perfect evening out, with the perfect guy, on a perfect summer night. The problem is... Preston's not her date. His real date is her B.F.F., and she's passed out in the backseat.

Wishing on Water by Liz Ashlee

After watching everyone's else's lives hit huge milestones, all Hope wants is to escape to her boring, unchanging, single life. So, where's the one logical place to escape to? *A retirement home.*

Art with a Pulse by Clara Winter

Artist Alice finds herself rescuing a seal on the sands of Laguna Beach with screenwriter Elijah. Can Alice put her past behind her and give Elijah the chance he deserves?

A Natural Passion by Tammy Mannersly

How will marine biologist, Dylan O'Day, solve the illegal poaching problem threatening the ecosystem he loves and protects when the gorgeous, new intern, Kyra Shine, is occupying his every thought?

You Had Me at Aloha by Sarah Vance Tompkins

Social media guru Vivienne Parker's dream trip to Hawaii turns into a nightmare when her roommate in the luxurious surf shack is the hot Olympic athlete who just got her fired.

More Than Puppy Love by Kitsy Clare

Fireworks spark when Arianna, a city girl with an elite pet portrait business is in a wreck and asks Dave a country auto mechanic for help, but can these two beagle owners from different worlds see eye to eye?

Stealing Haven by Mark Love

Sand, sun, romance and a mystery to solve. Sounds like a perfect vacation for Jamie.

Harmony in the Key of Murder by Melissa Kay Clarke

Summer in the South can mean a different type of heat when a newly appointed investigator and a mechanical genius cross paths leading to murder and love.

AVAILABLE AT ALL MAJOR BOOK RETAILERS.

ABOUT THE AUTHOR

Sarah Vance-Tompkins was born in a small town in northern Michigan. She received an MFA in Film Production from the University of Southern California, and went on to work in feature film development. Prior to film school, she wrote and produced radio and television commercials. A working writer, she has been paid to write everything from obituaries and press releases to breathless descriptions of engagement rings. She and her husband, The Handsomest Man Alive™, live in Southern California with three cats.

Website: http://www.sarahvancetompkins.com
Facebook Home:https://www.facebook.com/sarahevance
Author Page:
https://www.facebook.com/sarahvancetompkins

Twitter: https://twitter.com/sarahvtompkins
Instagram: https://instagram.com/sarahvantom/
Pinterest: https://www.pinterest.com/sarahevance/
Google+:
https://plus.google.com/u/0/+SarahVanceTompkins
Tumblr: https://www.tumblr.com/blog/sarahvantom
Amazon:http://www.amazon.com/Sarah-Vance-Tompkins/e/B00QSTJ3HS/ref=dp_byline_cont_ebooks_1
Snapchat: SarahVTompkins